SALT & STONE

THE SIREN'S CURSE, BOOK 1

A.L. KNORR

Edited by
NICOLA AQUINO

Edited by
TERESA HULL

INTELLECTUALLY PROMISCUOUS PRESS

1047512

I am a citizen of the most beautiful nation on earth. A nation whose laws are harsh yet simple, a nation that never cheats, which is immense and without borders, where life is lived in the present. In this limitless nation, this nation of wind, light, and peace, there is no other ruler besides the sea.

BERNARD MOITESSIER, A SOLITARY
TRANSOCEANIC SAILOR

BY A.L. KNORR

The Elemental Origins Series

Born of Water

Born of Fire

Born of Earth

Born of Æther

Born of Air

The Elementals

The Returning Series (Mira's Story)

Returning

Falling (retitled, was Returning II)

Surfacing

The Siren's Curse Trilogy

Salt & Stone

Salt & the Sovereign

Elemental Novellas

Pyro, A Fire Novella

Heat, A Fire Novella

The Kacy Chronicles

Descendant

Ascendant

Combatant

Transcendent

To be the first to learn about new releases, visit
www.alknorrbooks.com and sign up for AL Knorr's newsletter.

ONE

Georjie pulled her mother's SUV into the Sutherland's driveway, put it in park, and shut off the engine. We undid our seatbelts, but she didn't move to get out.

"Are you okay?" I asked, touching her shoulder.

She glanced at me, eyes moisture-rimmed and little red, but she smiled. Snatching a tissue from the box sitting in the console, she blew her nose.

"There's another of us gone," she sniffed.

We'd just returned from the airport, where we'd joined Saxony's family in seeing her off as she went to begin her grade twelve year at Arcturus, a school for fire magi in England. Saxony had come back from her summer stint as an au pair in Venice with a fire living inside her...like literally. When a mafia boss gave her contact info for a fire mage named Basil Chaplin who might be able to help her figure out what to do with her new firepower, she and her parents went all the way to Dover to meet him. The next time we saw her, she broke the news that she was enrolled in a secret school for kids just like her. She'd told us that in the nineties, Basil had opened Arcturus to provide a safe place for young fire magi like her to learn how to control their fire. There were a few private agencies who had agreements with Arcturus, according to Basil, who then offered employment to magi after they graduated. What Saxony's schooling might lead her to seemed exciting and glamorous to Georjie and me—secret spy work maybe, or joining a team of magi to fight terror.

"And you'll be next to leave, Targa," Georjie was saying. "So much has happened, so much has changed. It's been a little challenging to adjust, you know?"

I nodded. "I know."

"I never saw this coming. I thought we'd have our final year together."

"And we thought our high school would still be in one piece," I added.

She nodded. "Yeah. I mean, I'm sorry for Saltford and for what the storm did..."

'Storm' was a massive understatement. A corporation called TNC had tried to hire me, Georjie, Saxony, and another girl from Saltford named Petra. When Petra learned that genocide was their endgame, she destroyed their field station and accidentally released an invisible ancient demon called an archon. When it turned on Saltford, we did our best to battle it together, but we were losing until our dear friend Akiko—a demon hunter, appropriately—dealt the killing blow.

Tragically, her blow was a sacrificial one. We still could barely talk about what she had done without breaking down into tears. Since then, we'd agreed to refer to the archon as a storm, even while in private, so that we didn't slip up when talking in public. It seemed we were the only people in Saltford (besides my mom) who knew the storm hadn't been a freak natural occurrence.

"But we've weathered it pretty well, considering..." Georjie was saying.

"Considering that every time you visit the hospital, people have miraculous recoveries," I finished.

When we were sharing our summer stories, Georjie had referred to herself as a Wise, and she'd spoken of an incredible gift she had of pulling the healing qualities of the earth out of the ground and sending them into bodies that needed healing. Her elemental gifts had come in handy during the days immediately following the storm.

"And it's no coincidence that the media has been focusing on the disaster relief story, instead of hunting us down for interviews...thanks to you and your voice." Georjie shook her head. "I hate to think of what might have happened if you hadn't told that one kid to pull down and destroy the video of us on the beach."

"Things could be worse," I agreed.

Georjie nodded, but she still looked miserable.

"Do you not want to go to Scotland?" I asked, concerned. "Do you feel like you have to?"

She shook her head vehemently as she pinched her nose with the tissue again. "Oh no, I'm super excited to go to Scotland, and I'm really looking forward to seeing Jasher again. Saltford is the last place I want to be if my friends aren't here. I guess I'm just still in shock."

I leaned over the console and pulled her in for a hug. I'd already had my turn in this same state; I knew how she was feeling. Excited about traveling, sad about saying goodbye, maybe a little guilty about leaving Saltford while it was rebuilding. But we'd done all we could and now we needed to focus on the next thing—finishing high school and adjusting to our new lives.

"I can't believe you're leaving in three days," she said,

sniffling next to my hair. "And I can't believe I didn't get a chance to meet Antoni while he was here."

"There wasn't time." I pulled back as an idea struck. "Why don't you come visit me in Poland? You can meet Antoni, see where Mom and I will be living."

Her face brightened. "Why didn't I think of that?"

I paused, realizing she probably had thought of it, but was too polite to ask. "Maybe you were waiting for an invitation?"

"Maybe," her mouth quirked in a smile. "But I love the idea. Why don't I ask Denise to look into flights tonight while you're packing? Maybe it'll work out that I can come to Gdansk for a bit first, and then go on to Scotland from there."

"Great!" I mirrored her infectious smile. "Can we go in now? I'm starving."

She nodded. "Me too, actually."

The archon had destroyed our trailer. Mom and I had picked through the rubble of the trailer court along with several other families, rescuing what few belongings hadn't been totaled—which for us equaled Mom's winter tires, a rubber boot, and a barometer. At first Mom and I had stayed in a hotel, but then Liz and Georjie had insisted we stay with them for as long as was needed.

Georjie and I had registered for our grade twelve year through an online school and promised each other we'd be one another's motivation to do well and graduate with a bang. Saxony had also registered for some online courses but through a different organization—one that offered more flexibility, as she'd be studying at Arcturus at the same time.

"What time do you think your mom will be home tonight?" Georjie asked as we boiled water for spaghetti. "Should we save a plate for her?"

"I think The Bluejackets will have food at the goodbye party, and knowing my mom, she'll stay until she's eaten and then slip out."

Georjie laughed. "That sounds like her, all right. Was she surprised when Simon and the guys said they were throwing her a retirement party?"

She added salt to the pot of water and retrieved a jar of canned tomato sauce from the pantry.

I began to chop vegetables for a salad. "She was blown away. You know she and her colleagues never really got on."

"I know, but don't you think that secretly, they loved having her on their team? I mean, your mom is the opposite of dull." She pulled a second pot from the drawer beside the stove, then opened a jar of sauce and dumped it in.

"I think it was a true love-hate relationship." I added the chopped tomatoes to the greens and tossed them together. "One thing is for sure, they're in for a shock when their jobs don't ever go as smoothly as they did while she was there."

The front door opened and a voice called, "Hello?"

"Speak of the devil," Georjie said. "You're home early, Mira. Are you hungry?"

"We're making spaghetti," I added.

The sound of footsteps on the stairs preceded my mom. She entered the kitchen wearing a black t-shirt, a pair of jeans, and her hair in a topknot.

Georjie glanced at her, one fine eyebrow arched. "That's what you wore to your own retirement party?"

Mom looked down at her clothes. "What's wrong with it?"

Georjie and I shared a look.

"Nothing." Georjie picked up the spaghetti box and dumped a thick rope of pasta into her hand. "Dinner for three? Or did you eat?"

"I did, but I won't turn down eating with my favorite girls. How was the send-off?"

"Saxony was pretty excited. Couldn't blame her. Getting out of Saltford is the best thing for all of us right now." Georjie added the pasta to the boiling water. "How was the party?"

Mom gave a humorless laugh. "Everyone was miserable. Why do you think I'm back already?" She shook her head. "I told Simon a party was a bad idea. It would have been better if he'd just let me slip away quietly without making a fuss."

"Do you think maybe they were miserable because they knew they were losing a valuable teammate?" I asked. "It's probably something they never thought could happen. You were like Simon's star, he paid you better than anyone."

Mom shrugged a shoulder. "I don't know why they were miserable, and I don't really care. I was ready to leave a long time ago."

I tried not to let this statement make me feel guilty, but it was tough. Mom had worked for The Bluejackets to support me. When I finally had my salt-birth and became a mermaid, she'd been so excited about the prospect of the two of us going to sea together—experiencing a salt-cycle with her daughter, the way every siren dreams. But I couldn't have been less interested in leaving my human life. Even if I hadn't fallen in love with Antoni, I was committed to finishing school and maybe going to university, having some kind of vocation, a family. I loved swimming in the ocean, but I had a hard time imagining living out there for years at a time. For Mom, this was nearly impossible to understand.

So when Saltford High was destroyed by the archon, and the opportunity to move to Poland and take up our

Novak inheritance came sooner than expected, Mom accepted this as the next best thing to going to sea.

I suspected that she still hoped I'd come around, maybe after I graduated. But I couldn't imagine ever wanting to leave Antoni. My siren heart had chosen him—he was it for me.

Mom had been on a project when the demon struck, but she got on the first plane home as soon as she was able. By the time she'd arrived, teams were already organizing to rebuild. We'd helped our neighbors clean up as best we could. Mom didn't ask me for my version of what had happened, and I hadn't been ready to tell her, either. I was still in shock. But when she'd asked me when we were going to see Akiko, the silent siren-tears came and it all spilled out.

Mom had listened silently while I'd told her about the offer from TNC, delicately explaining why I hadn't notified her about the day trip and the proposal—I'd really felt we'd be in and out in a matter of hours and the whole thing would be over. I told her about Petra and the incredible hidden field station we'd been flown to, as well as the dome project and all the stuff Petra had unearthed about it. I went into detail about the attack of the massive demon TNC had made a pact with, and then our efforts to subdue it and Akiko's role.

Akiko...well, I had seen her little avian body disappear into the shadowy vortex of the creature. She never came out again.

It was too horrible, too final, too sudden, too unfair. It didn't fit with my sense of justice or my world view. I preferred to hope that I would see her again one day and she'd have some fantastic story to tell about slipping into another world. If I thought about her as dead, my heart became panicky and tears threatened to spill over, so in my mind, I had relegated her to 'ascended' and it helped me cope with the grief.

Akiko's home had been damaged but not destroyed by the archon, and when we realized Akiko was not coming back, Georjie and I sneaked into the house to retrieve her samurai swords. They were the only material thing Akiko had cared about. The swords were stashed in a locked box in Georjie's basement, in case by some miracle Akiko ever returned.

Beyond comforting me and listening, my mom couldn't offer up any insight about the storm-demon. She'd never heard of such a thing. She felt so guilty for not being there that she tortured herself for days over it. When I suggested we move back to Poland as soon as possible, she'd said yes right away.

Antoni sounded as excited as I felt that I was returning to Europe so soon when I called to catch him up. I'd carefully referred to the archon only as a storm so I didn't freak him out.

Mom and I worked through a checklist to ensure our emigration went smoothly. She gave her notice to a shocked Simon, arranged for our visas, closed down accounts, filled out a change of address card and informed acquaintances. I notified the Novak estate of our arrival, scheduled a flight with Novak's company pilot, registered with my online school, and sorted through our meager belongings.

In a matter of days, we'd be on a plane back to Poland.

TWO

For a mermaid, flying is torture. The best thing to do is to sleep. Any hopes I had that becoming an elemental would make it easier vanished as the imagined chains wrapped around every joint and threatened to pull me down through the floor. Mom and I had guessed that sirens were tied to the ocean in inexplicable ways, and flying thirty-thousand feet over the earth's surface was just too far from water. Thank goodness I never wanted to be an astronaut, I'd probably die a few minutes after take-off.

We staggered drunkenly off the plane and were met at the small Gdansk airstrip by a Novak driver. He introduced himself to us but I immediately forgot his name in my haze of exhaustion. Relieved to just be on the ground and in desperate need of a good night's sleep, even after all the hours we'd been unconscious, Mom and I leaned against one another's shoulders in the back of the limousine until we arrived at the manor. I sent Antoni a text letting him know we were on the ground and he sent back a heart and a 'see you soon.'

Somehow, we and our bags made our way into a suite in

wondering why I hadn't communicated this to my mother myself after I'd received her carefully structured and thorough email with this very information and itinerary.

"I'll make sure she does."

"Thank you." I rested my forehead against the wall beside the panel and grimaced. I wasn't making a good impression. She was probably questioning Martinius's good sense for the hundredth time. Why had he given over his company to these two daft Canadian women? Couldn't say I blamed her.

"Not a problem," she said. "See you in an hour."

I wanted to find my mom, just to make sure she was awake and indeed up to speed, but poking my head out of my suite door revealed a bewilderingly long hallway—in both directions—lined with many doors. I didn't have time to find her now.

After hopping in the shower and coming fully awake, I felt my spirits brighten. This was an exciting new chapter of my life, and Antoni was here somewhere. I could barely restrain myself from dancing for joy under the spray of the showerhead when I thought about seeing him soon. Butterflies took flight in my stomach when I imagined throwing myself into his arms and feeling his big, warm body next to mine again. My skin tingled with inspired gooseflesh and excitement, not just for Antoni, but for all of the recent changes for me...and Mom.

She no longer had to work in a job she hated, and she had control of the artifacts from *The Sybellen*. I could be with the man I had fallen so hard for only a few months ago, much sooner than I had ever anticipated. Of course, at the time, no one knew Saltford was going to suffer from a massive natural disaster (supernatural attack), or that my high school was going to be destroyed (pulverized by a demon), or that my friends had had their own transformative summers (becoming powerful elementals) and were changing their lives just as drastically as I was changing mine. It was scary and sad and exhilarating all at once.

Hurriedly, I toweled off and found a blow dryer in one of the many drawers in my rather large bathroom. Fumbling in my luggage, I found a brush and dried my hair before putting it up in a topknot. I applied a little bit of makeup, not knowing what to expect at the office. Were these offices dirty and industrial, or sleek and modern, or something else altogether? Marian hadn't told me how to dress, so I pulled out a pair of black jeans, my favorite ankle booties with a little bit of a heel, and paired them with a gray silk camisole and short black dress jacket. It was the best I had besides the gorgeous teal gown Antoni had gifted me with, and I wasn't about to wear that, so this outfit would have to do.

A final check in the mirror called for little hoop earrings, and then I felt ready to take on whatever was coming, especially Antoni. I took another peek at my phone to see that he still hadn't replied to my question. He was probably working.

Looking into the bright teal eyes of the young woman in the mirror—hair pulled up and back like she didn't need anything to hide behind, I smiled confidently. I grabbed my little purse and strode from the room in search of the dining room, where I hoped I'd find Mom. I had just pulled my door closed and was wondering if I was supposed to lock it, and whether someone had given me a key or not the day before, when Mom appeared beside me.

"Good morning, sunshine. You look nice."

I turned and gave her a kiss on the cheek. "You do too."

Mom was wearing black pants, flat Oxfords I'd picked out for her, a pale green blouse, and a black cardigan. Everything we wore was new, given we'd lost most of our clothing. Her hair was tied back in a low ponytail and her face bare of makeup.

"How did you sleep?" I asked.

"Like a dead log." She looped her arm through mine and steered me in a direction which I hoped led to the stairs. I didn't even know which floor we were on.

"I think the expression is either 'like the dead' or 'like a log,'" I replied with a smile.

"Why must you bore me with grammar?"

"Well, you know, you're the owner of your own salvage company now, not to mention a fine collection of really old soggy stuff you rescued from *The Sybellen*. I figured you might want to step it up a notch, is all."

"Ugh," she groaned. "Don't remind me. We could be exploring the Aegean by now." We came to the wide staircase I recognized and began descending. Mom cocked an eyebrow in my direction. "It's not too late to change your mind, you know. We could be braless and careless before lunch today."

I shot her a hybrid look of exasperation and amusement.

Mom had been more than incensed with me when I'd told her I wasn't interested in going to sea with her at this point in my life, and while some of that anger had fizzled after we'd inherited Martinius's fortune (manor, companies, and every other asset he and his family had worked so hard for over the last century and a half), it hadn't entirely gone away. Seeing the destruction in Saltford did put her ire to rest, and it wasn't hard to convince her to jet. But it seemed she was still hoping I would change my mind.

We were welcomed into the dining room by the smell of fresh baked goods, sausages, and eggs. While we filled our ravenous bellies, we speculated on what today might be like.

"Do you remember meeting someone by the name of Krulikoski, last time we were here?" I asked after swallowing a mouthful of scrambled egg and spearing a piece of cantaloupe.

Mom nodded. "The lady with the deep voice, from the party."

My memory finally opened and flooded with images of the elegant woman in the gray gown. I smacked my own forehead. "Of course! The CFO, the one who introduced Martinius."

She nodded. "Only I think she's the CEO now."

It came back to me. Hanna Krulikoski, she'd been given active control of Novak Stoczniowców Braciz after Martinius's death until the board made a decision about who would take the dead president and CEO's role. Marian had likely told me about the board's decision in an email, and I'd been too distracted to pay attention. I guessed they'd decided to make her position permanent.

I wondered where the chips had fallen for Antoni in the post-death shuffle of the Novak company roster. I hoped he'd done well for himself. He had big ambitions and came across as incredibly capable, but what did I know about what a company this size was looking for? I hoped for some kindly individual at Novak to take me aside and discretely fill me in on all the big players. A little bubble of anxiety threatened to inflate in my gullet and I shoved it down with a big gulp of orange juice. I was the owner of Novak now, but I didn't know what people expected from me. Were they going to be hostile? Did they think Martinius was a crackpot old guy who'd lost his marbles? I'd soon find out.

As we were finishing, a woman in a Novak household staff uniform came in and began to clean up. "Good morning," she said pleasantly. "I hope you slept well."

"Morning..." Mom looked mildly pained.

"Serafina." She smiled. "But everyone calls me Sera. Me and my husband Adalbert are your full-time live-in staff. Anything you need, just ask one of us."

We thanked Sera and made our way to the front foyer. Breakfast didn't settle happily in my stomach after all the mental speculation and I put a hand over my belly, feeling slightly nauseated. Give me a freaky demon-storm and I could stop a tidal wave, but put me in front of my 'employees' and my face went numb with trepidation.

A woman in a pantsuit and tailored jacket stood in the foyer holding a portfolio in her arms and chatting quietly with a fellow dressed in the navy Novak uniform. She brightened when she saw us coming.

"Here they are." She smiled warmly at us, the corners of her eyes crinkling. I liked her immediately. "Are you ready to meet your staff and see your offices?"

Mom and I glanced at one another. She tilted her head in my direction. "This is your rodeo, sweetheart. I'm just along for the ride."

I cleared my throat. "Ready as we'll ever be."

"Great." Marian turned to the fellow standing beside her with his hands behind his back and a serene smile on his face. "This is Adam Krulikoski, you'll remember him from yesterday."

Mom and I smiled politely at the gentleman neither of us could remember, but who more than likely met us at the airport the day before.

"Hello...again," I said, awkwardly.

He extended a hand and shook with each of us. "Anytime, day or night. If you need to be somewhere, I'm your man."

"That's very kind," I replied. "But we do have our

licenses, and thankfully you drive on the same side of the road as us here. Once we get settled in better, we'll look into getting our own vehicles. I'm not sure we require a driver."

"Mr. Novak did like to drive himself from time to time," replied Adam without missing a beat. "He has a small collection of vehicles in the garage. You could take your pick. They'll be yours now."

Mom and I shared another look and she murmured, "I'm not sure why we're not used to it by now. Private jet, personal driver, mansion on the beach. Why not a fleet of vehicles?"

"He has a 1969 Ford Mustang Shelby I'm rather fond of." Adam brightened. "Maybe I could pick you up in that one day?"

I didn't miss the warning look Marian gave Adam, and his resultant chastened expression.

"Sure, that would be fun," I said, and he smiled. "I don't know what a Shelby is, but Ford is American. That must have been expensive to bring over here to Europe."

"I'm sure it was," Adam said as we were escorted to the car and tucked into the back seat of its sleek black body. Marian slipped into the car with us and took the seat facing us.

"So, your last name is Krulikoski—are you related to Hanna?" Mom asked, peering at Adam.

Two spots of pink appeared on each of Adam's cheeks, and Marian gave a smile at my mother's nosiness, eyes downcast.

"Yes, ma'am. She's my mother."

"Cool. Call me Mira, though."

"Yes, ma'am. I mean, Mira."

Adam closed the door, went around to the driver's side, and got in. As the car pulled away from the front steps,

Marian put on her seatbelt and then opened the portfolio on her lap.

"I thought we could review the agenda on the journey," she said. "I'm sure that with the unfortunate natural disaster in your hometown, setting up your schooling, and all the preparation for the move, you haven't had much time to review my emails."

Mom and I looked at one another, mildly astonished. It was like Marian had anticipated precisely the state we'd be in when we arrived and pre-empted our embarrassment.

"She gets me," I stage-whispered, feeling grateful and wanting her to know it.

Marian chuckled. "This is what I do."

The car slipped onto a broader, faster moving freeway as we headed toward Gdansk. We could see the blue of the Baltic and the square peaks and troughs of the city, growing ever larger.

"First things first, you'll meet with Mrs. Krulikoski privately. She has a few things to go over with you, and she's also eager to get to know the two of you. After this initial meeting, you will have some paperwork to sign." She peered over her glasses at us. "You'll have to get used to that, I'm afraid. At least for now. After this initial meeting, Mrs. Krulikoski will introduce you to the board. Some of them you may have met briefly last time you were here, but there are also new faces, and people in new positions, so we'll get you up to speed."

"Will Antoni Baranek be there?" I asked.

Marian smiled pleasantly. "Ah, yes. Martinius requested he be your chaperone the last time you were here, correct? While your mother worked the salvage?"

"That's right." I bit my tongue against the urge to add

that we'd become close, or some other inane personal comment.

"I imagine the two of you became friends," Marian injected smoothly. "You'll be pleased to learn then, that Antoni has been promoted. He's on our international business development team, now."

"Good for him," my mother said softly, before bumping my shoulder with her hand and pointing out the window as the car exited the freeway and joined traffic on more historic and quaint streets.

Peering out of the window, I craned my neck to look at the tall, narrow buildings painted in different shades of green, blue, and orange.

"I thought the offices were at the harbor," I said as Adam navigated the car through the cobblestone streets.

Marian smiled. "Novak Shipping's first offices were near the port, but as the company grew and more offices were opened in Europe, the headquarters were moved to the downtown core."

We slowed as we approached a red brick building where a garage door was making its way open. The company logo—the one with the mermaid icon, rather than the old ship—had been painted over the garage and the main door. The red brick matched the manor, and the white trim around the windows was also the same as the Novak residence.

The car descended a short ramp and into the darkness of a small parking garage. We removed our seatbelts as Adam parked the car in a space marked 'reserved.'

"Everyone is ready?" Marian asked, a twinkle in her eye. "This is a big moment for us and for you. Novak Stoczniowców Braciz is yours now. The relationship between you and your company will last the rest of your lives, as you are the only living Novaks."

I wasn't sure what to say. There was no point in denying that we were Novaks. We'd already done that, and still been forced into claiming the Novak inheritance. If we hadn't accepted it, the whole thing would have gone to the government, all of what Martinius and his ancestors had worked for. It would have been enough to make Martinius turn in his grave. Still, it had sat uneasily with me and Mom ever since we'd signed the papers that day in our little kitchen, with Antoni looking on.

I smiled and reached for the door handle, but before I could get there, Adam was opening the door and extending a hand to help us out. It wasn't until we were headed toward the big silver elevator that I noticed my mother's face had gone pasty and she looked like she wanted to throw up.

THREE

We took the elevator up six levels. Marian used a keycard to take us to a floor labeled "NSB." I stood by Mom and put a hand on her back, concerned by her pallor. She gave me a wan smile, enough to say *I'll be all right.*

The door opened on plenty of natural light and a completely different kind of office than what I had been expecting. There were clear glass walls everywhere, white paint, and exposed red brick features. The brick pillars were home to black and white images of ships of all sizes and shapes. Some of the photos had the graininess of true vintage photographs and I assumed they had to be ships that the company had owned at some time in its long history.

The statuesque shape of Mrs. Krulikoski appeared in a doorway, silhouetted against the cityscape behind her. She looked the same as when I'd seen her at the party in the summer, but instead of wearing a gown she wore a simple gray pantsuit and white blouse with a ruffle at the neck. Her brunette hair was streaked with gray—an especially large shock of it over her right eye—and pulled into a low bun at the nape of her neck. Now that I was seeing her up close, I realized she was older than I'd first assumed.

"Welcome," Mrs. Krulikoski said, extending her hand to me first, then my mother. Her voice struck me again with its depth and warmth.

"Thank you, Mrs. Krulikoski," I said. "Lovely to see you again."

"Call me, Hanna. May I address you by your first names? Martinius and I always did, and we do prefer to be casual here."

We agreed and followed her into her office. Marian shut the door and we occupied the three seats in front of Hanna's glass desk while she went behind and sat in her office chair.

"Wow," my mom breathed, and I followed her gaze along the many photographs on the only wall that was brick. Mingled among the images of ships, ports and groups of people dressed in business attire, was a shot of Hanna and Martinius shaking hands. Then my eye found two black and white photographs which startled me right out of my calm.

"You have photos of *us*?" Getting out of my chair, I went closer to the candid shot of me and Martinius. Whoever had snapped the image had taken it while we'd been saying goodbye at the airport. He was holding my hand and smiling as the wind picked up my hair and blew it away from my face. In my hand was the envelope he'd just given me, the one containing the translated excerpt from his ancestor's diary—concerning Sybellen herself and the years leading up to the night *The Sybellen* had gone missing.

Reading Aleksandra's diary had been an emotional experience for me, and it had made me feel closer to the Novak family. Even though we weren't related, the fact that Sybellen was a siren tied me and my mother to the Novaks in a powerful way. Martinius's great-great-great-grand-mother never knew what Sybellen was, but what she'd written about Sybellen's behavior had been more than enough proof for me. The Novaks had siren blood, and now, Mom and I had inherited their legacy. I had to admit, there was a sense of poetic justice about it.

Below the photo of Martinius and me was a caption written in Polish, but my name was there, written as 'Targa MacAuley-Novak.'

"What does this say?" I asked Hanna, pointing to the Polish caption.

From her seat, Hanna steepled her fingers and smiled. "A long-lost daughter comes home."

Tears pricked my eyes and I looked away from Hanna. I hadn't expected that the new CEO of Novak really believed Martinius's claim that Mom and I were family, but it seemed she did.

The photo beside the one of Martinius and me was of my mother in her salvage gear. It was also candid, taken while she was talking with the dive team on the deck of *The Brygida*, their salvage vessel. She looked to be deep in discussion with Simon and Jozef, the weather-worn but handsome fellow she'd said goodbye to in a familiar way (out of character for my mother). They'd hugged, and my mother never hugged anyone except for me, my girlfriends, and Antoni.

She hadn't said much about Jozef since then, but I hadn't been imagining the connection between them. She'd admitted she'd felt something for him, but she cut me off whenever I had prodded for more. I glanced at my mother, relieved to see that normal color had returned to her face. She gazed at the photograph of her and Jozef, her expression closed.

There was no caption beneath the photo other than the date and a short phrase. I was able to translate the phrase as something to the effect of 'on board *The Brygida*.' My mother's name had been written 'Mira MacAuley-Novak.' 'Simon Nicholls' and 'Jozef Drakeif' were listed behind hers. Drakeif? What kind of last name was that? It sure didn't seem Polish to me, based on all the Polish names I'd been exposed to.

"It must have come as quite a shock to you to learn of your true heritage," Hanna commented from her desk. "It was quite a shock to us."

"I'm sure," my mother murmured as I returned to the chair beside hers.

"What did Martinius tell you about us?" I asked.

"Simply that you are his only living relatives and that you came from Sybellen's side of the family, of which there is almost no record."

"You had no trouble believing him?" my mother asked.

Hanna's dark eyebrows lifted a little, wrinkling her normally smooth forehead. Suddenly she laughed, as though the very idea of not believing Martinius was preposterous. "I have been part of this company for longer than you've been alive," she said to me, "and Martinius and I were friends for even longer. I would put more faith in something Martinius told me, even with no evidence to back it up, than a whole panel of people I didn't know who had reasons to believe otherwise."

Mom and I shared a startled look and I thought I could read her thoughts. We'd been expecting skepticism and resistance, but instead we were accepted as Martinius's bonafide heirs. It was baffling given that there really was no proven family connection between us.

"Shall we move on with the agenda?" Marian prompted.

"Let us do that," Hanna said, in that way that ESL speakers had of being technically proper. She glanced at me and I noticed that her eyes matched her suit, a light dove gray. "If you agree, I'd like to arrange a weekly meeting between you and me, as well as one between you and Marian. You and I will go over the important points about the company, whatever is the most valuable for you to know, as the owner." She nodded at Marian. "Then Marian can give you the company's background and history in detail. I think it is important for you to know the Novak story, because one day you might wish to work in some capacity. You may even want to take the position of CEO if you find yourself so motivated."

"I don't think that will ever happen. I can't imagine I would ever do a better job than you," I said, biting my cheek against a smile. The very idea was hilarious. "But I like the idea of meeting with you both. I'm interested to learn as much as I can."

"Good." Marian smiled and a dimple appeared in her cheek. "But we don't discount any possibility for the future. Agreed?"

"Agreed."

"You have your high school schedule settled? I understand you started a bit late?"

"I did, but it's going steadily now, with a slight blip as we prepared to move here."

"Excellent. You'll have to speak to our lawyer about the Novak family trust, but I know there is money set aside for post-secondary education, such as you'd like to pursue it."

I blinked and stared at her. The surprises had not ceased. "Really?"

"Yes, any school you would like. Do you have any particular one in mind? Any line of study?"

I hadn't thought that far ahead, and suddenly felt very ill-prepared, not just for this meeting, but for my future.

"I'm not sure," I replied, hoarsely, and felt Mom's hand on my shoulder.

I had thought that I would probably go to Dalhousie, in Halifax, or perhaps a local college near Saltford, maybe take a general arts program to start with since math and science weren't my strong suit. I'd always preferred history, English, geography, and the arts. But now, I could go anywhere. I had decent grades, and with the help of Akiko I had pulled my math and science courses up to B's and maintained A's in all other subjects—if by the skin of my teeth in social sciences and world religions.

Perhaps she sensed the borderline panic in my glazed expression because Hanna then said, "You don't need to make a decision right this minute. But in the new year it might be good to discuss some options with an academic advisor." She leaned back and put her hands in her lap. "I'm not interested in becoming involved in your personal life," she said, "but let me be clear that I will become involved should I sense any activities that might potentially be a threat for the company."

"What does that mean?" Mom didn't sound quite as alarmed as I felt by that statement, but close.

Hanna's voice softened. "I simply mean that because you are now the owner, and we are on-boarding you, so to speak, this is a fragile time in the company's history. This year will be defining, for the company and for both of you. We will need some time to learn how you are."

I still didn't totally understand what she meant, but her tone was not threatening, and there was something about

Hanna that I liked, something that I trusted. I nodded, not sure what else to say.

We talked about the schedule and selected some days and times that worked for all of us, before moving on to the matter of the staff at the manor.

"I don't know if you noticed, but we cut back on the staff at the Novak manor since Martinius's death, including the security at the front gate. It now operates by a remote, which Adam will make sure you have."

"I thought it seemed quieter than before," Mom said.

Hanna nodded. "It is, but now that you're here, you can decide if you'd like to bring any positions back."

"I don't think we need any staff at the house, really," I said impulsively.

There was a moment of silence while Hanna and Marian took this in. "With all due respect, some of those staff members have served Novak for a long time. It is old fashioned in your view, perhaps, but the manor used to employ a permanent staff of a dozen, plus casuals when we had a lot of guests, such as when you were here with The Bluejackets. We've cut the staff down by half, meaning those let go had to seek employment elsewhere. Are you certain you want to do all of the cooking and the cleaning yourself? Not to mention the maintenance of the gardens and the house? The yards are extensive..."

"It's okay," I said, holding up my hand to stop her as I realized my error. "We're just not used to being waited on, or living in a house of this size. We'll be happy to keep the staff that is left."

She nodded, satisfied. "Good, because I think you'll find that you're going to be quite busy between school, our weekly meetings, and various events and meetings throughout the year."

"More meetings?"

"I think it would be a good idea for you to attend our quarterly board meetings as well as our annual general meeting. If you find in the future that you simply have no interest in the company, then we can arrange to have you as a silent owner." She spread her palms up. "Totally hands off."

I nodded, although I wasn't sure about anything yet.

She gave me a serious look, one I thought was laced with nostalgia. "If you're anything like the stock you come from, you'll want to be involved up to your neck. Novaks are a very ambitious lot."

"What about Mira?" I asked, aching to get the spotlight off me after that rather pointed discussion.

Hanna's sharp, intelligent gaze landed on my Mom. "I understand you've chosen to retire from the salvage business? True?"

"It's true. I'm a little burnt out by the industry, if I'm honest," replied my mother, resting her hands on the arms of her chair confidently.

"If that is the case, then the salvage company can remain as is. We have a good team, and the company does well as one of our subsidiaries. If you ever change your mind and wish to become involved, just let me know."

Mira gave a nod. "I will. In the meantime, I'll support my daughter in the transition to European life, and in finishing her final year of high school."

This seemed to satisfy Hanna, but it made me feel like my mouth was full of sawdust. It was only a matter of time before my mother went to sea for her salt-cycle, and what would we tell people then? More importantly, how would I cope without her? I hoped her departure was still years away.

The rest of the meeting involved signing some documents and adding the board meeting dates into the schedule. When this was done, Hanna laid her hands on the desk and straightened.

"Very good. Are you ready to meet the board?"

We agreed and stood to follow Marian. She reached for the door handle but then stopped and turned to address Mom.

"I forgot to ask—one of the local museums here in Gdansk is curated by a lovely fellow by the name of Abraham Trusilo. He is looking to secure permission to feature the artifacts taken from *The Sybellen* in the spring. May I tell him he can borrow them?"

Mom blinked once vacantly as though she'd forgotten that the artifacts belonged to her, then registered understanding. "Of course. Please tell him he can. Any questions regarding the artifacts can also be answered by Targa; I'd like her to have control of them as well."

"Wonderful!" Marian scribbled in her portfolio. "I'll make a note of that and arrange a time for his team to come by the manor and collect the pieces they need."

We followed Marian into the bright hall and crossed to the other side of the building, Hanna following behind. Marian held open the door to a boardroom from which the buzz of casual conversation could be heard. Hanna walked past us and entered the room; we followed her. All conversation ceased immediately.

"Antoni!" I gasped, unable to stop myself.

He'd been standing by a small bureau where a coffee pot gurgled as it brewed next to a stack of cups. He'd been facing one of his colleagues and turned as we'd entered.

His cheeks reddened and he raised the coffee cup in his hand to salute me. "Hello, Targa. Nice to see you again."

I had to fight back the urge to leap across the boardroom table and fly into his arms, covering his face with kisses. The aloof tone in his voice and his carefully blank expression was the only thing that held me back. I had forgotten that Antoni was sensitive to how he was perceived by his colleagues—of course he wouldn't want to greet me affectionately.

"You, too," I murmured.

Mom poked me in the side and I thought I could feel her shaking from stifled laughter.

"Some of you will remember Mira and Targa MacAuley-Novak from the summer dive project and the party," Hanna said. "And all of you are aware that they've completed the big move from Canada and will resume life here in Gdansk."

I could hardly tear my eyes away from Antoni's face. It was only when Hanna began introducing the men and women in the boardroom that I forced myself to focus.

"This is Earnest Jurak, our CFO." Hanna gestured to a short, red-faced man in a suit that was a little too small for him.

"Pleasure to meet you, Miss Novak." His hand was cool and soft.

"And this is Hilary Osetek, head of mergers and acquisitions."

I shook five more hands until we came to Antoni, finally.

"You remember Antoni, of course." Hanna put a hand on his arm.

Antoni's hazel eyes met mine and a smile curved his generous mouth as my palm slid against his. He was as beautiful and enticing as I remembered him to be, and my fingers trembled.

"Congratulations on your promotion," I said.

"Thank you." He released my hand and it felt cold and bereft. "How are you settling in?"

I became aware that everyone in the room was watching us. "Great, thank you. Will we be seeing you later?"

A tinge of color revisited his cheeks and crept up from the collar of his shirt. "I... I'm sure we'll see each other around."

Hanna was introducing us to the remaining board members but I kept one ear on Antoni as he chatted quietly with my mom before she moved on to the next person.

After the introductions, the meetings were over and Hanna released us for the day as she and Marian joined the team for a meeting. I'd been hoping Antoni and I could slip away somehow for a proper hello, but he was needed in the meeting too.

As Marian led us away from the boardroom I looked back through the glass walls and found the top of Antoni's head. He looked up and caught my eye just briefly and I smiled at him.

"Miss you," I mouthed.

He'd already looked down again but not before I caught the smile on his face.

FOUR

A knock on my suite's door came while I was hanging the beautiful teal mermaid dress Antoni had given me. It was one of the few things that had survived the destruction of our trailer because I had taken it over to Georjie's house to show her. She told me she'd steam the wrinkles out of it. I left it in her hands, which had saved it from ruin. It had wrinkles in it once again from its journey back across the ocean, but it was in one piece and could be made to look as good as new again.

Going to the door, I found Adalbert, Sera's husband, in the hall. I was happy to find I did remember his face from my last visit. Finally, someone I didn't have to be reintroduced to.

"Oh hello, Adalbert!"

"Lovely to see you again, Targa. Welcome home. Antoni Baranek is downstairs waiting to see you. I'm sorry I didn't use the intercom, I had to come up anyway."

My heart leapt. "No worries. Thank you."

I left the suite and went down the main staircase to find Antoni still in his business attire, standing in the foyer.

He opened his arms and I flew into them. He kissed the side of my face and picked me up off the ground, crushing me against his chest. It felt so good to be held by him again, it felt like home, and the thought startled me.

Setting me down, he cradled my face in his hands and kissed me properly, softly and sweetly.

I couldn't help but smile when we separated. "Finally, a proper hello."

"Finally. Welcome home," he said, kissing me again. "I know it's late but I didn't want to wait to see you. We're working long hours at the moment as we're nearing the fiscal year end. I wish I still had the suite here, but that perk ended when I took my new position, and I can't stay, as I have an early start tomorrow."

My expression fell. "You tease."

I'd save the convincing him to move back in for when we had more time to be alone.

He gave a lopsided grin. "I know, I'm sorry. I can be back tomorrow evening around nine, if that works for you?"

"Nine?" I fought the urge to stick out my bottom lip. "So late?"

"I have a hockey game tomorrow night."

I brightened. "Why don't I come and watch? We can leave the rink together?"

"Really?" He looked delighted and bemused at the same time by this idea. "You'd really want to come watch me and a bunch of overgrown boys shoot a rubber thing around the ice for two hours?"

"Of course! You know it's Canada's sport? I got to see my dad play a couple times when I was little. I liked it, I would love to see you play!"

"All right, then. I have to be at the rink early and right after work. Can you get Adam to bring you?"

"I'm sure I can."

"Why don't you invite Mira to come, too?"

I said I would and we kissed one another good night. Dashing up the stairs to my mom's suite, I knocked on her door. When there was no answer, I went in.

"Mom?"

The suite was empty but I found a doodle on a piece of paper on the end of her bed. Picking it up, I smiled at the drawing. The message was for me and me alone, and it couldn't have been more clear. The doodle was of a little fish swimming in waves with a smile on its face, meaning: I've gone to the Baltic for a swim.

I HADN'T SET foot inside an ice rink since before my father died almost ten years ago. When I reached the rectangular, windowless building, I stood there looking at it for a few minutes before making my way inside. The smell of fries and sausages mingling with rubber and chemicals hit me as I stepped through the glass doors. The sound of people shouting, stick slashing on ice echoed through the metal double doors on the other side of a line in front of the snack bar. As rinks went, it wasn't so different from the ones we had in Canada, but they offered things like sauerkraut at the snack bar, and everything was written in Polish.

I stood in line for a hot chocolate and then passed through the double doors to find myself a seat. The stands were half full, leaving plenty of space for me close to center ice where I could see everything. Settling on the cold bench, I blew the steam off my drink and looked for Antoni.

Hockey wasn't a game I'd ever gotten into—actually, there weren't any sports that I'd ever become a fan of. But it was hard to avoid and if I had to choose a sport to follow, hockey would have been it, simply because my dad had loved it so much. It took me a few minutes of play to find Antoni, and even longer to recall the main rules of the game. Most of the players were tall and long of limb, and with their helmets on and the pace at which they skated, it was difficult to find him. My gaze repeatedly swept over the benched players and those playing until I found him. He was number 88 and once I realized that, it was much easier to keep my eye on him.

It didn't take long for me to learn that Antoni was a strong player, but that didn't surprise me. What did surprise me was that he moved with a powerful, almost predatory energy that I wouldn't have equated with him. Antoni was sweet, earnest, and gentle. This player was aggressive, bold, and full-on. He seemed to think nothing of elbowing his opponents, shoving them, charging through them, and yelling at them and the referee. Was I imagining it, or were none of his teammates playing with this same level of hostility? Puzzled by this, I became more engaged in watching Antoni's behavior than in watching the game itself.

When the clock ran out for first period and intermission began, I stood up on top of the bench so Antoni could see where I was. I waited while he was in conversation with one of his teammates and then waved when his eyes wandered up to the stands and landed on me. He lifted a gloved hand but didn't smile, and then filed toward the dressing room with the rest of his teammates. That confirmed my suspicion—something was wrong. Antoni always smiled when he greeted me, always.

I finished my hot chocolate over the middle period, watching with growing concern as Antoni's playing style seemed only to increase in hostility. He ended up in the penalty box near the end of the second period and didn't look my way before filing out for the second intermission.

During the final period, I watched completely bemused as he started a fight with an opposing player. The two big men grappled with one another, tottering on the ice and almost losing their balance before the referee stepped in and pulled them apart. There were a lot of shouted Polish epithets, at least that's what I thought they must be, as they were said with enough venom. Antoni served another penalty, but even assisting in the tie-breaking goal in the last three minutes of play didn't seem to cheer him up. He simply swung around the ice, stick out in front of him, not reacting while the fans (including me) celebrated in the stands. He touched gloves with a few of his teammates, but that was it.

I squinted at his face, hoping to detect a smile through his helmet, but there was no glimmer of white teeth. He looked up at me before heading for the change room. I sent him a thumbs up and he bobbed his head and gestured that he'd change and meet me in the lobby. I nodded and waved.

I amused myself by wandering along the glass cases filled with old black and white photos of hockey players from decades long past, tarnished trophies and medals, and vintage skates and hockey equipment. Players and fans talked and laughed as they left the building for the parking lot. The numbers dwindled and soon it was just me and the empty lobby.

The double metal doors clanked open and Antoni finally came strolling through, just saying goodbye to someone on his cell phone. There was a vein standing out on his forehead that normally wasn't there.

I turned and waited, letting him come to me. His short hair was freshly washed and spiked out from his head in all directions like he'd simply raked it over with a towel. He wore black jeans and white sneakers with a puffy bomber and carried a bulky hockey bag over his shoulder.

"That was quite a game," I said, deciding against asking directly what was wrong.

He tucked his phone away and met my eyes. His expression melted and he dropped his bag and reached for me.

Wrapping my arms around his neck, I felt him tuck his face into my neck. He smelled like soap and his wet hair left a damp mark on my cheek. He squeezed me hard and let me go.

"Thanks for coming, Targa. I'm sorry it wasn't one of my better performances."

"I beg to differ. I was riveted by the drama, the action, the intrigue." I smiled and touched his face and added, "The violence. I've never seen you like that before."

"I know." He bent to retrieve a hat from his bag, raked a hand over his hair and pulled it on. "It hasn't been a good day. Come on, I'll take you home."

He took my hand and we walked out to the emptying parking lot. Our breath hung in the air in front of our faces.

He opened the door to his car for me and I slid into the passenger seat. Popping the trunk, he dumped his hockey bag in the back, slid into the driver's side and started the engine. He pulled out of the parking lot and onto the road leading to the freeway heading south. I watched his profile in the darkness of the car, city lights blurring behind him.

I was about to finally ask him what was wrong when he said, "I've been thinking about Christmas. I have an idea."

"Okay. Proceed." I shifted a little to face him, curious.

"I was going to invite you to come spend it with my

family..." He opened his mouth to continue, but nothing came out.

"But? You hesitated like there's a but."

"Well, it's a little presumptuous." He shot me a sheepish look. "But Mom and my siblings already fill the place, and mine is just a little one-bedroom."

I thought I knew where he was going with this and my heart jumped with excitement. "Why don't you all come to the manor for the holidays?"

His hesitation morphed into relief. "Really? That would be so wonderful, Targa."

"Imagine the manor all done up with lights, that big sitting room with a fire and a tree. It's just been me and my mom for Christmas since my dad died, not including the one that Hal came to when I was barely old enough to remember." I almost bounced in my seat and was suddenly reminded of Saxony. Excitement had a way of reminding me of my wild-haired friend. "It'll be amazing. We'll make a turkey dinner and do it up properly."

Antoni was getting into the idea, his face brightening. "We can make coulibiac for Christmas Eve..."

"What on earth is that? It sounds like a sea creature, or a weed you can't get rid of."

He laughed and winked at me. "You'll see. I also have to take you to the Christmas market in Gdansk. You'll love it. Maybe your mom will come and I could bring mine?"

"Sure, that would be great." My mom hated shopping, and she sure didn't seem to be in much of a mood to do anything social these days, but maybe the festive season would help her feel better.

"This is going to be an amazing Christmas. Our first one." Antoni smiled at me as he guided the car around a turnpike. His hands had relaxed their grip on the steering wheel. "Christmas at the Novak mansion. How Martinius would have loved it."

The tension had gone out of his voice and I let out a breath. "You feeling better now?"

He shot me a look and then his eyes were back on the road. He took a moment before answering. "I am. Thank you."

"Are you going to tell me what's going on?"

He reached for my knee, his warm palm settling over the curve of my kneecap. I put my hand over his.

"Was it that obvious?" he asked.

I chuckled. "Antoni, you almost eviscerated one guy with your hockey stick, and I'm pretty sure the other one will be sporting not one but two shiners for the next two weeks. I've seen you step around a caterpillar on the sidewalk—imagine the difficulty I'm having putting those two concepts together."

He shot me a crooked grin. "Fair enough."

The car pulled off the freeway and onto the winding road which led to the manor. Dark trees over-crossed the road, throwing it into heavy shadow, while a line of white froth revealed where the water met the beach beyond.

Antoni had gone quiet and I wondered if it had been a mistake to ask him what was wrong.

Then he said, "What's a shiner?"

I laughed, relieved. "It's slang for a black eye."

"Oh."

Antoni entered the code at the gate and pulled the car into the driveway and up to the front of the manor where he put it in park.

"Not coming in?" I asked, hopeful.

He undid his seatbelt and turned in the seat. "I'd like to, but I have an early meeting tomorrow."

He looked down in his lap and looked as though he was thinking about what to say next.

"I'd like to say I won't keep you up, but we both know that's a lie," I said quietly, in an effort to lighten the mood. Antoni's resolve about us sharing a bed hadn't changed. He wanted us to wait. If it hadn't been the way my own father had been with my mother, I might have throttled him for being so frustratingly traditional. If I was human, I might have felt the same as Antoni—after all I was still only seventeen, but I was a siren, a creature whose main imperative while she was on land was to find a mate and have at 'im.

Antoni smiled. "I'll take you up on that one of these days."

"You'd better."

He smiled again, but his eyes were once again clouded with troubled thoughts. He rubbed a hand up under his cap and it slid off the back of his head. He set it on the console in front of the gearshift. "It's my sister."

"Lydia? What's wrong with her?"

He nodded. "I think she's fallen in with the wrong crowd."

"What makes you say that?"

"It might have something to do with her asking me for one thousand złoty to pay off a debt."

"That's not that bad," I replied, doing the math in my head. A thousand złoty equaled about three hundred fifty Canadian dollars. It was more than pocket change, but hardly a sum to freak out about.

"It's not the amount I'm concerned about, it's the frequency and the cause. This is the third time in as many months that she's asked to borrow money."

"Does she pay you back?"

He nodded. "Eventually."

"And what's the cause?"

"That's the thing. I don't know, she won't talk about it with me. I know my sister. She would only keep something from me if she was ashamed of it."

I frowned. "But you've asked her about it specifically, right?"

"I finally did, this time." He cracked one of his knuckles by pressing his thumb on the joint at the base of his finger, something I was coming to know he did when he was aggravated. "She basically told me to mind my own business. She says she always pays me back, so why should I care?"

"Have you asked Otto about it?"

Antoni waved his hand. "If she won't tell me then she won't tell Otto. They're not close and they don't move in the same circles."

"And your mom?"

Antoni's eyes widened. "Definitely I will not be bringing it up with our mother. Lydia would make shoes with my skin."

I bit my cheek to keep from laughing. I loved the way Antoni muddled English figures of speech.

"*If* she asks you again, say you'll give it to her only if she tells you what she needs it for. How about that? It's your money, you have a right to know where it's going."

"I will do that, but it might be another month before she asks me and what is she getting up to in the meantime?"

"You could always tail her if you were really concerned."

He blinked at me, astonished. "Tail? Like *follow*?"

"Sure." I shrugged. "She won't tell you, which makes you worry even more. What other way can you find out?"

"That's an invasion of privacy. You would do that?"

His scrutinous gaze made me shrink a little against the

seat, but I nodded. I would do that. I wouldn't think twice about it, especially if I thought a loved one was in trouble. But I lived in a world where demonic storm-ghouls attacked cities, and evil corporations plotted mayhem and chaos to feed their pet demons, not caring who they hurt to do it. I had to remind myself that most people lived in blissful ignorance about the preternatural world I was part of.

"And I thought your mom was the scary one," Antoni muttered.

I cleared my throat. "Well, I'm sorry to hear you're worried about your sister, but if you're not coming inside so I can pounce on you, then I'll say goodnight. We're polluting the yard."

"Right. Sorry."

"Don't be sorry." I smiled and leaned over the armrest for a kiss.

His lips were warm and pliant and the kiss lasted longer than I had been expecting. My body quickened, and I felt his breath come faster as I pulled away. I left my face close to his.

"You sure you won't come in?" I asked. My lips still tingled from the kiss.

His expression melted into one of tortured longing. "You're killing me."

"*You're* killing you," I replied with a smile. "It's your decision to wait, not mine."

He grabbed his knit hat from the console and smooshed it against his face and groaned in a comic gesture of tortured emotion.

I laughed and opened the car door. "Just remember, if you need help tracking your sister, I can move like a ghost through a back alley. She'd never even know I was there."

I got out of the car and peered in at him, one hand on the door.

He shook his head, gazing at me with something like admiration mingled with bewilderment. "Thank goodness we have no secrets between us, or I wouldn't be able to sleep at night."

My smile faltered.

"Good night, love," he said, his eyes soft and head tilted back against the headrest. My stomach gave a twist at the sweetness in his face. If he'd noticed my expression waver he didn't give any sign. I was grateful for the dim lighting.

"Good night, darling." I closed the car door and watched as he took the rotunda and exited through the gate.

No secrets? I had a whopper and had no idea what to do about it. It was a nice idea, to have a relationship without secrets, I thought. But it wasn't realistic for anyone, let alone a siren. A secret I had, and that was the way it had to be. My mother had lived with it while my father was alive, and I'd have to live with it too.

I went up to my suite, yawning with exhaustion. It seemed I could hardly keep my eyes open enough to crawl into my bed, but it took a very long time for sleep to claim me.

FIVE

Autumn became winter, the days grew short, and blustery gales blew in from across the Baltic. Sudden and intense winter storms left the coastline cities and towns coated in ice and out of electricity temporarily. The short-tempered fury of the Baltic stood in stark contrast to the deep cold Atlantic winter with which I had grown up.

The Novak mansion staff kept the rooms snug and cozy, with a throw on nearly every chair and couch, well-lit with yellow tinted sconces, and crackling fires in constant burn.

My weekdays became routine: breakfast at eight in the smaller of the two dining rooms, high school work alone or with an online tutor if need be (for math) until lunch. Lunch in the front room where the big picture window displayed the trees of the front yard and the thin line of the Baltic beyond it. After lunch, I would meet with either Hanna or Marian for a couple of hours, and after three, my day was my own again. Occasionally I would go for a swim with my mom, but more often than not she'd be gone already and I would be craving time with Antoni anyway.

On nights when he wasn't playing hockey, he would

come spend the evening at the mansion or he'd take me out in Gdansk, to a museum, a show, a restaurant, or just walking the historic center. Holiday lights appeared in the historic streets of the city, adding to its already considerable charm.

I adjusted to life quickly and I loved it, except for one thing—Mom's swims were getting longer and when she wasn't swimming, she was lethargic. She seemed apathetic about the details of my day. This was not like her. Mom had always been invested in conversation with me, in the details of my life and my friends' lives, but these days she was distracted in a way I had never seen her before. I started out concerned, but soon grew anxious.

One evening as I returned to the mansion, I spotted my mom talking to someone in the front yard under the cover of the gazebo. Squinting through the passing trees, I couldn't make out who it was she was with.

"Who is that?" I asked Adam as he pulled the car up to the front steps.

"Looks like one of the salvage team from the jacket, Miss Targa," he replied, bringing the car to a halt. "Only they have the crest on the shoulder like that."

"Right."

After saying goodbye to Adam, I went up the stairs to where the view of the front yard was better. Not wanting to seem like I was snooping, which was exactly what I was doing, I went inside the house. Leaving my winter gear on, I went into the front room with the huge windows and peered toward the gazebo again.

"Jozef Drakeif," I whispered, realizing that Adam was right.

It was the first time I'd seen him in the flesh since returning to Poland. I'd asked Mom once if she'd seen him and she'd said no and made some excuse as to why not—a reaction that seemed as much a part of this lethargy that gripped her as anything else.

I watched as Mom and Jozef stood and talked, until Jozef leaned in and kissed my mother's cheek before leaving. She didn't react to the kiss, only stood there and allowed it. Jozef hiked his jacket up around his ears and crossed to a black car parked in the manor's small visitor parking. He kept his head down against the wind, but the posture also made him seem defeated somehow. My mom watched him go, her face both impassive and yet sad.

I expected her to come into the manor, but instead, she turned for the path leading to the gate...and the beach.

I scampered for the door and took the front steps down in one big leap. Running across the grass, I caught up to Mom as she reached the gate.

"Where are you going?" I asked.

She turned back, one hand on the latch, and the look in her eyes made my stomach tighten. It wasn't the expression on her face, but the deep indigo color her eyes had become and the way the brows pressed down on them, the muscles tightening like cages.

"Swimming," she replied, simply. "Always swimming."

"You weren't going to..." I paused.

Maybe putting the expectation on her that she was always to share her secrets with me wasn't right. This new distant mother was unfamiliar to me, and made my heart ache, but I thought I understood something of what she was going through.

"I saw you with Jozef," I said, instead.

"Did you? Yes, he was here."

"Are you okay? He seemed upset." And she seemed upset, too, in her own quiet way.

"He came to ask me to accompany him to the exhibition in the spring, and dinner before that, so we could catch up."

My heart lifted a little. "That's great, Mom! You said he was one of the few people here that you liked."

"I said no, Targa."

My heart did a faceplant. "Why?"

Her hand still on the gate's latch, her exasperation broke free, and I felt glad for it. It was better than her introverted melancholy.

"To what end?" she snapped.

I had no answer to this. "But... you like him," I said, weakly.

"I more than like him, Targa. There is something connecting us that I cannot explain. The only way I can make it make sense is that if I were beginning a land-cycle, he would be my *one*, my love. My heart can feel it, but my body is pulling me the other way, to the ocean. There is no point in encouraging a relationship with him that I am unable to partake in. It would only break his heart, and mine."

Every word struck my chest with a fist of truth, and every sentiment sat in my mind like a cold brick. Another lash of suffering to add to what she was already bearing. She couldn't move on with her life until she went to the sea. It wasn't a matter of just changing our lives, keeping her distracted or entertained, or being able to go swimming as much as she wanted. She was inside a body that needed things to happen in the right season, and she was in the season of salt and fighting it. Worse, the fight was getting harder.

I couldn't think of what to say. She reached up and touched my face.

"You know where I'll be," she said.

I watched her pass through the gate. Her shadow grew thin as she hurried in the direction of the ocean.

"How long," I whispered. "How long can she do this?"

But this was not the question that I should have been asking and I knew it. My mother was the strongest person I knew, and she would deny herself everything to be with me if she thought I needed her. The question I wasn't brave enough to find the words to voice was: How long would I keep her from her fate?

SIX

A few nights later, I woke to the shushing sound of distant waves and an eerie quiet in the empty manor. The light of a half-moon fell across the floor through the warped glass of the old window nearest my bed. Feeling small and a little spooked, I threw the covers back and fished under the bed for my slippers. It would be nice to share a bed with my mom, and I wondered why it hadn't occurred to me when we'd said goodnight. There were fewer than four of us in the huge house at night these days and tonight, though nothing had changed about the building itself, the thought of being alone in this ancient and towering home made me think of ghosts, which in turn made me think of Georjie, which in turn made me homesick.

Padding softly on the carpeted hallway, I made my way to my mom's suite. The door was ajar and I pushed it open and entered.

"Mom?" I whispered into the gloom, hoping not to startle her. She'd always had reflexes like a cat and a preternatural awareness of what was going on around her, even at night while she was asleep.

No answer.

In the dim shadows I peered at her bed. The coverlet and sheets were rumpled and disorderly, as though she'd had a nightmare and thrown the blankets off in frustration. But she wasn't in the bed. I frowned, approaching the bed and resting my hand on the divot created by her body. It was cold.

"Mom?"

The old fears of my childhood emerged slowly, languidly. Memories of sitting outside my parents' room at night, with one eye leveled at the crack in the door, watching their sleeping forms, came to my mind. Fear opened in my heart—a blossom that only blooms in the darkness of night, by the cool blue light of the moon. In the dark, my anxieties magnified and my rational mind took a back seat to the horrible imaginings of my worst fears.

I searched her small suite of rooms, stumbling over a pair of shoes as I reached for the light switch. Electric brilliance flooded the space and I looked down to see that it was her everyday sneakers I had stepped on. Panic rippled up and down my spine and I took a deep breath in an effort to squash it. She was here. Somewhere. She had to be here.

I called twice more, louder each time but not so loud I'd wake the others asleep in the manor. Swallowing down a cold terror, I ran down the hall and to the main stairway. The foyer was a den of shadows, with only one dim and flickering electric bulb glowing from the sconce closest to the front door. They were closed and locked.

Mentally talking myself through my search, I told myself that there was no way she would leave without saying goodbye to me. She wouldn't do what Sybellen had done to her family—just vanish in a splash of seawater.

Would she?

As I took the narrow passageway leading to the back garden and private beach, my heart threw itself against my ribcage like a trapped animal. My mouth became an arid wasteland of panic as I threw the door open wide and yelled for my mother.

Only the wind answered. Heedless of the chill, being barefoot wearing only my pajama shorts and t-shirt, I ran across the yard to the gate leading to the beach path.

My vision blurred as tears of worry filled my eyes and spilled over, running down my cheeks and neck. Angrily, I brushed them away, straining to focus on the path ahead. The sound of the waves grew loud as I sprinted to the beach, stumbling in the coarse sand and weeds. Tough grasses ripped at the tender flesh between my toes. I barely noticed and staggered onto the beach, calling for Mom, throwing my words out over the Baltic with desperate abandon.

"Mira!" Her name ripped from my throat and the sound was a plaintive, agonized cry, even to me. I raked my hair back from my face, holding my head and biting my lip to keep from screaming uncontrollably. I tasted blood. "Please don't leave me. Not yet. I can't..." I took a shuddering breath. "I can't handle it. I don't know what to do without you."

I paced along the beach, frantically skimming the black horizon where the sea met the moonlit sky, helpless, not even knowing where to start searching.

"I'd give it all," I whispered aloud to any deity who might hear me and have power to help. "I'd give up all my elemental power, even my fins, to have her back. Please."

A shiny black head broke the surface in the distance, followed by her wet, white face.

I gasped, nearly choking on my relief. Sprinting into the

waves, I ran forward to meet her as her feet hit the sandy floor and she stood, naked and pale and beautiful.

"Mom!" I threw myself into her arms and she clutched me tightly, one hand against the back of my head, the way she used to hold me when I was upset as a child.

"Shhhh."

The taller of the two of us, she lifted me off the sand.

"I'm here."

The vicious pounding of my heart began to slow, and along with it my breath. Relief coursed through my limbs, making me feel weak.

"I thought you'd gone," I said, steadying my voice as I realized that if I fell apart on her in this moment, it would make the inevitable even more difficult...and dangerous.

"I wouldn't," she whispered, hugging me close and then releasing me as we were pushed around by the cresting waves.

She turned to face me and the moonlight illuminated her face fully.

What I saw there ran me through like a frozen blade. Her eyes were glassy and bloodshot, the skin of her cheeks had a stiff unyielding quality I hadn't seen before, like marble, as though expression was more difficult than normal. Lines of stress bracketed the sides of her mouth, making her look old, and her hand trembled as she lifted it to push her wet hair from her forehead.

The sight of that tremor in a body that had always been steady and more than strong—formidable—nearly undid me. My knees buckled.

She grasped my forearms and lifted me easily to set me on my feet for a second time, demonstrating that she was still powerful. "Hey, it's all right. I'm all right. Are you?"

The tears were still streaming down my face and I put

on a smile for her and brushed them away. I nodded. "I could use a fortifying swim, though."

Her brows rose a fraction, her eyes widening. "Now?"

I nodded, fighting a lively internal battle to keep the worst of my emotion from my features. "Now. Let's go. Please? Let's go..." I paused, searching for an idea, a distraction, something more than just a desperate swim in the dark trying to get away from my terror. "Let's go visit *The Sybellen*. I haven't seen the wreck since last summer, I would really love to see it again."

"Are you sure?" She brushed a wisp of my hair from my cheek.

I nodded, already taking my t-shirt off. "It's exactly what we need, to forget and enjoy for a little while."

She smiled. Some of the age vanished from her face, and some of the glassiness faded from her eyes. I tossed my clothing onto the windswept beach and without another word, my mother and I disappeared beneath the waves, leaving the human world and its many worries behind.

THOUGH THE WATERS of the Baltic were so low in salt as to almost qualify as fresh, they still offered the soothing, stabilizing effect I so needed. My heart resumed its regular rhythm as we swam through gloomy waters. Shoals of fish caught the moon and starlight as they flickered out of our way, and a grayscale sea bed offered up swaying tendrils of seaweed which reached up like an adoring crowd of fans as we swept by.

The swim to the wreck worked its miracle on me, and by the time we saw the mast in the gloom, all of my cares had shrunk to a manageable size. My mother regained her ageless beauty and powerful grace. I became more entranced by watching her than I did about the details of the wreck.

Her skin glimmered with a pearlescent sheen, and her torso seemed almost to glow preternaturally in contrast to the dark blue-green shades of her fins. Her long black hair fanned around her head, a shadowy halo swaying and darting in response to the elegant movements of her head and neck as she swam. Her face and its delicate features seemed so ethereal with its supernatural beauty that she hardly seemed to look like her human self.

Her expression was marred for a moment when her brows drew together and I followed her gaze.

"The foremast wasn't like that before," I observed, always a little amazed at how well our siren voices allowed us to talk underwater. The words came out clear, and without bubbles to garble them. "It must have collapsed since we were last here."

She made a thoughtful noise and swam closer, floating over the wreck's hunched and angular shapes. Detail became clear as we approached, and I noticed that other things had changed as well.

"Look." Mom pointed out a thick, algae-coated three-cord rope, coiled and scattered over the deck like intestines. The rope had clearly been moved, because nearby was a void in the algae marking where it had used to sit. The wood of the ship was bare where the rope had once sat, and little drifts of algae and particulate snaked their way around the deck, framing its old resting place and providing clear evidence that it had been recently disturbed.

Now that I was really looking, there was evidence of disruption all over the deck. The juxtaposition of items' current resting places and the outlines of their previous places came into focus like a three-dimensional drawing.

"Someone has been here," Mom said, her voice soft and calm. "Recently."

"Treasure hunters? Come to scavenge and see what might have been left behind? The location of the wreck is no longer a secret; anyone who wants to can dive on it."

She made a disbelieving sound back in her throat. "Maybe."

"Let's look inside," I suggested, my siren tones floating from my mouth and spreading around us like a musical chord that then faded slowly.

The last time we'd been at *The Sybellen*, Mom hadn't allowed me to go inside. She'd said it was dangerous, and because I was still so new, I didn't have the control over my body that I needed to have in order to fit into such a tight space without disturbing the things inside. But a lot of things had happened since we were last here, not the least of which being that the wreck had already been salvaged and I had mastered my mermaid tail. She didn't protest when I followed her through the hatch and into the belly of the wreck.

My eyes adjusted quickly to the dimness inside and I couldn't swallow down my startled, "Oh!" When Mom didn't say anything right away, I added, "Is this how you guys left it?"

"Absolutely not." Her voice was tight and not a little dismayed.

"Good, because what a mess."

We drifted through the first level where it appeared that someone had raked over every single surface and corner. The salvage team had done its best to disturb the wreck as little as possible as they retrieved the items of value, and my mother had made this task even easier for them by carefully positioning the artifacts so they'd be easy to spot and even easier to extract. This was what my mother had become so skilled at. I wondered how she felt to see that whoever had been here after the salvage dive had rendered all that fastidious work futile.

She didn't say anything as we combed over the deck and dropped into the next level, and then into the hull. Even the belly of the ship—which was smothered in silt and algae and littered with jagged, broken beams—had been torn apart by someone.

"What were they looking for?" Mom muttered, her gaze falling on a large wooden trunk. Someone had wrenched the lid off its hinges and cast aside the top. Now the trunk sat upside down, displaying an underside which had yet to become home to the Baltic's microscopic creatures.

I gave a little gasp as something shiny beneath the rubble beside the trunk caught my eye. I drifted over and picked up a small candle-snuffer with a delicately made handle.

"It's silver, right?" I held it out to Mom.

She didn't take it, but nodded. "Yes. I found it last summer, but it wasn't on the manifest, so I left it. Why wouldn't whoever was searching *The Sybellen* have taken it with them? It's definitely worth something."

"Maybe they weren't looking for treasures," I mused, unsure of whether or not I should put the candle-snuffer back. I elected to keep it unless Mom told me I should leave it behind. It would become my own private artifact.

"What did they want, then?" she asked.

"You know more about this wreck than I do. Was there anything else significant on the manifest or in the reports that Martinius gave to Simon?"

I followed Mom as she turned toward the hatch opening, clenching the candle-snuffer in my fist. When she didn't answer immediately, I continued, "Maybe paperwork? Legal documents of some kind? Proof of ownership of something valuable, like property or a bank account?"

Mom looked over her shoulder and gave me a bemused smile. "My, you have an active imagination."

"You said that sometimes even paperwork can survive underwater if it's protected well enough—tightly wrapped in leather or closed in a safe. Right?" I had to admit I was loving the mystery of it all, and my joy at being distracted mingled with the relief of seeing my mother appear as though all was normal once again. "What else would they be after if it wasn't leftovers?"

"I'm more concerned with *who* than *what*," Mom said as we retraced our path through the open hatch and out through the largest exit. "No salvage diver that I know, and no treasure hunter either, would ever do this to a wreck, not because they're good people, but simply because it would take too much energy for almost no reward. Not only that, it's *the way* in which it was done. Human eyes cannot make out details well enough in this gloom to dismantle things so expertly, and even a diver who has lights would be hard pressed to do this much damage, even on purpose."

A chill swept across my skin and I almost forgot to swim. "What are you saying?"

"I'm not saying anything for certain," she replied as she hovered over the foredeck and peered down at the wreck below us. "But I suspect this was done by a siren."

SEVEN

When Mom and I returned from our swim, I watched her carefully for any signs of that glassy-eyed look I'd seen when she'd come out of the water. Thankfully, her eyes seemed clear enough.

I went to my room to put on my pajamas and stash the candle-snuffer in a drawer. Grabbing my toothbrush, I brushed my teeth in her bathroom with her, instead of in my own. I poured her a glass of water and set it by her bedside table as she slipped into fresh pajamas. I even fluffed up her pillow and tucked her in once she was under the covers. Normally, my mother would laugh at these protective and motherly behaviors. She'd tell me to stop worrying and remind me that she was the parent and I was the child.

But she didn't laugh.

She gave no indication that my behavior was out of the ordinary. This scared me as much as the expression on her face when I'd finally found her.

Instead of returning to my own bed, I crawled in with her.

As the moonlight shifted the shadows of her room, I watched her as she slept. Eventually, I drifted into my own restless dream, one where I was still watching her face.

In the dream, her expression appeared peaceful enough, but a damp circle spread slowly from under her head, darkening the fabric and seeping across her pillow in all directions like blood from a slowly leaking wound.

THE NEXT MORNING, a sharp buzz from the intercom in my suite came as I was zipping up my hoodie and jamming my toes into my sneakers. I went to answer it.

"Mr. Trusilo is here, Miss Novak."

"Be right down," I replied. "And call me Targa. Is Antoni..."

"He's already in the foyer, Miss Novak...Targa."

"Great, thanks." Blowing a stray lock of my bangs away from my face, I threw open the door and padded down the carpeted hallway to the grand staircase.

When Mom and I had woken up, I was dismayed to find that she was complaining of a slight headache. Given that she never complained about anything, I suspected that the 'slight headache' was actually closer to 'apocalyptic migraine.' She begged me not to turn on any lights or open the drapes. I fetched her some ibuprofen from the first aid kit in the bathroom—though I knew she would never take it—placed a fresh glass of water on her nightstand, and told her to go back to sleep. I put a hand-scribbled 'do not disturb' sign on her door before closing it quietly and retreating to my own room to get dressed for the day. I would ask Adalbert to take her some breakfast later.

But as I closed the door, I heard her murmur something unintelligible. I opened the door again.

"What?"

She mumbled something again. Still I did not understand her. I walked back into the room and sat on the edge of the bed. "I'm sorry, Mom, I didn't hear you."

Without opening her eyes she said, "Amiralyon."

For a moment, I had no idea what she was talking about, but a second later it clicked. "You heard your name," I whispered, the hairs on my arm standing up.

She didn't respond and I realized she'd been talking in her sleep.

Amiralyon.

Every siren had two names, the one given to her by her parents, and the one the ocean eventually christened her with, which swallowed up the human name. I had heard mine whispered to my soul by the ocean after coming back from Poland at summer's end—Atargatis. Mom had complained that she'd never heard hers, which was strange for a full-grown mermaid. Now, finally, she had, and I wasn't sure how to feel about it. Had she heard her siren name because the ocean was calling her to it? Or did the timing have nothing to do with her salt-cycle?

Taking the wide steps down two at a time, I couldn't resist patting the shiny head of the mermaid sculpture on the landing. The gesture might have suggested to anyone observing that I was in a sprightly mood, but in reality, I said a prayer under my breath on behalf of my mother that she'd be feeling better by the time I was done dealing with the museum.

Turning the corner and continuing down revealed Abraham Trusilo, the museum curator, and Antoni, standing in the foyer and in conversation.

Abraham stood with his hands behind his back and round specs perched on the end of his nose. He was nodding and leaning forward on the balls of his toes and listening attentively to something Antoni was saying.

Both men's eyes caught upon me as I hit the main floor.

"Morning, Abraham," I nodded, then smiled at Antoni and reached up, intending to give him a kiss on the cheek. I stopped at the look of consternation which crossed his handsome face, and the nearly imperceptible shaking of his head.

"Good morning, Miss Novak," said Abraham. "It is remarkable, the resemblance between you and your mother. If it were not for your difference in height, I might simply mix you up." He chuckled. "Is she also to join us? I was hoping..."

"I'm sorry, but she's not feeling well," I replied. "She won't be with us today."

Abraham frowned and pushed his glasses delicately up the bridge of his nose. "I'm sorry to hear that."

"Me too." Antoni peered down at me. "Can we have something sent to her room? Does she need anything?"

"I've taken care of her already, but thank you." I took Abraham by the crook of his elbow. "I'll show you to the artifacts. They've been lovingly packaged and are ready to load."

"Okay." His brow furrowed, even as his cheek dimpled. "Uh, thank your mother for me, then. My team is in the van; let me get them."

"Antoni can tell them how to get around to the back, and we can meet them there." I crossed the foyer toward the rear corner where a small, ornate door led to a narrow hallway, which in turn would take us to a private stairway.

Out of the corner of my eye, I caught sight through the window of the front door of a familiar shock of blond hair and an even more familiar blur of blue jacket. Even warped by the glass, I would know that particular shade of azure anywhere, but I could not believe what its presence might mean.

"One moment, sorry," I murmured to Abraham and Antoni, waiting as Adalbert welcomed in the entrepreneur who had started Bluejacket Underwater and Recovery. I blinked in astonishment as Simon Nichols stepped across the threshold, doffing his blue baseball cap. He muttered a 'thank you' to the man who had let him in and seemed about to make an inquiry when his eyes fell on me. His expression brightened, but also seemed a touch sheepish.

"Simon!"

"Simon," Antoni said quietly under his breath, so only I and Abraham could hear. "As in Mira's old boss."

Abraham peered at Simon with a fresh curiosity. "How interesting."

Simon held the brim of his cap in front of his stomach now, his fingers bending it nearly in half. He was nervous. He approached, chin tucked down, almost like a puppy who knew he'd been bad. "Hello, Targa. How are you? How has the move been? I know this is a bit of a surprise."

"A *bit*? What are you doing here?" My voice had taken on a cast of the old siren brassiness, and I smiled in apology. "I'm sorry, I'm just very surprised to see you. What brings you to Gdansk, and our doorstep?"

"Hello again, Mr. Baranek." Simon extended to Antoni.

Antoni grasped it and the men shook heartily. "Nice to see you again."

I introduced Simon and Abraham to one another, both of whom had heard of the other through their proximity around the salvage of *The Sybellen*, but had never met.

Simon turned to me. "I'm here for an industry conference." His bushy blond eyebrows stitched together with concern. "I've been trying to reach your mother to arrange a time to come and see her, but her Canadian phone number no longer works and she hasn't been replying to my emails. Please, tell me she's all right?"

"Actually, she's not well, apparently." Antoni answered for me.

I agreed. "I'm sorry, Simon. It's not a good time for her to take visitors."

Simon looked alarmed. "I don't mean to pry, but it's nothing serious, I hope?"

It rarely gets more serious, I thought, *for a siren.* "No," I answered aloud. "She'll be fine. May I pass a message to her for you?"

"Uh..." Simon looked utterly nonplussed.

An arrow of understanding struck my mind, and I suddenly knew what Simon wanted. My eyes narrowed suspiciously and he seemed to wilt under my gaze like a daisy on a frosty morning.

Antoni glanced back and forth between us with curiosity, trying to read the unspoken exchange which had just passed between Simon and me.

Outside, there was a short toot from the horn of the a navy van with the museum crest emblazoned on the side. The driver peered out through the window.

"I'll give them directions." Antoni went to inform the museum staff how to access the rear of the manor.

"We're sort of in the middle of something," I said to Simon, not doing a lot to prevent an icy film from coating my words. "The museum has come to gather some artifacts for an exhibit in the new year. We'll be busy with this for most of the day."

"Could I offer my help?" Simon perked up, his gaze

swinging to Abraham. "After all, I already know the arti-facts and how they must be handled. I ran the salvage oper-ation." He said this as though he was terrified history would forget his place in this story.

"And a splendid job you did, too. We'll be discussing it as one of the best examples of this kind of work ever in the history of salvage for many years to come. You sir, must have a good luck charm stashed in some secret place."

Abraham beckoned Simon to join us and before I could protest, we were on our way to the rear of the manor through the narrow passageways. Simon and Abraham struck up a lively conversation about the unique quality of Baltic finds, while I shot daggers with my eyes through Simon's back. It was surreal, seeing my mom's old employer here, unexpected, unannounced, and in my view, a little unwelcome if all he was after was attempting to draw my mom back into his employ. It wasn't going to work, and if I wasn't so annoyed with him, I'd feel sorry for him.

But as we made our way into the depths of the Novak manor, I began to understand how I might be able to take advantage of the situation. My expression softened toward Simon, and pity crept into my heart. Perhaps his unex-pected arrival here was just what I needed.

We met Antoni at the loading bay in the rear and swung the doors wide, locking them into place. The Novak manor's ground floor was a big concrete box used mainly for storage. There was a cold cellar full of preserves and root vegetables, dusty old bicycles, and a door leading to the garage where the vehicles and a small vehicle repair shop were housed. The nicest part of the basement was a large workshop with wooden shelving, drawers, worktables, and woodworking tools no one used anymore. One part of the large workshop had been converted into the storage area for

The Sybellen's artifacts. Abraham's team moved into the storage space and pored over the carefully boxed and labeled items from *The Sybellen*.

While Abraham was directing his team on which items to load first, and Antoni stepped in to help, Simon sidled up beside me.

"So, how's life been for you guys? Are you missing Saltford?" He jammed his hands into his jean pockets and swayed forward onto his toes. It was painfully obvious to me that he wasn't here because he was concerned about how Mom and I were settling in.

"Guile doesn't suit you, Simon," I replied, softly. "Why don't you tell me what you're really doing here?"

We stepped back to make room for the museum team as they passed from the loading van to the storage room and back again.

Simon looked crestfallen. "Is it that obvious?"

"Yes."

He seemed taken aback, but his consternation didn't last long and he considered me in silence for a moment. "What else should I expect from Mira's daughter? You're as blunt as she is."

I gave him a close-mouthed smile and crossed my arms. "Some might say I'm even more blunt." This was true, but it hadn't been before I'd had my salt-birth; becoming a siren had a similar impact on my personality as it had for my mother—we could be candid bordering on tactless.

Simon blew out a breath and seemed to surrender himself to the cause. "I was never much good at being sly, anyway." He looked me in the eye. "Truthfully, things haven't gone well at Bluejackets since your mother left."

"Oh?" I'm sure my face failed to register surprise.

He shook his head. "I had three jobs lined up already,

before she gave her notice. The first two jobs both came in behind schedule and over-budget, and the third one backed out when they saw how things were going." He chewed his lip and shifted his weight back again, leaning against the beam behind him. "Your mother is the greatest salvage diver I have ever known, but there is something even more to her than just skill. She's like a..." he colored.

"What?" I pressed.

"A good luck charm," he mumbled, his cheeks flushed. "I never believed in that kind of nonsense before meeting her, but..." He shrugged.

Antoni passed by carrying one of the larger boxes stamped with the Novak emblem and labeled with its ID number and particulars of the wreck. He glanced at me with concern as he walked by, cocking an eyebrow. I knew what he was asking. Was everything okay?

I gave him the subtlest nod.

"You don't think your mother would be interested in becoming a partner with me, would she? I mean, I was kind of looking forward to making her an offer in person, something special. But from the look on your face when you saw me, I have a feeling she might not be so keen."

I tried to look thoughtful.

Simon responded to my silence with a hopeful expression. "I'd give her the most flexible position anyone could ask for. Bluejackets would fly her out for the important jobs, taking care of every cost, she'd join the team for the duration, and then return to Gdansk to be with you for a long break in between." Simon's words flowed faster now as he described what I'm sure he thought was an ideal scenario for Mira. He'd do his absolute best to schedule the bigger jobs with a long break in between, and he'd bid on more European jobs so that she wouldn't have to travel so far.

They'd buy or lease an apartment in Saltford for her, for times when she needed to do prep work with the team, or consult, or come to team meetings...

I listened as though I was actually considering his offer, but inside I knew that Mom would never entertain it, even if she didn't already own her own salvage company and wasn't wrestling the call of the ocean. The very idea of flying all over the place to work, of donning all that gear, of spending more time with the team she'd never gelled with... it was preposterous.

Preposterous and fortuitous.

"I'll talk to her for you," I finally said, once Simon appeared to have exhausted his pitch.

"Would you?" The look on his face sent a dagger of guilt into my heart, but I forged onward. Mom needed this.

"Sure. I can't make any promises..."

Antoni passed by again, and I knew he was catching bits of our conversation, though he feigned as much disinterest as the museum employees. He shot me a look and winked without smiling, which had the strange effect of both compounding my guilt and making me feel grateful that he was here.

"I understand that," Simon was saying, palms out in a gracious gesture. "I'm just so happy you'll mention it."

"How long are you in town for?"

"Uh..." Simon's expression froze in a locked expression of fear for a moment before it passed. "How long *should* I be here for?" He blushed again.

"There is no industry event, is there, Simon?"

"No, there is," he stuttered. "It's just not *my* industry." He laughed but it was awkward, and stilted. He cleared his throat. "Is there no chance I can see her later today, or tomorrow?"

I shook my head, expression stony. "I can call you once I've spoken to her."

"If that's the best we can do, I'll take it."

Simon moved to help Antoni and the museum team finish loading the van and then dismissed himself, making sure I had his number before he left.

We said goodbye to Abraham and the team, and Antoni pulled me into his arms after we closed the rear door.

"What was that all about?" He kissed me softly and his enticing natural scent settled over me, making my head spin.

"Simon wants to offer Mom a partnership, one with quite a few perks and the flexibility to be here in between contracts." It had been a struggle to get all the words out without sighing with pleasure at Antoni's close proximity. I stepped back and slid the bolt on the back door home.

"Really? Do you think she'd go for that? She's got a salvage team here which she can run if she wants to." Antoni followed me up the stairs.

"It's not quite the same, and I'm not sure Simon knows about that. She has been missing her team," I lied smoothly. "It hasn't been all that easy, adjusting to life in Gdansk. It's so different from what she's used to."

As we crested the stairway and stepped into the dimly lit hallway, Antoni peered down at me skeptically. "I'd believe the last half of that sooner than I'd believe the first half. Don't forget I spent some time with The Bluejackets during the salvage, and I didn't see a lot of love between Mira and her colleagues." He raised his brows and shrugged a shoulder. "Just being honest."

"Do you see much love between Mira and anyone, except for me?" I shot back my own cocked eyebrow. "You might think you know my mother, but you don't."

"Touché," he acquiesced, his expression turning thoughtful, like maybe I was right and he'd misjudged the situation.

Feeling bolstered, I carried on. "She worked with those guys for almost seven years, she was the Rockstar of the Deep, don't forget. The North American industry press called her that. Here, she's nobody."

"She's not *nobody*," Antoni protested with vehemence. "She's a Novak, she's an owner of the famous ship *The Sybellen*, and president of one of the better European salvage diving operations this side of the Atlantic."

"You're just as bad as Martinius was. We're *not* Novaks. We're MacAuleys, and she doesn't know any of the Novak team," I protested. "She has history and camaraderie with The Bluejackets." I twined my fingers through his and his hand enveloped my own with its heat.

"She does know them," he disagreed. "What about that fellow she seemed to take a shine to last summer, as much as she can take a shine to anyone who isn't you," he added as an afterthought.

"Jozef?"

"Yes, him. I thought they had sparks, even if they were only professional ones, but maybe that was just me."

My face was a mask, but Antoni was actually impressing me to the very soles of my feet with his insightfulness. He didn't miss much, this love of mine.

"Unfortunately, they're not getting along so well anymore."

"What?" Antoni rolled his eyes and let out an exasperated sigh as we came through to the front foyer again. "I swear, it's like a sitcom around here," he muttered. "Or, a soap."

One of the Novak staff crossed from the east wing to the west, and Antoni let my hand fall.

I frowned at him, not hiding my displeasure. "Speaking of a soap."

He gave me a withering but good-natured look and deftly skirted the topic of us-in-public. "So you're going to tell Mira what Simon said? See what she has to say?"

"Of course. I said I would. As soon as she's feeling better."

"And what do you think she'll say?" Antoni seemed apprehensive about my answer and I was struck by a second guilt-blade in the gut. How could I continue to deceive him like this? Especially considering how hard I had tried not to use my siren voice on him in the past, and how I'd vowed not to use it in the future.

"I'd say the odds are pretty good that she'll be interested," I said, hating myself for how easily the fiction dripped from my lips. "It's a very tempting offer."

"Damn," Antoni said, softly. "And I was just getting used to having her around again. Your mom is a special lady, intimidating as hell, but special."

I smiled. "That she is."

EIGHT

Mom was special, and she was also suffering in a special hell reserved for sirens coming to the end of their landcycle. Winter transformed into the holiday season, and my hopes that my mother would pass through the call of the ocean and come out of the other side relatively unscathed were still unmet. She could swim whenever she wanted, and did so, frequently and for long periods of time, but her lethargy only grew.

Weeks passed with a routine that steadied me. Meeting with Hanna and sometimes Marian to learn about the Novak business, doing my online classes, studying for tests, having video calls with Saxony and Georjie every couple of weeks, and spending as much spare time with Antoni as I could while keeping an eye on my mother—it all made the time fly by.

When Mom was at sea, I couldn't sleep and was never quite at ease. The haunting fears of my childhood had come back with an intensity that took my breath away. During the day, I could fight them back with the belief that my mother would always come back, she would never leave without saying goodbye. She hadn't even brought up the possibility, didn't so much as suggest that it was on her mind to leave. She wouldn't slay me by doing something so cold as going for swim and not coming back. This I knew, during the day.

But at night...

At night, my mind became an eerie place full of tormented visions, irrational misgivings, hag-ridden by vivid imaginings of my worst fears come to life. The mind is a powerful thing, and as potent as it was in the daytime matched how vigorous it could be at night when the shadows were deep and long—when it slipped out of its tethers and frolicked without restraint.

Antoni, Hanna, and Marian frequently began to ask me how I was sleeping and if I was feeling well.

Mira never asked if I was feeling well, and that was only one of the breadcrumbs she was leaving for me as the ocean's briny fingers slowly wrapped themselves around her mind and began to squeeze.

By the time the Christmas holidays were upon us, I knew it would to be our last together, possibly ever. What I would have paid to give my mother the gift of freedom from her siren cycles, I would have given everything: sold Novak Shipping to the highest bidder, auctioned the house and all the artifacts from *The Sybellen*. Maybe she would make it to my February birthday, maybe she'd even make it to my graduation, I didn't know. But this Christmas I would not waste. I would soak up every minute I could have with her.

Antoni and his family arrived at noon on Christmas Eve. Lydia and Otto were there more in body than in spirit. Lydia turned out to be a tall and slender girl with a punk hairstyle. She wore mostly black with heavy black eye make-up. Her one colored item of clothing was a plaid coat with a skull patch on the shoulder. Any hopes I had of becoming friends with her, and maybe helping Antoni figure out why she'd been asking for money, evaporated as soon as I met her. Coolly detached, Lydia spared me only weighing glances that seemed to say she wasn't certain I was worthy of her handsome, successful older brother. She made more of an attempt to talk with Mom, who'd achieved some small level of celebrity status in Gdansk since the salvage, but soon gave that up when Mom gave her as cold a shoulder as she was giving me. She soon retreated to chairs situated in corners and glued her eyeballs to her phone.

The familial resemblance between Antoni and Otto was obvious, though Otto was a little shorter in stature, a little more baby-faced, and with gray eyes instead of green. He was shy and also mainly absorbed in his phone. Much to Antoni's chagrin, Otto politely injected into conversation that he'd been invited to a party that night and would probably slip out after dinner.

But Antoni's mother, Waleria, brought a warmth and sweetness to the house that put me at ease. She spoke no English, which left Antoni to do a lot of translating, but she oozed kindness. She was a tall, slightly stooped woman, with very short silver hair and glasses with a chain to hold them around her neck. She brought three traditional Polish dishes to add to the turkey, scalloped potatoes, and pie I had suffered to make, using online video tutorials every step of the way. I had found the cooking and baking a good distraction. Mom even chopped the apples and potatoes for me, while Antoni grated cheese and fried things as required. Adalbert and Sera had gone to Sera's family in Warsaw for the holiday, and though we were lost in the gigantic kitchen, we started early and fumbled our way around until good smells began to fill the manor.

The six of us sat down to a very enticing meal, Antoni at

my right elbow and my mom directly across from me between Lydia and Otto. Antoni's mother was seated at the head of the table, against her many protestations.

"Is your mom okay?" Antoni leaned in and whispered to me over the dessert. "I've never seen her eat so little, and she hasn't even touched her pie. She's usually ravenous."

Mira's eyes flicked to Antoni's face. She hadn't missed a word he'd whispered. She sent him a stiff smile and picked up her fork.

"She's all right," I said, quietly. "Maybe just a little tired."

"What's she been up to? She's never here when I visit and she clearly hasn't taken The Bluejackets offer. What's keeping her busy?"

"She's still considering it," I said, glancing quickly at my mother. I hadn't told her about Simon's visit or offer because I knew she'd never take it. She'd heard what Antoni had said, but hadn't reacted, not even a little. "She's got her own projects."

"Like what?" he persisted. "Maybe it's something I can help her with?"

Lydia's chair squeaked against the floor as she got up, leaving her napkin on her plate. "Thanks for dinner. I'm going to catch a ride with Otto and meet up with Makary, wish them a happy Christmas and all." She touched a finger to her forehead and looked at me, as though saluting me. "Enjoy your evening, nice seeing you again."

"You too, Lydia," I murmured.

"Really?" Antoni frowned at his sister, unimpressed. "You're not even finished with your dessert."

"I told you I wanted to go out."

"No you didn't. Otto did."

Otto stood also. Picking up his plate, he said, "Where should I take this?"

"It's all right, we'll look after it," replied my mom. My gaze darted to her again, for I thought I'd detected the faintest multi-layered siren sound leaking into her voice. Had she meant to do that, or had she slipped?

As though she'd had the same thought, my mother's lips pinched shut and she looked down at her plate. Her throat moved as she swallowed.

Waleria spoke to both of her younger children in Polish and they each kissed her on the cheek before leaving. No one protested any further, whether it was because they'd thought there was no use arguing for the kids to stay, or my mother's possible siren slip-up had soothed the tension in the room, I couldn't tell.

After dinner, we put on some vintage Christmas music and cleaned the dishes and the kitchen before slipping into the living room for the evening. Antoni stoked the fire already crackling in the hearth and I plugged in the lights and decorations Adalbert and Sera had put up. The room glowed with white and blue holiday lights and the fire threw a warm glow over everyone's faces. Mom had suggested in early December that we donate money to a charity rather than giving gifts as we had everything and more that we could ever need, and no one protested, so there was nothing but tinsel under the tree.

Waleria sat in the rocking chair and pulled out a minia-ture quilt she was working on. Antoni taught me a few confusing Polish card games, teasing me when I didn't catch on very quickly, until I taught him one of mine and the tables turned.

Antoni's gaze kept flicking to Mira where she sat in one

of the overstuffed brown leather chairs near the window, looking deeply lost in private and serious thoughts.

"Did I tell you that one of my best friends is coming for a visit in the spring?" I said.

Antoni's eyes came back to mine. "No, that's nice. Who is that?"

"Georjayna Sutherland."

"The redhead with the temper?"

I laughed. "No, that's Saxony, and her temper isn't so bad anymore. Georjie is the tall blond one."

"Has she ever been to Poland before?"

I shook my head. "No, and she's not going to stay any longer than a week. She's detouring in this direction to meet you and hang out with me before going on to Scotland."

"Scotland." He brightened. "I have always wanted to go there."

"Me too. Perhaps we should go sometime."

"I'd like that." His eyes flicked to my mom again. He leaned in. "I'm sorry to harp on this, but Mira just isn't herself tonight Are you sure she's all right?"

Though she was across the room, her siren hearing meant she'd heard, Mom got up from her chair and came over to Antoni and me.

"I have a little headache, sunshine," she said, touching my hair. "And Christmas always makes me miss your father," she added, purely for Antoni's benefit. Not that she wasn't missing Dad, we both felt his loss keenly during the holidays, since it had been so close to Christmas, and on his birthday, too, but Mom never talked about it, never used it as an excuse for behavior. Just the way she never talked about suffering through the pull of the ocean, or complained about bodily pains or emotional turmoil.

Antoni nodded and smiled at her. "Understandable. Have a good sleep and see you in the morning."

Mom said goodnight to Waleria, kissed my cheek and headed to bed.

"I get it now," Antoni murmured.

I nodded. Mom had saved me from having to make another stupid excuse for her. Always thinking of me.

Hope glimmered with a hard bright flare as my thoughts wandered back to Georjie. She had helped all those people after the disaster in Saltford—was there something that she could do for Mom? Could my mother even last until Georjie arrived? It seemed like our only hope. Georjie was an elemental, and what ailed my mother was magical in nature. Perhaps Georjie was just what Mom needed to be free.

The rest of the holidays passed uneventfully, and as we rang in the new year, Antoni went back to work and I tackled another semester of school. Life seemed an endless roundabout of routine, one my mother became more and more absent from as her lethargy grew. Helplessly, I watched for her return from her swims, coaxed her to eat, and felt despair hook its talons into me as she slipped into a place where I could not reach her.

NINE

Something was desperately wrong, I knew it before I even opened my eyes. My body went from asleep to tense and fully awake in the length of one sharp inhalation. My head came off the pillow and my eyes found the digital clock on my nightstand: one thirty-three in the morning.

My room was painted in a million shades of indigo and black, and the barest of starlight cast a shadow on the carpet where it pooled in a soft rectangle. A figure in my periphery brought me all the way up to sitting, in full alarm and with my siren voice swelling in my throat.

At first it seemed a specter from a horror movie—a pale-skinned girl with her head bowed and her long black hair obscuring her face, her posture not just broken-hearted, but broken-of-spirit. My heart leapt into the back of my throat and trembled there with fright, my fingers became spindles of ice. I knew this pale broken-spirited woman.

"Mom?"

I could hardly equate the figure standing at the end of my bed with my powerful, fearless mother.

Slowly, she raised her face and her hair fell away. "I'm sorry," she whispered.

Half convinced I must be dreaming, because surely this stooped and defeated creature was not Mom, I scrambled over the covers and across the bed to her—afraid of touching her but more afraid not to. I desperately hoped I was still dreaming, and that I'd reach for her only to wake up and discover it was all a nightmare.

"Sorry for what?" I put my hands on her arms, slid them up to her shoulders, to her neck as she raised her eyes and looked at me.

Those piteous orbs made my throat close in on itself, choking back a scream.

"I need you to lock me in." Her whisper became a soft-spoken supplication.

The flesh of my entire body crawled with gooseflesh. "What?" I couldn't have heard her right. My own voice sounded high and fearful, I barely recognized it, and despised it at the same time.

Her siren voice filled my room. "Lock me in my room," she said beseechingly, her siren violins grating in an ugly dissonant way. Her command had no effect on me, but my body shuddered at the sound. Her formerly beautiful voice was raw, damaged, and desperate. She sounded *out of tune*.

The diary of the long-dead Aleksandra Novak came rushing back to me, ice-water flooding my brain and making it ache. She had written of this very thing. The siren ancestor of the Novaks, Sybellen, had also asked to be locked in, not long before she'd vanished for good.

"Lock me in," she croaked again. "Please."

Her voice broke on the word *please* and I began to tremble, quaking in my knee joints, in my shoulders and elbows, at the base of my neck.

I had to lower my own face to hide my expression from her. I had never, until that moment in time, felt such self-loathing. I was a disgusting, selfish, wretched, and pathetic excuse for a daughter. Tears of rage burned behind my eyelids and I took a slow, deep breath and fixed my expression. Aiming for pleasant and probably falling somewhere in the vicinity of pained, I looked up at her. The corners of my mouth were quivering, and I hoped she couldn't see it in the dark, though I knew I was fooling myself.

"Come on, Mom. We're going down to the beach."

Silently, without any shoes or warm clothing, we slipped from the sleeping manor like the ghosts that we were. That's what my mother had become, I thought bitterly as we crested the dunes and approached the sacred place where the water met the sand.

My mother said no words as I led her to the Baltic. She moved like a vacant body, a shell with no thoughts of its own.

By the time we were standing in the surf and facing one another, siren tears were pouring down my face. I put my arms around her and pulled her close. She moved to hug me back, but too slowly, and her lack of 'self,' the pure absence of her 'Mom-ness,' brought a fresh wave of salt water flowing down my cheeks.

"Mom, it's time." My voice was steady, and I was grateful. "You've done everything for me, you've sacrificed so much. I'll probably never know how much."

Her eyes were limpid pools in the moonlight, huge orbs expressing a struggle to understand, a slow dawning realization of what I was saying, what was happening here.

My heart broke when I looked into those eyes and it gave me the will to go on. My breath hitched.

"You taught me what love is, you made me who I am

today. You gave me independence and resourcefulness. Your strength has made me strong."

"Targa—"

"You are not you, and I won't have you with me as a shadow of your former self. I can't bear it. You have to go. Be free. I hope that you can forgive me one day."

"Forgive—?" Her hand drifted slowly toward my face and she began to shake her head, *no*.

I nodded. "Yes, I need your forgiveness. I'm sorry I wasn't strong enough to let you go before it came to this."

"No." Her eyes seemed to clear a little and she pulled me into a hug as I fought back the sobs threatening to wrack my body. She whispered against my hair as the surf swirled around our ankles. "Shhh. There is nothing to forgive."

She was wrong, but we weren't here to fight, and I was quickly losing my resolve.

"I love you, Mom. I'll always love you."

"I love you, too, Targa." Her words came very slowly, almost slurring, like it cost her physically to say them.

I kissed her on both cheeks before stepping away. "Please, go. Go, now. You're free."

My knees were shaking so hard, I thought that if she waited another second, I would collapse, and then she would never leave.

Her own siren tears were slipping down her face now, and she gave me a lingering look as she walked backward into the water, the Baltic soaking through her clothing.

"I love you," she whispered slowly, but with a gathering power, "more than anything."

She tipped her chin up as the water reached her neck, and the moonlight bathed her face with light. For one moment I saw the potent, beautiful being that she was, her eyes clear, her expression lifted. She was a goddess, a deity of the underwater realms and all their mysteries. She was not meant for the land, not right now.

The water closed over her, and she was gone.

I stood there on the beach, hugging myself, tears pouring down my face. My knees finally did give out, or perhaps it was just the will to hold myself upright. I collapsed on the sand and wept in earnest.

I MUST HAVE MADE it back to the manor at some point, as daylight found me waking in damp sheets and with my face pressed to a wet pillow. I might have laughed at what a nuisance siren tears could be, but I felt too hollow and too sad inside. Mom was gone and I didn't know when, or even if, I'd ever see her again. As I thought about it, my tears began to well up again, blurring my vision and threatening to dehydrate my body further.

I threw the blankets off angrily. I grabbed up the glass of water on my bedside table, opened my throat, and swallowed it in one big gulp. Clacking the cup down on the wood, I tore the sheets off my bed to let the mattress dry out. Dumping the wet linens onto the floor, I changed from my damp pajamas into jeans and a red zip-up hoody. Moving a little too fast and with a little too much vigor, I jammed my feet into a pair of boots, grabbed all the laundry, and left my suite.

After reaching the laundry chute, I crammed the bedding and clothes into the rectangular hole and sent them tumbling into the laundry room three stories below. I took a shuddering breath as thoughts of my mother's face disappearing under the waves invaded my mind like a floodlight.

Slamming the laundry chute door, I turned away and almost ran smack into Antoni's chest.

"Good morning. I came to find you when you weren't waiting for me in the dining room. I thought we'd agreed to meet for breakfast." His expression told me he'd been watching me long enough to notice that something wasn't okay.

His voice rolled over me like a hug and I didn't back up, or apologize, only pressed my face into his cotton shirt and closed my eyes. His gorgeous, comforting scent filled my nose and my frayed nerves relaxed a little. The desperate urge to sob in his arms like a little kid passed. My hands crept around his waist and I bunched his shirt up in my palms, squeezing the fabric and him, feeling the solidity of his body underneath.

His arms wrapped around me and he held me and kissed the top of my head. "I'm sorry?"

I gave a strangled chuckle and sniffed. "I'm not mad at you."

"That's a relief." When I didn't volunteer any information, he prodded, "But, something *is* wrong."

Yes and no. She is free, and that is right. But will this vacant space in me ever feel warm and full again?

"Yes."

His arms tightened and he waited. When more moments ticked by and I didn't explain, he said, "You'll tell me if I should be scared, right? Or if I need to have someone..." he lowered his voice to a conspiratorial whisper, "killed."

Thankful that the tears had not begun to fall again, and feeling more in control, I pulled back and smiled. "No one needs to die."

We turned and walked down the stairs together, headed

for the dining room and breakfast. I remembered that I'd asked him to join me for breakfast because he was going to Germany for work and would be away the rest of the week.

Antoni waited, watching me, hand in mine. He didn't even pull away when a member of the household staff walked by.

"My mom left for Canada early this morning."

Antoni's face expanded with surprise. "Is she going to look at a job, or something?"

I shook my head. "She's taken the partnership with The Bluejackets." The lies were coming smoothly off my tongue, but I hated lying to Antoni; it made me want to send a fist through the wall. Antoni was my family now, even though we weren't even engaged yet. My girlfriends were living their own lives, and though I knew we'd always be there for each other, they weren't in my daily life anymore. Antoni was. He was my home now.

So why was I lying to him?

I knew why. Fear. Plain and simple. Fear, and the promises I had made since I was old enough to remember making promises. Fear, and the ironclad siren's credo to keep her identity secret—it had been instilled in me since the very first time I had ever seen my mother's beautiful tail.

But Antoni had stopped on the step, and I had continued on until I realized he was no longer beside me. I paused, too, and looked up and back at him. He was staring at me, unblinking.

"What?" I asked.

"You must be joking with me. Tell me you're joking." He cracked a crooked smile in anticipation of me admitting that I'd been having him on.

"It's no joke. What's the big deal?"

"She didn't even say goodbye." He joined me on the

step where I'd stopped, then took another step down, bringing our eyes level with one another.

"Simon had an urgent job, she had to leave immediately." I shrugged, hating myself even more for the cavalier gesture. "Why stick around?"

Antoni blustered. "Maybe to tell us all to our faces that she was leaving? Maybe to get some help packing, have dinner with us all one last time."

"Us all?" I cocked an eyebrow.

"Well, my family at least, and the staff would have liked to have seen her off. She's part of the Novak clan now, and that's how they feel about her."

"There wasn't time." I took his hand, my voice had gone soothing and he relaxed a fraction, but he still was not happy.

"She couldn't even stay for your birthday," he grumped.

"Hey." I touched his cheek. "You of all people should understand commitment to work. She's passionate about what she does, she missed it. I told you that. You knew it was a possibility."

Antoni didn't believe this, and it was written all over his face. "There was nothing in the world more important to her than you, Targa. Nothing and no one. I don't believe for a second that this job was more important than you, than being there when you turn eighteen."

I tugged on his hand and he reluctantly continued down the steps beside me. "We'll see. Maybe she can come back. I'm sure she'll do everything she can."

I said this knowing full well that she wouldn't be here for my birthday, but I wanted to soothe him for now and deal with the reality of the situation later, when the sharp pangs of loss had eased to blunt ones.

Antoni continued to protest my mother's decision to

leave, and I continued to defend and make excuses for her. By the time we were sitting down to breakfast, I had lost my appetite.

It wasn't right, not being able to share this huge development in my life with Antoni. Lying to him tasted like acid on my tongue, and the worst of it was that he was slowly coming to believe me, to accept it. That made me feel like a total heel.

I forced the eggs and toast down because Antoni would definitely have been worried if he saw that my huge appetite had dwindled to nothing, but it tasted like chalk.

By the time we were clearing our plates from the table, Antoni believed me, but he was not impressed with my mom. He made a few comments that he never would have suspected she'd make such a decision, he was shocked, and maybe he didn't know her as well as he thought he had.

Really, he didn't know her at all.

And he didn't know me, and that sat on my chest like a bag of cement.

THE REAR PATHWAY to the beach had become my favorite escape route. During the day, I had classes and the business sessions with Hanna and Marian, and I was grateful for the distraction. I found the company's history interesting and though the shipping industry was not one I'd ever be passionate about, it was interesting enough to keep my mind engaged while Antoni was working.

In the evenings, if I wasn't with Antoni, I would dress for the weather and walk along the beach until I reached a rocky promontory, which was really a man-made break. Huge black boulders clustered at the water's edge kept the sea from eroding the tender earth on the other side. I liked to climb these rocks and step along their tops, watching the glittering pools of black water reflect the stars. At the very end, one could lean forward and almost not see any of the lights of civilization in their periphery. The floating twinkles of lit barges and passing ships moved quietly in the distance, dwarfed by a black sky scattered with stars.

I loved the night sounds of the Baltic, the sweet sway of the waves and the crashing of the larger ones over the stones, the hollow sounds of water pouring over the spaces between the rocks only to drain back into the sea.

Mom was ever on my mind. I wondered where she was. How far had she gotten in the days since she had left? Was she happier? Of course, she was happier. She was free. She was living how she had been craving to live ever since I had been born. What was she doing? Did she think of me, or was she now so far away and so accustomed to the salt water that I was a distant memory? Would she forget me entirely? Would I one day be a sealed envelope from her past, locked away from even her?

The waves slipped past the break, gathering speed and seeming to softly call to me, its voice lifting to a crescendo before descending again. Its sound was haunting, melancholy, somber. I had never known the ocean, or any body of water, to sound this way. It possessed me, and for some unknown amount of time, I stood there no longer thinking, only listening to that eerie, mournful song.

When I came to myself, my face and the collar on my coat were wet. I took a shuddering breath and sent loving thoughts to Mom, wherever she was, whatever she was doing.

The sound of a foot scraping on stone made me turn.

The silhouettes of two people stood like black cutouts against the lights of the shoreline, still and slender.

My body tensed, but the tension dissolved when one of the people sniffed and a hand journeyed to her face with a white thing I realized was a tissue.

I moved closer and their faces became a little clearer. I started when I realized it was Adalbert and Sera.

"That was the most beautiful thing," Sera said, "that I've ever heard."

I realized then that she was crying.

Adalbert wrapped his arm around her shoulders.

"Please don't be angry, we've just been worried about you since Mira left. When we saw you out here while we were walking, we followed." He hesitated. "We didn't mean to intrude on your private time. That was some...singing."

Singing?

I opened my mouth to protest when it came over me like a tsunami. The swelling feeling in my throat had just begun to fade. I hadn't realized that I'd been singing...singing in my siren's voice.

I didn't know what to say.

"I've never heard anything like that," Sera said, and Adalbert was nodding. "Truly, you have a gift. You should be on a stage. You could move a statue to tears. I thought while I was listening to it that I was never going to be happy again."

Adalbert nodded again. "It was remarkable, but I hope you don't mind that I was relieved when you stopped. I felt like I couldn't move until you finished, like your voice was holding me captive."

Finally, I just said, "I'm sorry. I thought I was alone."

Sera shook her head. "Never apologize for having such a talent."

I allowed them to escort me back to the manor, but I was too lost in my own thoughts to converse with them. I had been singing without even realizing it? Was this just a symptom of my grief, or was something else going on? Another thin layer of mystery fell away from my siren identity. When I was very, very sad, I sang to myself, or to the ocean. I didn't know to which because I didn't know I was doing it. I hoped these two weren't adversely affected by it, but I didn't think they would be. I'd said no words, given no orders, erased no memories. Surely the singing was harmless, and simply part of the grieving process. I wondered if my mom ever sang to the ocean after my dad died.

Thinking of my mom made my throat swell, and I swallowed hard, grateful Adalbert and Sera weren't making conversation either.

Remarkable. I would have loved to share this discovery with my mother. Even more remarkable, I found that I actually felt a little better than I had before I had left the manor for my walk along the break.

TEN

Adam navigated the Novak limousine to the opening of the museum exhibition. The evening was drizzly, the sky was an angry boil of dark clouds. The occasional flash of lightning over the Baltic lit the seams in the heavens to a bright white, illuminating the churning waters in the distance.

"I hope this weather isn't a sign that something disastrous is going to happen with the exhibition," Antoni said, putting a hand on my wool-dress coat where it covered my knee.

"I love this kind of weather," I replied, gazing out the car's windows as the lights of the city slid closer and lightning flashed over the beyond. "It's passionate, melancholy, romantic."

"And freezing." Antoni pulled his scarf up around his jawline and tugged his collar up as though wishing it could cover his ears. He sent me a sideways glance. "You know what I've noticed about you now that we've been able to spend an extended period of time together?"

"Hmm?"

"You never complain about the cold." He shuddered and rubbed his gloved hands together. "It doesn't bother you? Our damp Baltic winter?"

I laughed. "You haven't lived through winter in Atlantic Canada. The Baltic is a pussycat by comparison." Shrugging, I added, "Sometimes I feel the cold, but I guess I have a pretty good internal furnace."

Antoni snuggled closer, turning his face toward me. "I can't say I've ever noticed your body producing an excessive amount of heat."

I captured his lips in a kiss, cradling the back of his neck with my hand. His lips were soft, and melted against mine like butter.

When I drew back, he had a little smile on his mouth as he gazed at me through hooded eyes.

"I take that back." He tucked a small box into the palm of my hand. "Happy birthday, Targa."

I gave a soft gasp at the surprise and looked down to see a teal box with a matching ribbon. "Aw, thank you. You didn't have to get me anything."

"Don't be silly, of course I did."

"Should I open it now?"

He gestured impatiently and comically to get on with it.

Untying the bow and lifting the lid revealed a little fabric sack. Upending the sack into my palm, a gold bangle tumbled into my hand. Holding it up in the light of the streetlamps going by I noticed an engraving. It was simple, our initials stamped into the gold with a heart in between.

"Do you like it?"

"Very much," I replied, smiling. I slipped it onto my wrist and tucked the box into my clutch. Leaning forward again, I gave him a lingering kiss. "Thank you."

His eyes flicked toward the tinted glass which hid us from Adam in the front seat.

"I know what you're thinking," I teased. "You're an open book."

He chuckled. "Come now, I'm your date tonight, aren't I? That's progress, right?"

"I'll be forever grateful." I fluttered my eyelashes at him in an expression of satiric appreciation.

He shook his head. "You've got a lot of your mother in you, you know."

I looked out the window as the buildings of the old city in central Gdansk passed by. "I hope so."

"Such a shame she couldn't be here for your birthday, and the exhibition," Antoni muttered, still sour at her. "You'd think she could take a few days off to enjoy the fruits of her labor. Everything in the exhibition is now hers, people will think it's very odd that she's not here."

"They'll have to be satisfied with me," I said, my voice sounding more clipped than I meant it to.

The car slowed as we approached the front doors of the museum. Antoni leaned over me as we peered out my window.

"Look at the crowd," he said. "Wow. They did a good job with the publicity. Looks like half the city came out."

This was an exaggeration of course, but there was quite a crowd of elegant looking guests in dark dress jackets and sophisticated updos clustered under a temporary awning which had been constructed to cover the sidewalk. Stanchions had been erected to guide the crowd to the open double doors where tickets were being scanned.

"A red carpet?" I blinked at Antoni in surprise. "They put down a red carpet?"

Adam snugged the car close to the taillights of the vehicle in front of us, where a beautifully dressed older couple stepped out onto the carpet. A valet in coattails held their door open and welcomed them.

"Who are they?"

"That's Pawel Adamowicz, the city mayor and his wife. Did Mrs. Krulikoski not tell you who'd be coming?"

"No, she did," I answered absently, touching up my lipstick and watching the elegant woman with short silver hair wave to the crowd standing on the other side of the stanchions. "I just saw the list of names, not their photos."

"We're next. You ready?"

I dropped my lipstick into my clutch and nodded as the car inched forward and the valet reached for my door handle.

"Still not fair that I haven't gotten to see you in that dress before anyone else," Antoni whispered, and planted a kiss behind my ear.

I smiled over my shoulder at him. "That's what happens when you don't live with your date. Just sayin'. Benefits, you know?"

"Very funny." He grinned.

The valet opened the door and I stepped out of the vehicle, clutching my long coat and dress so they didn't land in the gutter. A few people called my name from the other side of the stanchions and I looked up, surprised. Smiling faces greeted me, hands waving. I waved back, smiled, and tried to look like I belonged here.

"They know my name," I muttered so only Antoni could hear as he got out and followed me up the red carpet.

Flashes of light from a small group of journalists went off.

"Of course they do. The Novaks are as much a part of

the fabric of Gdansk as the canals. Most of these people didn't come to see some rotting artifacts, they came to see Targa Novak in the flesh. Martinius Novak's long lost heiress."

I swallowed down a cold feeling at these words and resisted the temptation to say, "I'm not a Novak." It would be a bad idea to even mouth the words when so many eyes were on us. Instead, I forced my lipsticked lips into a smile and stood for the cameras for a minute, wanting to shrink inside my coat and slink into the museum.

"Targa!" One of the journalists caught my attention as she held a small recording device out toward me. "Where is your mom, Mira Novak—will she be joining us tonight?"

Antoni put out a hand and spoke to her politely in Polish; the journalist nodded and asked another question back in Polish. She and the others looked as though they wanted to ask me more questions, but with a hand at the small of my back, Antoni guided me into the museum.

"The media isn't allowed inside at this point," Antoni whispered in my ear. "Don't worry, you won't have to run from them all evening."

I was stunned at the realization of how many people wanted to know more about me. I wasn't anybody but a teenager from a small coastal city in Canada that most of the world had never heard of. I felt like a fraud just being here, pretending that I was who they thought I was. I deeply wished from the very soles of my high heeled shoes that my mother was beside me. It was an ache that took my breath away with its intensity. If she were here, I wouldn't be left feeling like a fraud all on my own; someone who knew and shared the truth of me would be here, and that would be such a comfort.

I watched Antoni's face as he held out a hand to take

my coat. Unbuttoning the long wool coat, I wormed out of it unconsciously, wishing suddenly and earnestly to spill all of my secrets out to him. With my mother gone, I felt isolated and burdened under the weight of what I was, under the weight of who all these people thought I was. The one person who knew absolutely everything about me, who knew what had brought me to this moment in my life, was gone.

"Wow, Targa."

Antoni's words snapped me out of my wistful thoughts. "What?"

"What do you mean, *what?*" His eyes combed my body from the top of my updo to the hem of the turquoise and blue mermaid gown he'd gifted to me. "You look like a woman out of a fairytale. You don't even look real."

"Thank you."

His words reminded me to relax, and that I was supposed to enjoy myself, not torture myself with thoughts of being a fraud all evening.

I took a breath. "You look gorgeous, too."

"Oh, you haven't even seen... wait." He handed my coat to the smiling man behind the coat check counter and unbuttoned his own coat. Shucking it with a knowing look, he turned his body in a little 'ta-da' posture, palms out.

His suit was dark gray, perfectly tailored to complement his shape. Beneath the suit jacket he wore a navy vest and tie; on the tie, embroidered in the centre, was one of the Novak logos—the tall-masted ship.

"Very appropriate," I said. "The man knows how to dress."

He gave a little bow, handed his jacket over to coat check, said thank you, and put out his elbow for me to take. We passed through the foyer and into the museum together.

"Miss Novak, welcome!" Abraham, dressed in a tuxedo and looking dashing, called to us from across the room. He crossed the foyer, dodging waiters carrying trays of champagne and canapés. Taking my hand, he smiled down at me. "You look simply enchanting." He shook Antoni's hand as well. "There are so many people I would like to introduce you to, please come."

For the next hour, I rubbed shoulders with the who's who of Gdansk—old families with old money, supporters of the Novaks in some form or another. Even though I'd met some of them at the gala in the summer, I wrestled with matching names with the right faces. I plastered a smile on my face, sipped small amounts of champagne, ate interesting snacks from a high-quality fabric napkin, and tried not to say or do anything stupid or trip over the hem of my dress.

"How unfortunate your mother couldn't be here," Hanna was saying to me. Her long tapered fingers shone with a French manicure as she held the delicate stem of an empty wine glass. "It must be quite an all-consuming job she and her team are working at the moment. Where did you say it was?"

"Uh...I didn't say. Sorry, I'm not sure if it's confidential or not."

Hanna looked taken aback and blinked like a startled doe. Couldn't blame her. Salvage jobs weren't usually confidential, but it wasn't impossible.

"How intriguing," she finally said, moving closer and lowering her voice. "It's not got something to do with that Vanderbilt yacht accident, has it?"

"I wouldn't know." I smiled nervously. The last thing I wanted was for Hanna to be 'intrigued' about where my mother was and what she was up to.

I felt Antoni's hand at my back as a waiter came with a tray to retrieve Hanna's empty glass. While she was distracted by choosing another drink, I took the opportunity to move away.

"How are you doing?" he asked.

I smiled and said through my teeth, "If one more person asks me why my mother isn't here, I'm going to throw a perogy at them."

He chuckled and made to respond when a gorgeous, willowy young woman with auburn hair and a porcelain complexion appeared from out of nowhere and threw her arms around him, speaking in Polish. She wore a strapless, peach satin gown. A fine necklace graced her collarbones and chandelier earrings dangled beside her jaw, glittering in the light. It took me a moment to recognize her as Antoni's sister.

"Hi Targa," Lydia said in breaks between streams of Polish.

"Hello, Lydia." I wondered how she'd snagged a ticket. It wasn't the sort of event I had thought would interest her. I stood for her cool assessment of my dress, hair, and makeup.

"You look sweet," she said, tilting her nose up a little. She surveyed the room through eyes hooded by extravagant false lashes. "Is your mom here? I'm dying to see what she's wearing."

Antoni gave me a sympathetic smile. He'd told Lydia long ago that my mom had moved back to Canada for work. I wondered if she'd forgotten or if she was rubbing it in, then I decided I didn't care either way.

"If you'll excuse me," I said through a tight jaw, "I haven't seen the exhibition yet. I keep hearing Martinius's voice and have been wanting to watch the video the museum made."

I excused myself, leaving Lydia and Antoni to talk. Passing from the foyer through a set of double glass doors, I entered the darker, cooler exhibition area.

The recorded sound of Martinius's voice grew much louder over a soundtrack of soft music and waves. On several screens scattered throughout the exhibition space, which was more of a maze than a wide open room, Martinius was being interviewed by a Polish TV personality about the salvage and the story of *The Sybellen*. It was in Polish, but small English subtitles scrolled across the bottom of the screen.

I stared at Martinius's kind, weathered face for a while, not really paying attention to what he was saying. It was easy to miss him. Once we'd figured out that he wasn't the enemy, he'd become a good friend for the short time he'd been alive after we'd met him. He was the only man who knew our secret, and he'd gone to the grave with it. Seeing Martinius's face again reminded me of removing the figurehead from *The Sybellen* with my mom, and a wave of sadness washed over me.

The museum had created a serpentine path across the exhibition floor, guiding people through display cases and educational showcases. Though the exhibition was primarily about *The Sybellen*, the story and the artifacts, numerous other shipwreck salvages were referred to, and finds brought up from those Baltic wrecks were also displayed.

Through a crack in one of the displays, I caught a glimpse of Lydia laughing and flirting with a man in an ill-fitting tux. He was handsome, though he seemed a lot older than her. Stepping closer to the crack for a moment, I watched as he put an arm around her waist and nuzzled her just below the ear. Confused, I thought Antoni had said her boyfriend was a young blond guy from her grade—Makary, the fellow she'd mentioned at Christmas. I shook it off and moved on. It wasn't my business, anyway.

While I was poring over the case of jewelry recovered from *The Sybellen*, I felt a presence move beside me and a shadow fell over the glass casing. I looked up and was taken aback by the man's appearance.

Tall and lean, he towered over me, and may have even stood taller than Antoni. His hair was the color of snow and cut very short due to the thinning crown, yet his face was mostly unlined. His eyes were a bright crystal blue, different from mine because they seemed faded, like denim that had been washed many times. His skin was pale but bright, and his expression seemed fixed into a permanent small smile, the corners of his mouth turning up naturally. High cheekbones and a wide mouth spoke of youthfulness, but the white hair and thick glasses belied age.

He glanced at me as I looked up, and crooked a polite nod in my direction before bending at the waist and peering curiously at one of the pieces in the showcase.

"Gerland Chamberlain," he said, surprising me.

I looked around, thinking that he must have been addressing someone else, but there was nobody but us in the vicinity. He didn't look like a fellow who might be interested in conversing with a teenage girl, more like a stuffy scholar who enjoyed brandy and cigars in a library at a gentlemen-only type of club, but I couldn't discount the wild card in every encounter I had—my siren appeal.

"Targa MacAuley," I replied, scrutinizing this interesting character with an intense inquisitiveness. "You sound Swiss," I guessed.

"I grew up in Switzerland. Very good." He smiled again.

"But Chamberlain is English, isn't it?"

"Ah, but there you are wrong. It is actually rooted in old Norman French. 'Cambrelanc' is what my ancestors would have said."

I liked the rasp of his voice, and thought from its rough timbre, that he was more old than young.

"What are you doing in Gdansk?"

His thin white brows crept up a notch. "Why, I'm here for this." He plucked the spectacles off his face and held his hands out, indicating the display. He put his fingertips on the edge of the display case. "And in actual fact, this, in particular."

"The jewelry?"

"Yes, I have a particular interest in pieces with," he paused, "let's call it historic significance. Most relic aficionados are interested in value. Cut, color, and clarity, and all that." He pushed his glasses up his nose. "Not me. I am interested in something like this, for example." He pointed to a pendant in the middle of the case.

The pendant was nothing spectacular, but it was interesting to look at. A long chain held a unique design wrought in gold and set with a small teal gemstone.

"What is that? Turquoise?" I squinted at the stone.

"Turquoise is opaque and a deeper blue, so no, this is aquamarine. A very small piece, but interesting nonetheless, don't you think?"

"Sure." I humored him. Scanning the rest of the case, I found numerous other items to be more eye-catching. A set of large amber pendant earrings, a ring made from an old coin, a choker set with opals and onyx in an alternating checkerboard for the neck. "Why are you interested in this one?"

"It's the stone itself that I find most fascinating, and also the glyph it is set in."

"What does the glyph mean? It almost looks like a letter from a foreign alphabet."

"It does, I know. To be honest, I am not sure, but it gives me something to research." Gerland produced a cell phone from his breast pocket and took a photo of the pendant.

I opened my mouth to tell Gerland that photography was forbidden by the museum when...

"Here you are," Antoni said as he joined us, slipping an arm around my waist. "Sorry about my sister."

"Family problems?" Gerland's white brows jerked up a notch as he tucked his cell phone away.

"No, everything is fine." I replied. "We were just looking at this pendant," I explained to Antoni, "the one with the small aquamarine. Wondering what the glyph meant."

Antoni's eyes landed on the pendant and his face became very still. Eyes glued to the twisted gold symbol, it was several moments before he finally responded. "It means 'anything for you.'"

Both Gerland and I looked at Antoni with surprise.

"How do you know that?" I asked.

Antoni took a breath. "I...I'm not sure. But I've seen that shape before, and that's what it means. I'm almost positive."

"How intriguing." Gerland's bright gaze locked on Antoni's features.

"Would you excuse us?" Antoni addressed Gerland. "There's someone else who would like to meet you," he said to me. "You can finish the exhibition afterward?"

"Okay." I nodded at Gerland. "Nice to meet you, Mr. Chamberlain."

"Charmed," he replied, still staring at Antoni.

I let Antoni lead me from the exhibition room back to the foyer to talk to a historian who was writing about Martinius's life. For the next hour, I juggled answering questions with vague, evasive answers—normally my mother's specialties, and wondering when Antoni and I could go home and finally be alone.

ELEVEN

"You looked amazing tonight," Antoni murmured into my hair as he helped me out of my coat back at the manor. "I haven't had a chance to give you proper birthday kisses, at least eighteen...hundred of them."

He hung my coat, then picked me up and swung me around until we almost fell into the living room, giggling as he kept his arms wrapped around my waist.

"Who *are you?*" I squirmed in his embrace, wrapping my arms around his neck. I toed out of my shoes and stood on tiptoe, pulling his face toward mine. His eyes were hooded pools of desire.

"Still me." His lips traced my jawline and I shivered.

"Is this because I just crossed over into a certain legal bracket?"

He pulled back and gazed at me and I could see the gears in his mind rotating slowly and steadily, choosing how to answer.

"Yes?" he finally went with, but said it like a question.

I burst out laughing. "You're so predictable. So conservative and proper."

He went back to nuzzling my neck. "Do you have any more attractive descriptors to add?" He nipped my earlobe.

"Like what? Good in the kitchen? Bilingual?"

"I'm trilingual, thank you very much." His voice was muffled in my neck as he stepped around me and started pulling me toward the stairs. My heart skipped and I wondered if it was finally, actually going to happen. It seemed my thinking slowed down suddenly, like a record flipped to half-speed.

"You are?" I droned.

"Mm-hmm."

"English, Polish, and...?" I waited for him to fill in the missing language but I tripped over the hem of my dress as we reached the top step and Antoni hugging me to him made my thoughts fly apart. I couldn't remember what I'd just asked. Wait, *had* I asked a question? Oh, who really cared.

"It's an ancient, very important language. Spoken now only in the sitting rooms of prestigious libraries and universities."

I had no idea what he was talking about anymore. As he opened the door to my rooms with one hand, I lifted a finger to trace the line of his lips, dumbfounded by the simple beautiful curves I found there. We almost fell into my bedroom.

"Wait." Antoni took a half step backward. "I'm mad at you."

I blinked, some of the fog of desire clearing. "What?"

The sudden vacancy of his warm bulk made me feel abandoned. I reached out for him, but he pulled away, gazing down at me.

"Why?"

"You've been keeping secrets from me," he stated softly, and took his own turn tracing the contours of my face.

I shivered with pleasure at the touch of his fingertips but his words had jolted me out of my hunger for him. I sat down on the bed, trying not to let the alarm show on my face. "What are you talking about?"

"All this time and you've never told me you could sing." He shook his head like he was chastising me, but there was a twinkle in his eye.

I allowed a small smile to creep onto my face, but I wasn't sure I liked where this was going. "I can't really sing."

Antoni laughed. "And she denies it. I knew you would. You can. I have it on good authority that your voice is rather remarkable, so good in fact that it brought my witness to tears."

I looked down, shyly. "I didn't know anyone was listening."

"You have to sing for me."

My eyes flew open. "No way. Uh-uh. Not going to happen." I got off the bed and walked to the window. I hadn't even known I'd been singing, but if I told Antoni that, I'd look like a crazy person.

"Why not?" Antoni looked genuinely taken aback. "I'm the one person you're supposed to share everything with. You can sing for the fish, but you won't sing for your sweetheart?"

He made an adorable pout with his lower lip.

I shook my head and pinched my lips in on themselves. I pulled the curtains. "By the way, who was that older man Lydia was hanging out with tonight?"

"Don't change the subject," he muttered, but glowered. "That's Adrian."

"Who is Adrian?"

"I don't know, I just met him tonight in passing, but I suspect he's bad news for Makary." Antoni made a comical tsk-ing sound. "But why are we talking about my sister's dalliances? You are not allowed to dodge my request. Tell you what." He put his palms together and rubbed his hands like he was preparing to negotiate. "I'll make you a deal."

I cocked an eyebrow. This was interesting.

"I'll reveal one of my hidden talents," he said, "and you sing for me."

"You have hidden talents?"

He chuckled and posed in a cocky manner which I'd never seen in him before. I liked it. "What is the ridiculous nickname that they give girlfriends in North America? Baby?"

I burst out laughing at the way the pet name sounded in his accent and coming from his lips.

He smiled but didn't break character. "Baby, I'm a wealth of hidden talents."

He gestured along his body with his fingers as though showing off merchandise and I laughed even harder.

"How can a girl turn down such an offer?"

"That's what I'd like to know." He grasped my shoulders and shuffled me around him to sit on the bed. "You, sit there, and just give me one second."

He pulled his phone out of his pocket and appeared to be looking for something online.

"I give you, the Allman Brothers," he said, pressing a button on his phone.

A bluesy, fast-paced tune poured from the tiny speakers and he began to bop with his shoulders.

I leaned back on my elbows, grinning from ear to ear and nodding in time to the beat. "Oh, this is gonna be good."

Antoni set the phone down on top of the dresser and

did a little turn on one foot before breaking into a tap dance. The soles of his shoes didn't make much sound on the carpet but it was easy to see that he knew what he was doing. I gasped in delight and sat up.

"No way! You can dance?"

He grinned and did an impressive step combo across the floor, adding in what I could only assume was an 'air-banjo' to the mix. The color rose high on his cheeks and down his neck and a thin sheen of sweat highlighted his forehead.

My body felt warmer and a wave of his scent washed over me, making me feel dizzy. I was thankful he'd made me sit down. Watching him spin and shuffle across the room like he owned the music filled me with an intoxicating kind of joy, and suddenly I was overwhelmed with the emotions of all that had come to pass since I'd returned to Poland. My eyes welled up, my mouth opened.

Antoni stopped dancing and looked up at me wide-eyed before diving to his phone to shut off the jazz tune.

The slow haunting melody filled the suite, my siren voice pouring from my throat like a multi-stringed orchestra. Every note labored to carry the heartbreak and grief I held since losing my mother, and the love I'd found in Antoni.

His expression grew still and astonished, like a parody of shock frozen in time. His eyes grew soft and liquid.

Still singing, I closed my eyes and listened to the sound of a fathomless sea cascading from my lips. It rose from the very bottom of my soul and poured from my throat and mouth like a fountain—a love song for Antoni, no words, just my multi-layered strings rising and falling like a symphony.

Antoni was suddenly there, kissing my face, my neck, my lips like he was afraid I could evaporate at any moment. My song came to an end as my heart beat only for him in grateful pulses. I had lost someone I loved dearly, but life had found a way to provide another beloved to fill my heart and help me survive.

Heat unfurled in my belly like a fragrant rose opening to the sun and I returned his kisses urgently, pulling him toward me. Something broke open inside both of us, desire gushed from the rends and mingled as we came together.

MY PARENTS WOVE through my dreams that night, as Antoni finally slept beside me.

I was no stranger to grief. I had been young when my father died, and the grief was softer-edged, a muzzy pain that manifested in a simple desire to smell him, be in his arms, hear his voice, just sit with him and be with my father.

The grief for my mother was an entirely different species—hard-edged, acute, sharpened to a needle-fine point as moments came that I wished she could be part of and knew she would not want to miss.

Dreaming she was with me—talking and laughing and listening in a way only she could—nearly crushed me with disappointment when I woke to discover she was still gone, and would likely never return. Waking with a start, my eyes found Antoni's shape in the soft dark shadows of night. My heart was a tumult of feeling as I set a hand over his where it lay on the sheets. Love for him oozed from every seam within me, and it was heightened by the hollow sadness that always followed waking after dreaming of my mother.

Slowly and quietly, I slipped from the sheets, pulled on the jeans I'd tossed over the back of a chair when I'd dressed for the exhibition, along with a hoody and my sneakers. With a hand against my heart and wondering when I'd wake to not have this pain, I sneaked from the house and made my way down to the only place I knew I would find comfort like no other—the sea.

My feet found their way to the rocky promontory that reached out into the Baltic like a finger. I sat down and crossed my legs, taking deep breaths and willing myself not to cry.

Missing her slipped between my ribs like the cold blade of a knife. How badly I wanted to tell her everything, what I'd experienced with Antoni, about my birthday, about the exhibition. Just to have her company, be cradled by her unconditional love.

Closing my eyes, I imagined her swimming, carefree and happy—free from the torture of her life on land, the salt healing her wounds and giving her what she needed right now.

My cheeks and lap were wet as I realized I'd lost the battle against my siren tears. Letting them stream without staunching them, I visualized her playing with dolphins, exploring wrecks and caves, sunning herself in clear teal waters.

My mind reached for hers, searched for her over the expanse of waters between us.

Mira.

Where are you? What are you doing? Will you ever return to me?

Amiralyon.

A high soft song played on the wind and I realized I was singing again.

No, not singing.

Calling.

Amiralyon.

My siren voice rose and fell as the wind lifted it from

my lips and carried it over the Baltic to the mermaid it was meant for, but it was not just my siren sound, I realized, it was *elemental*. It was intended, it was a message, it was a request to come back to me.

Amiralyon.

The Baltic rose to help me, the call stretching out from a single point to unfold and fan out in all directions...wherever there was water. The beckoning transmitted through the Baltic and beyond. Out to the Gulf of Bothnia, west to the North Sea, spreading past the Norwegian Sea, searching, seeking—out into the Atlantic, my elemental calling spread. Every molecule of water had become my mouthpiece, transmitting my desire.

In the Bay of Biscay, I found her and knew she heard me. I could feel her pausing, listening, turning—startled and confused. She became frightened, did not understand what was happening. As though not powered by her own will any longer, she began to slide through the water back the way she had come, hands and arms searching for control.

Both hands clamped over my mouth to shut off the sound I had barely any control over. My chest and shoulders rose and fell as I panted through my nose. Siren tears still coursed from my closed eyes, and my heart fluttered like a frightened caged bird.

The sound of the waves reached my ears, calmed me. The song had ceased.

I let my hands relax into my lap as I digested what had just happened. I'd found her, I'd found my mother, I knew exactly where she was. She was in the Bay of Biscay. The water told me she was fine, she was whole, she had been happy before my calling had disturbed her. And while her mind had shifted, she was not salt-flush.

I couldn't hold in a surprised laugh of delight over my newfound ability. Discovering my siren abilities had so far been an amazing ride, but becoming acquainted with my elemental powers was a whole different world.

For the first time since I had said goodbye to her, that sharp knife-edge of grief backed off a little. I had a way of knowing she was okay, of knowing where she was, and even of drawing her home if I wanted.

The temptation to call her again rose swiftly up in me and I worked to rationalize. She had only just begun her salt-cycle. She needed this time; it would only be selfish of me to bring her home for my own comfort. I would not do that to her, especially not after all she'd sacrificed for me, all the years she'd suffered for me.

But perhaps one day, years from now, when her salt-cycle had had its time, when she was ready for life on land again, I could.

I could call my mother home.

TWELVE

Antoni picked me up at four on the afternoon of Georjie's arrival.

"You're vibrating," he said, flashing me a grin. "Excited?"

"You have no idea." I buckled my seatbelt and settled in as Antoni pulled around the rotunda and guided the car through the gate and onto the road.

"It's been hard not having your mom around, I know. I'm sure it's a bit lonely sometimes."

"It's not just that. I mean yes, I do miss my mom, of course. I miss her like crazy. But Georjie and I have been best friends since preschool. We grew up together."

"Like sisters."

I nodded and swallowed down the lump in my throat. The emotion startled me. Maybe I had been hiding my own feelings of loneliness and missing my friends from myself. "Yeah. She's family."

As we hit the freeway heading to the airport, Antoni asked, "You spend a lot of time doing your schoolwork and meeting with Hanna and Marian, and spending time with me. After Georjie leaves, why don't you sign up for Polish classes, or join a group in Gdansk, meet some locals and start making friends here? After all," he reached over and took my hand, "this is your home now, right?"

I nodded. Though I loved Gdansk, it didn't quite feel like home because my mom wasn't here, and none of my friends had visited yet and were so far away that it seemed like they didn't have any significant place in my world anymore. Antoni was the only thing that felt like home.

"It's a good idea," I murmured, squeezing his hand. "Thanks."

We pulled onto the airport road and Antoni guided the car into short-term parking. Making our way to the meeting point for arrivals, my heart beat faster and felt lighter than it had since my mom had left. We bought a bouquet of yellow roses from one of the airport shops and waited. My eyes barely left the sliding doors through which tired looking passengers wheeling bulky bags continuously passed.

When I spotted Georjie's blond head I leapt up, Antoni following.

"Georjie!" Putting my hand in the air, I waved to get her attention.

She heard her name and scanned the waiting crowd. Her big brown eyes fell on me and a grin burst across her face. She was half a head taller than everyone around her so it wasn't difficult for her to spot us.

Leaving her luggage near a wall, she swept me up in a tight hug. The lump in my throat was back and I hid my face in her hair, a little embarrassed for being so teary-eyed. Georjie didn't know I was mourning the loss of my mother yet, she wouldn't understand why I was crying and it would upset her, because it was very unlike me to show emotion in public. I brushed a hand over my eyes as I pulled back, clearing the moisture.

"How was your trip?" I asked. "Are you exhausted?"

"I'm okay, I slept on the plane a little, but yeah, I'll sleep well tonight, I think." Her eyes went to Antoni, standing quietly with his hands in his pocket and a smile on his face. "You must be Antoni?" She held out a long slender hand.

"That's me. Welcome to Gdansk." Antoni shook her hand.

"Thank you. I've heard so much about you," Georjie said as I grabbed her luggage and we made our way to the parking lot. "You know that you broke the curse, right?"

I shot a surprised look at Georjie.

"Broke the curse?" Antoni unlocked the trunk of the car and we deposited Georjie's bags into the back. "What curse?"

I opened the door for Georjie and put my hand on her head the way a police officer does to a criminal as they shove them in the back seat. "Watch your head," I said, mussing her hair, "brat."

Georjie laughed and pushed her tangled hair out of her face. "Yeah. Before you, Targa thought she didn't have the ability to fall in love."

Antoni's amused eyes fell on me. "I didn't know that," he murmured.

I gave him a smug smile over the roof of the car as we both slipped into our seats. "Thanks, Georjie," I muttered.

"You're welcome," she said sincerely.

"Tell me more." Antoni started the car and we began the journey home.

"I think that's enough for one day," I said.

"I'd really like to hear more about this curse," Antoni teased. "I mean, if I broke it, it would be nice to know by what magic I did such a thing. Was this an ancient family curse?"

We chatted all the way home, with teasing me as the brunt of the conversation. It seemed Georjie and Antoni were bonding over a common hobby—making fun of Targa.

As we unloaded Georjie's bags and Adalbert came out to shuttle them upstairs, Antoni slid back into the driver's seat.

"You're not coming in?" Georjie asked.

He closed his door but rolled down his window. "I have a hockey game and a late dinner with my mum after that. But I'll see you both tomorrow."

I kissed him goodbye through the window and he smiled at Georjie. "Have fun catching up."

Waving him off, Georjie then turned and looked up at the red brick mansion. "Wow, it looks even bigger in person than in the photos. What a cool place. Look at all those vines. Are there underground tunnels or secret passageways?"

I laughed. "Probably. I haven't had time to explore the whole building, yet."

"I can't believe this is yours."

We passed into the foyer and I led her up to show her to her suite, where she could rest and unpack, then took her to my suite so she would know where to find me.

"I know you said your mom was on a job right now, but when is she back? And I thought she quit salvage diving?"

"Yeah, about that..." My voice trembled and I stopped talking as my throat closed up. Georjie was behind me as I walked into the suite.

"Whoa, it's like your own apartment!" Georjie tossed her purse on the couch and began to explore. "Are all the rooms like this?" She caught sight of my face and her expression melted into concern. "What is it? What's wrong?"

"My mom is gone, Georjie. She went back to the sea. I didn't want to tell you over the phone. I couldn't say it out loud." I felt my lip tremble and my face crumple, but there was nothing I could do to stop it. Sometimes you have control over emotion and other times emotion has control over you, and I had just lost the battle. Tears began to course down my face and it was not the kind of cry I'd be able to stop; it was a siren's weeping. "I don't know if I'll ever see her again."

"Oh, Targa." Georjie pulled me into a hug, arms firmly around my shoulders. "I'm so sorry. I wondered when that might happen. You poor kid. Why didn't you say?"

Streams of salty tears coursed down my cheeks and I released Georjie to get a towel from the bathroom. I mopped at my face and neck, unable to answer Georjie yet as grief had throttled my voice.

Emerging from the bathroom, I sat on the couch beside Georjie.

"You'll see her again, Targa," she said, rubbing my back.

"You don't know that," I choked out. "What if I kept her out for too long and she goes salt-flush? She could lose her memory, even her identity."

Georjie was silent for a moment, then said, "Salt-flush?"

I had never explained salt-flush to my friend before. "Mom told me that if a siren delays having a salt-cycle for too long, then when they finally succumb to what their body needs and go to the ocean, it can cause a kind of backlash. The salt erases more than just their memories, but their humanity as well. They become like any other animal in the ocean, just surviving day to day."

Explaining it to Georjie, saying it out loud, made me

picture my beloved mother as just that—vacant expression, just existing in the ocean like a tuna, neither happy or unhappy, all traces of Mira MacAuley gone for good if she was never exposed to fresh-water again. Fresh tears coursed down my face at these thoughts.

"I have all these amazing powers, Georjie." I looked at my friend, miserable, wretched. "But there was nothing I could do to save her from her fate. She just got worse and worse, until it would have been cruel to do anything but take her to the water's edge and say goodbye."

Georjie's brown eyes had darkened with moisture and her own tears slipped down her face. "I didn't know."

"I never explained it to anyone before, and with all the crazy stuff that happened in Saltford before we said good-bye, there was no time. And I wasn't thinking it would happen so soon anyway. I thought, deep down, that maybe she would be strong enough to push through it, or that I might be strong enough to prevent the ocean from taking her. But I was wrong."

Georjie didn't know what to say, she just held me while I wept.

It took some time for the tears to dry up enough for us to venture down for dinner. We barely spoke over dinner, and Georjie threw a lot of concerned looks my way. By the time I felt good enough to talk again, Georjie and I were in pajamas and in my suite lying propped up against my pillows.

"How is Liz?" I asked.

Georjie closed the book she was reading, something to do with the Scottish highlands, which made sense considering that was where she was headed next. "She's really good. She's still part of the disaster relief crew, though she donates money more than time because her clients keep her as busy as always."

"She'll miss having you around."

She shrugged. "Yes and no. We've come a long way, and our relationship is better than it's been since I was a little kid, but you know we'll probably never be best friends. I think we're both okay with that."

I nodded. "What are you going to do in Scotland?"

"Besides classwork?" She laughed. "Tour the highlands, I guess."

I nodded, but could tell that Georjie didn't want to talk about herself because she was worried about me.

"Antoni doesn't know anything?" Georjie ventured, quietly.

I shook my head. "How can I tell him the truth?"

"I understand why you're scared to, Targa," she replied, turning and drawing her knees up so she was sitting on one hip and facing me. "But if you want to have a life with him, how do you think you can keep your identity a secret forever?"

"My mom did it."

"Yeah, but your mom lost her husband about nine years into their marriage. You don't know what would have happened if your dad had lived."

I knew this also, and I did have my doubts about any mermaid's ability to keep her identity a secret for any extended period of time to the person she was closest to. Trina, my grandmother, had needed to use her voice on Hal to keep her secret.

"You said you never wanted to use your voice on him ever again," she reminded me.

"I know what I said."

"Do you still feel that way?"

"Of course, I do. I already had to tamper with his memory once just to get him to stop asking questions about the day we both drowned." It made me ill to think about it. Messing with someone's thoughts and memories made me feel like an abuser.

"What is the downside of telling him, Targa? The worst thing that could happen?"

I didn't answer. She knew what the worst thing was—losing Antoni.

"Now think about the worst thing that could happen if you don't tell him, but he discovers it on his own, as he's likely to do if you're together for long enough." She paused. "You'd be forced to use your voice on him, or face how he'd feel when he discovers that you've been hiding your identity from him since the night you guys drowned."

I shot her a venomous look, not intended for her but at the thought of that very scenario. "I thought you were on my side?"

"I am, Targa. And I think you're making a mistake if you don't tell him."

I couldn't turn the question around on her, ask her if she'd tell Jasher her secret, because Jasher already knew. Envy for her situation filled me like a mouthful of lime juice.

"And if you and Jasher don't end up together, and you met someone new, would you tell them what you are?"

"I would," she said, easily.

"But it's not the same," I almost wailed. "You don't shapeshift into something totally different from what you are right now. You draw healing power from plants, and watch fairies hatch from water droplets. You're... quaint."

Georjie laughed, and I might have too if I didn't feel sick at the thought of telling Antoni what I was.

"What is so repellant about what you are?"

"I'm not fully human, Georjie. You have magic, too, but you're still human, you and Saxony both. If Antoni and I have a baby, and that child is a girl, she will only be half human, too. Don't you agree there is a pretty significant risk that Antoni won't be happy about that?"

Georjie's brows shot up. "Absolutely!"

I rolled my eyes. "You're not helping."

She shook her head. "You misunderstand, Targa. There is absolutely a risk in revealing your true nature to the man you love, I do not deny that. And yes, that risk is bigger than the risk Saxony or I would ever take. But if you don't tell him, then you're making that decision for him, and if he ever learns that, he might resent you for it. Wouldn't you?"

I couldn't answer out loud because I knew that I would. I would be extremely upset with Antoni for taking such a choice away from me.

"If you were the human, and he was a... mer-dude," Georjie went on, "and he told you what he was, would you leave him?"

"There are no mer-dudes, Georjie."

"Humor me. It's hypothetical." She studied my face. "Would you leave him?"

I thought about this but found it difficult to put myself in the position of being only human, of remembering what that felt like. "I don't think I can honestly answer that because it's one of those things where you have to be in the situation to know what you would do..."

She sensed the answer waiting in the wings. "But?"

"But, no. I don't think I would. He's Antoni, and I adore him."

Silence stretched out between us before Georjie said, "Well, that's something then, isn't it?"

I nodded, but it wasn't enough. It wasn't a guarantee, and if it wasn't a sure thing that Antoni wouldn't abandon me and break my heart, then it wasn't enough. I had just lost my mother, I couldn't bear to lose him, too.

Finally, Georjie and I said good night to one another and she slipped out to her own suite, she to her dreams, and I to mine.

THIRTEEN

Georjie's visit flew by. We minimized the time we spent doing school work and I canceled all my business meetings with Hanna and Marian in favor of spending time with my friend. I took her to all my favorite places in Gdansk, enjoying showing her around my new home city and delighting in how much she enjoyed it. We had dinners with Antoni, and long walks along the beaches and canals. Georjie's friendship was a balm to my heart and our holiday was just the peaceful break I needed...until it wasn't peaceful anymore.

"Targa," Georjie's whispered call and touch at my shoulder woke me with a startle. "Sorry," she said, "but do you hear what I hear?"

I lifted my head from the pillow, now wide awake and body tense, more from the alarm in Georjie's whisper than anything else.

Distantly, there came the sound of breaking glass through the open window.

"That was downstairs," Georjie said. "Like down-downstairs."

"Ground floor storeroom?" I guessed, wondering if Sera or Adalbert were up looking for something and tripped in the dark. I was used to hearing the occasional sounds of one or the other of them moving about late at night or early in the morning, which might explain why I'd missed the sounds but Georjie hadn't.

There were a few dull thuds, muffled by distance and levels of building, but unmistakable. It sounded like wood hitting against wood. Okay, those were not normal 'staff' noises.

Like a couple of ghosts, Georjie and I padded to the window to listen, where more distant sounds could be heard. We stared at one another in the dark, wondering what to do. I didn't want to call the police until I was sure it wasn't a staff member fumbling in the dark.

Without speaking, we made for the door, me in plaid cotton pajama bottoms and a t-shirt, and Georjie in a pair of knee-length sleep shorts, a long-sleeved t-shirt and slippers. I slipped my toes into my sneakers when we got to the door.

Opening the door a crack, we listened for sound in the hall, but all was quiet. Walking down the hallway to the main staircase, Georjie followed me silently. When we reached the doorway to the private passage and steps leading into the ground floor, I paused to turn the handle slowly.

Swinging the door open, we listened.

Nothing.

I didn't turn on the light as we made our way downstairs, but went slowly. I avoided the step which I knew to be a squeaker, warning Georjie with hand gestures to do the same. She nodded and stepped over it with ease, those long legs coming in handy.

"It came from that side," Georjie mouthed at me in the gloom, as she pointed to the workshop.

I nodded. Whatever we'd heard, it had been coming from that corner of the house.

Tiptoeing to the door leading to the workshop, I put my hand on the handle and listened. Still nothing. I began to turn the handle.

Georjie put her hand over mine and sent me a questioning look. I knew what she was thinking. Were we being stupid? If we were regular teenagers, I might have thought so, but we were supernaturals. True, there was no plant life on which to call for Georjie, but my siren voice was powerful enough to stop anyone except another siren or a descendant of a siren in their tracks. I also had superhuman strength, and wasn't afraid.

I gave Georjie a look that I hoped translated as 'it'll be okay,' and she lifted her hand from mine and nodded.

Opening the door in a quick movement, my hand darted for the light switch.

The workshop flooded with artificial light.

There was no one there, but it was clear that there had been.

Georjie and I entered the workshop and surveyed the evidence. Drawers had been left open, and boxes carried to tables and rummaged through, their contents spread across the tabletops. Cupboard doors were open and things had been pulled out. Two sprays of broken glass lay at the base of the door leading to the backyard, and the two window panes closest to the inside lock and handle were broken. The door was still open.

I moved toward the door, and Georjie said quietly, "Watch yourself, there. Looks like some oil was spilled on the floor."

A small bottle of overturned machine lubricant dripped a stream of clear oil onto the floor, and it was slowly spreading.

Georjie grabbed some rags from one of the open drawers and dropped them on the oil so it wouldn't spread farther. "Did they take anything?"

"I really can't tell. Last time I was down here was the day the museum guys came to get the artifacts for the exhibition."

"The artifacts were down here?"

I nodded. "Yeah, they were all packaged and labeled. They took up most of this wall." I gestured to the largest of the wooden shelving units, the one where most of the drawers and cupboard doors were open, revealing only emptiness.

Georjie made a thoughtful sound in the back of her throat. "Why isn't there more security?"

"There is more than you think," I said, pointing to the broken padlock and chain on the inside of the door. As I really focused on it, a chill settled over me. I nearly picked up the broken chain, but stopped myself when I realized I shouldn't disturb the evidence. The broken ends revealed metal that had been bent and stretched, as well as a warped padlock. "Look at this."

Georjie stepped over the mess of oily rags on the floor and came over, brows drawn. Bending at the waist to get a better look, she inspected the metal. "That wasn't snipped with bolt-cutters. It looks...almost like pulled taffy."

Our eyes met, the consternation on her face matched my own.

"Who could do that?" I asked.

"A supernatural could do that," she said quietly, putting words to my very thoughts.

Fear kindled in my gut the way it hadn't earlier. Even when we'd heard someone breaking the glass and thudding around down here, I hadn't been afraid. What human being should I be afraid of? The only human I should fear was the kind I couldn't see coming, couldn't anticipate. But this was different, the evidence pointed to someone with a very strange tool for stretching and twisting metal, or someone with the ability to do such a thing with their bare hands. I swallowed, and rubbed my arms with my hands.

"We'd better let the police know," I said.

Georjie nodded. "It's too bad this isn't a dirt floor. Is there dirt outside the door?"

I shook my head, and knew why she was asking. If there was earth for her to pick up, Georjie could look back in time and see the residual of what had happened here.

"The walkway leading up to this door is paved." Hope sprang in my chest. "But there's lots of grass and dirt beside it that they could have stepped on. What if they didn't follow the path? What if they scaled the hedge or something?"

We went outside into the cold cloudy night. A motion sensor light blinked on above our heads as we stepped into the back yard.

The path of paving stones led from the backyard, across to a patio where a covered seating area held patio furniture stacked and covered for the winter season. The path branched from there, one leading to the front of the house, and the other to the rear gate I used to get down to the beach.

Georjie's slippers went from paving stone to paving stone until we were halfway to the back gate. Bending, she scraped at the dirt beside the pathway, trying to get enough together for a handful. The ground was hard-packed and difficult to penetrate. She squatted, working at it until she had a small pile of the stuff in her palm. Standing, we both stared at the little lump of dirt.

"Is that enough?"

"I don't know," she said, "but it's worth a shot."

I took a step back, mesmerized. Georjie had explained to Saxony, Akiko, and me that this was one of her gifts as a Wise, but I'd never seen her use it. A small gasp issued from my lips as her closed eyelids popped open, the irises gone and replaced by a blue-white glow. Her blond hair lifted from her shoulders by a preternatural wind I couldn't feel and blew back from her temples and cheekbones, revealing her face in a way I had only seen in a photo. Her hand held steady in front of her stomach, the little pile of dirt sitting benignly in her palm.

I couldn't see her pupils anymore, but it seemed as though she was scanning the yard. She turned in a circle, slowly, while I stayed still so as not to distract her.

Suddenly, her other hand snaked out to grab me by the wrist and she yanked me across the pathway to the grass, her lips open with a quick intake of breath. My heart leapt into my throat and began to sprint.

"What is it, Georjie? You're freaking me out here."

"Sorry." Her hand upturned and the dirt fell to the ground. Her eyes lost the ethereal glow and her focus returned to my face. "A residual passed right through where you were standing, and I didn't think, I just moved you. It's too weird seeing a residual pass through a living body."

"So it worked? You did see someone?"

She shook her head. "Only a momentary flash. He came from that gateway and must have used the path except for a second where his foot hit the ground right there," she pointed to just beyond where I'd been standing. "I only saw him for a flash, the time it took for him to take half a step. And he had his back to me."

"Well, it's something. We know it was a man. Did you see anything else? What color was his hair?"

She shook her head. "I can't see in color, but he had a hood on anyway, so I can't even tell you if it was dark or light colored."

We gazed at each other, disappointed. "Shall we try outside the gate?"

"There's nothing but sidewalk out there, it's all paved."

Her shoulders drooped a little. "Well, we got something anyway."

"Yeah," I muttered. "Something we can't tell the police."

"Why not?"

"They'll ask us how we know, and what are you going to tell them? That you have magical powers gifted to you by the fae? They'll think you're crazy."

"No, of course not," she replied, as we moved back inside the building. "But we could say that we saw something from your window. It looks into the backyard, so it's plausible, right?"

"But how are you going to explain that you saw him only from the back?" I closed the door behind us.

"I'll say I saw him leaving."

"And when they ask you the color of his clothing?"

"I'll just say it was dark, and I couldn't tell."

"There's a motion sensor light out there."

"Right." Georjie frowned. "Well, his hoody was dark, it could have been navy or brown, black or gray, or maybe really dark red or purple. I'll tell them that it all happened too fast for me to register the color, just that it was a dark tone. Plus we were frightened."

"You were frightened," I knocked her on the shoulder, playfully. But I agreed her explanation to the police could work

"I was, actually," she admitted, dimpling. "But kind of excited, too. Is that wrong?"

I shook my head and chuckled. "I wasn't frightened until I saw the chain. Still a little freaked out. Next time, it'll be a code or a combination."

"I don't think that would make any difference. If they can bend metal like this, why couldn't they do that to a combination lock too?"

"I was thinking one of those electronic panels where you have to punch in a code."

"You'd have to change out the whole door for that," she said.

"Exactly. What are glass window panes doing in a ground floor door, anyway?"

"This door could be eighty years old for all you know, and you said the vehicles were kept in a super secure garage, so I guess this old workshop wasn't really in need of better security until now."

"Yeah, I guess. They're going to examine the lock. The police, I mean."

She nodded. "I know. But there's nothing we can do about that." We scanned the mess. "Better leave everything be for now. It's a crime scene, right?" Georjie crossed her arms. "I'm freezing."

"Let's go. I'll call them right now."

"What do you think they were after?" Georjie asked as we made our way upstairs.

"From the fact that nothing was taken, and the only things of much value in that room were the artifacts from the wreck, that's my guess. They wanted the stuff from *The*

Sybellen. There were some valuable pieces, so it kind of makes sense."

"I guess it was all over the papers," Georjie surmised in a whisper as we closed the door. "Everyone in Poland would have known that this house probably had valuable stuff in it."

I frowned. "Maybe."

I didn't know if that was a detail that had been printed in any articles, but it was a fact that wouldn't have been difficult to find. Novak staff, salvage team staff, journalists, museum staff, lots of people knew where the artifacts were stored. I made a mental note to check the press articles. Martinius had a scrapbook with them in his office, not to mention all the digital files which had been pulled together for a slideshow for the party. If it was noted publicly, that would throw a discouragingly wide net, but if it wasn't, then at least the police could narrow their search a little bit.

"I have to wake up Adalbert and Sera," I said as we made our way back to the main staircase.

"Right. They speak Polish," she added. "I'll come with you."

We crossed the manor to the suite Adalbert and Sera shared so they could call the police.

FOURTEEN

The police sent two officers to inspect the scene and take our statements. We brought Adalbert and Sera up to speed —they were both more shaken than either Georjie or I had been, and we didn't even tell them about the way the metal was broken. The police inspected the metal and took photos of it, conversing quietly among themselves about it in Polish. Georjie and I, now bundled up against the cold, watched from the doorway, sharing glances and observing their reactions. If they were shaken by the evidence, they did a good job in not showing it.

Adalbert had a contractor on the scene by late afternoon, installing a new door with an electronic code lock on it. I doubted a code would stop someone with supernatural strength who was determined to get inside, but it was better than the previous door with the glass windows.

Georjie and I went for a beach walk before lunch, and afterward curled up in the big parlor on the main floor with books and tea. It had begun to drizzle while we were on the beach, and as the gloom of a tenacious storm settled in, the early spring rain came down in fat drops. We were putting off the inevitable—Georjie's packing—and were seated on one of the big sofas together, facing each other with our backs against the armrests and our noses in our respective books, Georjie's legs against the edge of the couch, and mine against the inside. I was just thinking of adding another log to the fire when we heard a car pull up in the drive.

Hoping irrationally for it to be Antoni, whom I had called about the break-in, I leapt from the couch and headed to the window. He wasn't due until evening, but my heart surged with hope anyway.

"Easy there," Georjie said, "the springs in this couch are already poking me in more than one unwelcome location. Is it Antoni? I thought he would be at work."

"He is, and no, it's not him." I frowned through the wet glass at the blurry figure of the slender behatted museum curator as he stepped from the car and an umbrella blossomed over his head.

We met him in the foyer before he had a chance to ring the doorbell and call Adalbert or Sera to the door.

"You're on top of things today," he said, index finger pointed at the doorbell. He put his hand down. "Sorry for the sudden appearance."

He didn't smile, and his dark eyes held a grim, troubled expression.

"That's all right, Abraham. Come in out of the rain." I stepped back to leave room for him to pass and shut the door. "You seem upset."

"That's because I am. I don't suppose there is a way to reach your mother?" He set the pointed end of the umbrella into the oversized vase meant just for the purpose and took his hat off, cradling it to his chest. He looked hopefully into my face.

"She's working on a containment job, and not available,

I'm afraid. But I can pass along any news as soon as she reaches out."

Abraham was unsatisfied by this, but didn't push it. He ran his fingers through the thinning hair at his scalp. "I feel badly. Your mother put her precious artifacts into my care, and we've had something terrible happen. At the same time, I'm baffled by what has transpired, and hope that perhaps you might be able to shed some light on the situation."

Georjie and I shared a look at this. I suddenly remembered my manners and introduced her to Abraham.

Abraham took the brim of his hat between both index fingers and thumbs, fingers splaying out. He looked sheepish and contrite. "The museum had a break-in last night."

"Abraham, we had a break in ourselves here, also last night."

"Yes, I know. That's part of why I came. I wanted to make sure you were all right. The police told me when they came to take our statements, that the Novak manor had likely been breached by the very villain who had successfully breached our own security."

"Yeah." Georjie crossed her arms. "How much are you willing to bet that it was the same person?"

"That does seem likely at first blush," the museum director replied, letting his hat fall to the side. "But there are strange factors at play. The police said that you had glass windows smashed, and a padlock broken."

Georjie and I nodded.

"But whoever broke into the museum had the code."

There was only the sound of the rain while that sank in.

"That's whacked out," said Georjie, finally breaking the silence. "Why would they bother coming here if they had the code for the museum?"

"Yes, this situation is most bizarre, not the least of which is that only one item was stolen, and not even the most precious item, at that."

This was news. "What was stolen?"

"A pendant set with an aquamarine."

"I remember it," I said, surprised. "There was a lot of nice jewelry in that case."

He nodded. "Indeed, but nothing else was taken, though they just as easily could have cleaned out the entire display. The thief had access to everything in the case, and yet took only the pendant. There were several more valuable pieces left untouched." Abraham took a breath. "Could I ask you to either allow someone to go through the Novak family archives, or would you be willing to do so yourself, to look for anything that might shed some light about the pendant?"

"Isn't that something the police should do?" Georjie asked.

"Perhaps in cases where the value of what was taken was greater, yes," Abraham replied. "But the police are hesitant to put more resources than they deem necessary toward this particular scenario. They believe the perpetrator to be one of our own staff, or one of your own staff, someone who knows the Novak family history and might want the pendant for personal reasons."

"But the pendant wasn't necessarily Novak property," I ventured.

"That's true, but it quite likely was, given that the manifest contained only a small amount of jewelry and the pendant was not listed as cargo. Also, none of the history we have of the sailors on board points to families of affluence."

"Even if they had the means to own such a gem,"

Georjie ruminated, "why would they bring it on board a ship?"

"A good question," Abraham agreed.

"I don't mind looking," I said. "Martinius's office is full of interesting stuff, and I suppose someone will have to go through it sooner rather than later."

Abraham nodded and put his damp hat back on his head. "Thank you. And could I ask you to call me should you find anything of interest?"

"Sure."

"That's all right, then." He gave a nod and reached for the door. "I won't keep you any longer, and I can sort the details out of any insurance business with Marian. No need to trouble you with that."

"Thanks, Abraham."

"Least I can do." He turned to leave.

"Do you mind if I ask," Georjie said quickly, "how the thief broke in?"

"Through the back alley access, the same one the staff use." Abraham paused, his hand on the door. "Just walked right in." His face paled as though saying the words out loud made it even more embarrassing. His shoulders stooped and he seemed aged and weary. "I've never seen anything like it in all my days. I am very disappointed in my staff, I just don't know who to direct my ire on just yet. The police are arranging to question everyone. It's most disruptive, as you can imagine. Most upsetting."

"I'm sure. Mr. Trusilo, is there any green space by the back door? Perhaps a little garden, or a patch of bare ground?"

He looked bemused, but nodded. "There is, actually. Why?" His face changed expression as a breeze of understanding blew across it. "Oh, for footprints?"

"Yes, exactly," said Georjayna, face smooth as butter. I had to bite my cheeks to keep from smiling.

"There were a few dirty marks, but unfortunately not enough to leave a full footprint so they weren't of a lot of help to the police."

"What a shame," she intoned.

"Yes, well." Abraham readjusted the hat on his head and flicked the brim with his finger sending a little spray of droplets into the air. "I've taken up enough of your time this afternoon." He nodded at me. "Do let me know what you find, if anything, Targa."

"I will."

We said goodbye and he headed out into the rainy day. I closed the door behind him and leaned against it with my back. My eyes found Georjie's.

"Up for a little after-dark investigation?" she asked, one fine eyebrow twitching up mischievously.

I smiled at my friend. "I almost pity the fool. Now, let's get you packed and ready for tomorrow."

───

ONCE ANTONI and I had kissed one another goodnight, he turned to Georjie. "Have a good time in Scotland, whatever you get up to. I'm a little jealous. It was really great meeting you. I can see why Targa is so fond of you."

Georjie colored a little. "Likewise, Antoni. Maybe I'll see you among the highlands one day." They hugged, and as she stepped back, I heard her say, "Take good care of our girl."

As soon as Antoni slipped out the front door, Georjie and I put our outdoor gear on and went to the garage. Flicking on the light switch just inside the door flooded the six-car garage with fluorescent light. The cold concrete space smelled like rubber, oil, gasoline, and diesel, but it was shiny and clean. Four vehicles sat under custom black fabric cozies, and several times more than four sets of keys dangled from hooks on a corkboard over a workbench along one wall.

"Wow," breathed Georjie. "So, these cars are all yours now? Your life is so weird." She walked around one of the mysterious shapes and lifted the corner of the fabric to peek underneath.

"Says the girl who can see the past and turn into a tree," I replied, lifting my own corner of fabric.

"Touché. Have you ever driven in Poland before?"

"Yes, but only an old truck to the dump when I was collecting garbage from the sea. They drive on the right-hand side of the road here, so I should be fine."

"This is Europe, though, they don't build cities on a grid. It's more like someone threw a bunch of super-long spaghetti down on the terrain and then just paved it the way it fell...with cobblestones."

I grinned. "That just makes it more fun."

"Right." Georjie didn't look like she agreed with me.

"Do you want to drive?"

Her head was invisible beneath the fabric of one of the vehicles as she peered in through the window. "Nope. I don't drive stick shift." Her head appeared, her blond hair mussed. "Good thing your mom always drove stick."

I agreed. "Which one looks the least expensive?"

"I'd say the little Fiat."

"Fiat it is." Rifling through the keys on the wall, I found the Fiat's key fob while Georjie pulled the fabric off the sleek red body of the little car.

We got inside and I adjusted the seat, the steering

wheel, and the mirrors. The little black device hooked to the sun visor was easy to spot, and I pressed the button on the remote. An electronic hum and movement in the rearview mirror signaled the rising of the garage door directly behind us.

Georjie took my phone from my bag and punched the museum's address into the GPS. Backing the little Fiat out of the garage, I took a steadying breath, wheeling the car around to face the hill leading from the garage level to the main level and out the front gate. I guided the Fiat out onto the deserted nighttime street. The rain had let up a little, and now drizzled lazily against the windshield.

Georjie navigated us into Gdansk and to a side street not far from the museum. The night was cool and wet, the cobblestones of the downtown glimmered in the light of street lamps and broken patches of moonlight. After climbing out of the car, I could hear distant noises of laughter and music from the direction of the theatre district. Quietly, we slipped into the alley behind the museum and found the rear entrance. A small parking lot with a single car sat nestled against a narrow strip of scrawny saplings. The pavement ended and a short patch of earth sprouted with patchy grass below a rear door with a sign which read 'staff entrance' in several languages. The light of a single bulb over the door cast its eerie glow over the parking lot and patch of ground. A recycling bin sat against the fence separating the museum's lot from its neighbor, an art gallery.

"We should have asked Abraham if the police were watching the museum," Georjie muttered quietly as we approached the back door.

"I doubt they are. What's the point of watching where

the crime was already committed? The thieves got what they were after, so they won't likely be back."

"I guess. But if I was in charge, I'd double up security just because it would seem stupid not to after a break in."

"You have a point, and there is one car here." I put a hand on her arm, holding her back as I scanned the visible windows for lights. "If someone does bother us, I may have to use my voice on them."

"Fine, but if you addle my wits, you have Liz to answer to."

"That's a scarier prospect than it used to be," I joked.

The soles of our shoes squelched onto the grass and Georjie bent down and drew out a handful of soft wet earth. "Ending my visit on a bang," she muttered. "All right, Dark Hoody, let's see what your face looks like."

Her eyes phased to white and her lips parted as she faced the doorway. Her eyebrows shot up sharply and she uttered a surprised, "Oh!"

"What? What did you see?" I almost danced in place in my desperation to know.

"It's not a guy, it's a girl, and a young one!"

"What? Really?"

Staring at the residual I couldn't see, Georjie described her to me. "She's tall, almost as tall as I am. She's got brown hair, shoulder-length, and a piercing in her right cheek."

Shock sent the blood tumbling from my brain and I swayed for a moment from the surprise.

Georjie stood up and the white cleared from her eyes. She looked at her dirty hands and glanced around for something to clean them with. Dipping them in the rain-barrel under the drainpipe, she faced me. "Abraham was right, she had the code written on her hand. She walked right in."

"Was she wearing a plaid coat with a skull patch on the shoulder, by chance?"

Georjie blinked in surprise. "You know her?"

I nodded, feeling sick to my stomach. My mind could not grasp why she would possibly have robbed the museum. "It was Antoni's sister, Lydia."

FIFTEEN

I elected to drive Georjie to the airport myself rather than have Adam drive us, so that we could talk freely. The day was a rare one for winter on the Baltic, bright though not cloudless, the sunlight streaming through a wispy bank of cloud over the city was bright enough to require sunglasses.

Georjie and I drove in silence on the freeway toward the city's international airport, both lost in a thoughtful silence. The morning traffic closed around us and cleared out again as the majority of vehicles headed for the business center of Gdansk.

Feeling Georjie's eyes on me, I sent a smile her way.

"You're not fooling me, Targa," she said, lifting her sunglasses off her face and into her hair.

"I know. I'm not trying to." My knuckles were nearly white on the steering wheel, and I'd skipped breakfast, an act that alarmed even Sera and Adalbert, for I'd become famous for my appetite. I had tossed and turned all night, too.

"What are you going to tell him?"

I took a bracing inhale and let it out slowly. "I have to tell him the truth."

"Even without any proof? Or any explanation?" Georjie reached for the handle above the Fiat's passenger window as we took a curved ramp a little too fast. I eased off the gas a little. "He's going to ask you how you know it was her."

"I know." I frowned. "I almost wish we hadn't discovered the truth. That way someone else could tell Antoni."

"You could call the police and give them an anonymous tip..."

I glanced at my friend, hearing the doubt in her voice that her suggestion would be well taken. "That's the action of a coward."

Georjie lifted a shoulder. "Maybe, maybe not. We used a supernatural ability to discover her. Maybe it's just smart to keep yourself out of it? Avoid the questions you can't answer."

We lapsed into a thoughtful silence while I tried to follow the alternative paths into the future depending on which door I went through. An anonymous call to the authorities, who would subsequently question Lydia, who would more than likely lie to protect herself. And then what? Would they apprehend her? I didn't watch enough crime television to know what they had a right to do, but I assumed they'd look for evidence and once they had it, they'd arrest her. She'd have to hire a lawyer, and most likely Antoni would have to pay the legal fees, since it appeared she was already having money troubles. Ugh. The more I thought it through, the less I liked option B.

But where did option A lead?

If Antoni believed me, it would give him an opportunity to talk to Lydia before the authorities got involved. Maybe she'd be honest with him, tell him why she'd done such a bizarre and stupid thing. I could only hope that she'd be honest with her brother, though her behavior of late wasn't encouraging. It just didn't make any sense. Why steal a moderately valuable item from a collection of them, while leaving the rest behind? She obviously had the key to the case which held all the jewelry from the wreck, so if she was hard up for cash, why wouldn't she just take all of it? Was it a prank? Some inane dare that her friends put on her?

Taking the airport exit, I slowed the Fiat and guided it into the short-term parking lot. Turning off the vehicle, we got out and went around back as I popped the trunk with the button on the key fob.

As I reached for Georjie's carry-on bag, she stopped me with a hand on my arm.

I looked up into her concerned face and she pulled me into a hug.

"I don't like to leave you like this. Look at you." She squeezed me and kissed the top of my head the way my mom used to do. The gesture made my eyelids rim with moisture. How much I wanted my mom with me today.

"I'll be fine, Georjie. I am glad you were here when all this went down."

"You call me anytime, okay?" She released me and stepped back. "I know you a little by now. I understand that you won't take the easy way out—it's part of what I love about you."

I gave her a shaky smile. "Thanks, Georjie."

It was on the tip of my tongue to ask her to stay a little longer, but that wouldn't be fair. Georjie was looking forward to getting to Scotland, and someone she cared about was waiting for her.

We rolled her luggage toward departures.

"One day I'd like to meet your cousin," I said.

She wrinkled her nose. "I don't like to think of him as my cousin, anymore."

"Sorry. One day I'd like to meet this Jasher fellow."

"Why don't you come for a visit sometime?" she said. "And I was thinking that you, me, Saxony and...we need to get together to celebrate our graduation, since we kind of lost our final year together."

I didn't miss the pause where she'd wanted to include Akiko. My heart gave an ache of a different kind.

"That would be fun."

She brightened. "We could do our own little international prom night, meet up somewhere none of us has ever been, a girl's trip."

I nodded and agreed that it sounded like a good idea, but I was too distracted by my present problems to allow myself to get too excited.

"We'll all be legal by then." Her voice softened. "We can have a toast to honor our departed."

I nodded but didn't trust myself to speak. The departed no longer referenced only Akiko, but also my mother. I tried not to let my misery claim all of my expression, but I wasn't sure I succeeded.

Georjie checked her bags and we stood outside of security.

"Text me when you land in Edinburgh, let me know you're safe," I said.

"Sure thing. Are you going to talk to Antoni today?"

I nodded. "I want to give him a chance to talk to Lydia before the authorities figure it out."

"Then how about I call you once I get settled and you can let me know how that went?"

"Sure."

Georjie took out her phone and took a selfie of the two of us to send to Saxony. We hugged again, and I watched her go through security until I lost view of her behind the opaque glass walls.

Striding back to the Fiat, I braced myself for the difficult conversation still ahead.

AS I WAS MOUNTING the stairs from the garage and turning the problem of how I was going to tell Antoni about Lydia over and over in my mind, my cell phone rang. I retrieved it from my bag as I stepped through the door into the foyer. It was a local number.

"Hello?"

"Targa?"

I recognized the museum curator's unique voice. "Abraham?"

"Yes. There's been a development I thought you should know about," he said.

Yeah, you're not kidding, I thought, but kept my news to myself. I didn't want anyone to know before Antoni did. "What's going on?"

"There was a strange fellow here less than an hour ago. He came in and bought a ticket for *The Sybellen* display. He was alone. He asked one of our staff members about the pendant specifically, saying that he'd heard it was part of the display but he was wondering where to find it."

I stood there with the door open as this sunk in, until a cold draft hit my back and I remembered to shut the door.

"He was wearing a maroon hoody. Your friend told the police that the person who broke into your house was wearing a dark hoody, correct?"

"Yes." My voice came out hoarse and I swallowed.

"I immediately sent Helen to call the police, hoping they'd get there in time to question him. She called from my office but I swear it was like the guy had supersonic hearing or something. We tried to keep him there, get him to casually talk about the pendant, what he knew about it, why he was interested, but he flew out of the museum pretty quick and we weren't able to detain him. If the police had gotten here faster, maybe we could have caught the perpetrator by now. I thought you should know."

My mind whirled. Whoever this guy was, was not the perpetrator, but he more than likely was the one who had broken into the manor. I couldn't say that to Abraham though. "What did he look like?"

"Dark, almost shoulder length hair, blue eyes, Caucasian. Medium height and with a lean build. Hard to tell his age. He could have been twenty or forty. You know how faces can sometimes be like that."

"Yes, I do. Okay, thanks for letting me know, Abraham. I'll keep an eye out and let the staff know."

"No problem. I don't suppose you've had time to do any searching in Martinius's personal records for anything relating to this pendant, have you? This whole thing just gets stranger by the minute."

"I have looked a little, but I had a friend here until this morning, so I didn't want to spend all of yesterday searching," I admitted, stretching the truth a bit. The one half-hour I did get to snoop around Martinius's office produced nothing of interest. "I'll look again this afternoon."

"I appreciate that, Targa. I'm sure the Novak heiress has more important things to be doing than going through a bunch of old boxes and paperwork."

"Not really," I said with a smile. "It's a good excuse for avoiding writing my history paper on the Celtic holocaust."

"That does indeed sound grim. I'll leave you to it then, and Targa?"

"Yes?"

"Just...be careful." There was a pause, then, "I have a daughter about your age. I wouldn't be sleeping very well if I knew that her apartment had been broken into." He chuckled dryly. "I don't sleep well anyway, but that's beside the point. It comes with the territory of having a teenage daughter."

My thoughts flew back to Lydia and my heart sank. "Thanks," I said. "I'll be as careful as I can be."

SIXTEEN

After lunch, I changed into warmer clothes and got to work searching what used to be Martinius's office. Though it was technically mine now, I doubted that I'd ever think of it as anyone's other than his. I started with the desk. In the back of a drawer I found a brass key etched with the symbol of *The Sybellen*. A quick search of the room didn't turn up a lock to use it in.

Hefting the old brass key in my hand, I left Martinius's office and made my way to the main staircase. Padding down the stairs until I reached the foyer, I heard movement from the large sitting room at the west corner of the manor. Poking my head in, I saw Sera kneeling at the fireplace, adding wood to the fire crackling away merrily in the large grate.

"Hi, Sera." I crossed the room, weaving my way between the antique furniture.

"Hello, Miss Targa."

"Mr. Truliso called to tell me someone wearing a dark maroon hoody was asking about the pendant stolen from the museum."

Her green eyes widened and she got to her feet, dusting her hands off. "Really?"

"Yes. That's why I'm looking for anything in Martinius's family records that might help the police figure out what's so special about that pendant. I found this." I held out my palm, showing her the brass key. "I'm wondering if you know what it unlocks?"

She frowned, picked it up, and studied the imprint of the ship on the handle. "I've never seen the key before, but I have seen this symbol. I have a feeling I know exactly what it opens."

"Really!"

She gave a nod. "Shall I show you?"

"Please."

I followed Sera down the hall to the servants staircase and we climbed to the third floor, where she led me into the old part of the house. We passed Martinius's office and when we reached the end of the hall, there was a low, narrow doorway with a brass plate under the door handle.

"Here. See?" Sera touched the brass plate where the same ship had been etched into the brass. "It's the only door in the whole house that has this. I think they all must have had them at one time, but as the house was renovated and added to, they did away with the old doors and locks. All except for this one. This is just a storage room, though."

"That sounds exactly like what I'm looking for, Sera. Thank you."

My heart had sped up a notch. Inserting the key into the lock, the unused mechanism was tight, but the bolt came free. I opened the door and we stepped inside. The room had one small dormer, similar to the one in Martinius's office, only this window was dusty and the light in the room was dim. The space was similar in size and layout to Martinius's office, but where his office was clean and cozy, this room was cobwebby and the air stale. There had been a fireplace at one time, but someone had bricked it up. An old writing desk sat in front of the dormer, with no chair and a few boxes stacked on top.

"This looks like it was an office, too," Sera said, eyes sweeping the shelving against the wall, which was stacked with boxes with handwritten labels on them.

"The company's old business files?" I stepped closer to the stacks of boxes and blew the dust off one of the labels. The ink was faded but I could make out a row of numbers which looked like a code for month and year all run together in six digits.

"I don't think so, or if they are, they're very old. Everything to do with the company was moved to the downtown office archives back in the seventies." Sera waved a hand in front of her face and gave a cough. Then she sneezed. "Awfully dusty."

Glancing up at her, I asked, "Allergies?"

She nodded, a finger under her nose.

"Don't worry, I don't need help, Sera. And I didn't mean to interfere with your day. I can look. You go on."

"You sure?"

I said I was, and she left me to it.

Scanning the boxes and looking at what I assumed were dates, I found that there was no order to the way the boxes were stacked. Here was a box labeled 10-1945, and on top of it was a box marked 06-1892.

"Wow," I whispered. I didn't know any families in Canada that had family records or documents dated back this far. Maybe there were North American families who'd colonized on the east coast and brought documents with them, but it was more likely that many of their belongings were left behind. "It's a museum, with even older stuff than the rest of the house."

I continued to search for a box dated from before *The Sybellen* went down. She had sunk in the spring of 1869, so anything dated after that wouldn't likely be of much help in solving the mystery of the pendant. When I found a box labelled 031867, I almost whooped for joy. Hauling the box from its pile, I took it to the desk, opened it, and began to look through the contents.

It didn't take long for my heart to sink at the daunting task. All of the documents were in Polish, naturally, so even if something was written here about the pendant, I wouldn't be able to read it. It crossed my mind to ask Sera to do this job, but it would take her days, if not weeks, to read every-thing. And what a monotonous and possibly meaningless task.

What I needed was access to old photo albums. Perhaps there was a photo of someone wearing the pendant.

Putting all the documents carefully back, I closed up the box, returned it to the shelf, and looked for another box with any date before the spring of 1869.

My stomach was beginning to complain for its dinner by the time I had repeated the process with other boxes three more times. I gave a sigh and stretched my back after sliding the last box back onto the shelf. No photographs, and if there had been something written about the pendant, any evidence of it in a letter, I would have just passed over it anyway. I gave a growl of frustration. This was useless.

I locked up the storage room and went back to Martinius's room to return the key to safe-keeping.

His office was almost as gloomy as the room I'd just left and I wished there was a fire in the grate. I also wished

Martinius was there, sitting on his chair in front of the fire, telling me about the mysterious pendant.

My eye fell on a row of thick red matching spines on the far end of his bookshelf. Squatting in front of the low shelf, I retrieved one of them and flipped it open. Photographs. This was more helpful, except that the people in the photos were dressed as though it was the eighties, so way off in terms of era.

Quickly, I flipped through all of the photo albums, looking for somewhere with a year inscribed. The photos became black and white, then yellowed with age, but the oldest year I could find notated was 1923.

I shoved the last photo album back home with a sigh. No dice.

Sitting in the dormer seat, I pulled my legs up under me and frowned at Martinius's office.

"Can you give me a clue, old fella?" I asked the room. "What's the significance of this pendant?"

As I looked around, I spotted the old leather-bound journal, the one Aleksandra Iga Novak had written in, the one Martinius had had translated so I could read it in English. It did not have any title on the spine but I recognized it because of that. Curious to handle the original, I got up and retrieved it, returning to sit under the window again. I smiled as I rubbed a hand over the old leather, cracked at the seams. I brought it to my nose and inhaled the smell of old paper, one I'd come to appreciate.

A yellowed slip of paper fell from between the cracks and landed in my lap.

My heart lurched as the drawing on the page caught the light from the window. It was just a rough sketch, but there was no mistaking it, it was the pendant. That same oblong shape, and even the strange glyph cradling the aquamarine.

A bunch of Polish was scribbled on the page beside the drawing, as well as a tally of numbers. If I wasn't mistaken, this was a receipt of purchase. There was no vendor name or address, so I wasn't sure. I needed to get it translated.

Heart pounding, I took the page and tore from Martinius's office. Taking the stairs down two at a time, I landed in the foyer.

"Sera?" I yelled, and paused to listen, chest heaving and heart pounding.

"Here!" Came the borderline alarmed reply, and she appeared in the hallway to my right. "I'm here. Everything okay?"

We met halfway in between and I handed her the paper.

"Can you translate this?"

Her brows drew together as her eyes scanned the drawing and the writing. "Is this the pendant?"

"Yes, the very same."

She glanced up, shocked. "You actually did it. You must be some kind of magician. Where did you find this?"

"It was inside Aleksandra's journal. It's a receipt, right? For the purchase of it?"

She read the note a second time, brow furrowing. "Interesting. It is a receipt but not the way you think." One tapered finger traced the handwritten scrawl beside the drawing. "Someone paid this fellow, Rainer Veigel—that's the recipient—a finder's fee for the necklace."

"A finder's fee?"

She nodded. "That's what it says under 'services rendered.'" She handed the receipt back to me. "And no surprise that it was definitely a Novak, look at the signature on the bottom."

My eye found the messy scrawl on the line at the

bottom of the receipt and goosebumps rose on my skin like a ghost had breathed across my neck. If I had looked more carefully before I had barreled out of Martinius's office, I would have noticed it myself.

The signature on the bottom was the hand of Sybellen's husband—Mattis Novak. I stared at the name, mouth hanging open.

"The date, Sera," I whispered, hoarsely. "Look at the date."

Peering over my shoulder she read aloud, "May seventeen, eighteen-sixty-nine."

I stared at her, and at first her expression did not convey any comprehension. Then the moment of realization struck and hers eyes found mine in disbelief.

"That has to be significant, no?" she said, in awe.

"I don't know, but if it's not, it's one hell of a coincidence."

The receipt was made out on the day before the ship went down.

SEVENTEEN

I tried to wait until after dinner to break the news about Lydia to Antoni, but failed to act natural before we'd even started eating. He'd asked me three times if I was all right by the time we reached the dining room, which I'd tried to deny twice, and the final time, I had asked if we could talk after dinner.

He grabbed my hand and pulled me around to face him. "Are you trying to torture me? No, we can't wait. If there is something wrong and it's something you can share with me, then please share it now. What is the point of waiting until I have food in my stomach? So I can feel sick afterwards?" He put his warm hands on either side of my face. "Is it something to do with your mom? Why we've hardly heard from her since she left?" His hazel eyes were dark with worry, and his brow wrinkled as his concern deepened. "Are you going to join her?"

I put my hands over his. "No, it's got nothing to do with my mother." As always happened when she came up in conversation, my belly filled with guilt.

"Then what?"

I sighed, and the muscles of my stomach trembled with fright. I could face a storm-demon, a tidal wave, a selfish shark-finning bastard, but I could hardly handle the fear that accompanied telling my love something that I knew was going to hurt, and something that he might choose not to believe. I tried not to think about the possibility that he wouldn't believe me, about the truth it might reveal—that he would sooner believe I'd tell a horrible lie than try and give him an opportunity to talk to his sister before the authorities got to her.

But I had told him a horrible lie. My entire relationship with him was based on a lie. He believed me to be fully human, and I was letting the deception stand. Clenching my eyes shut against the awful feelings all of this torturous self talk roused in me, I asked, "Can we talk upstairs? Somewhere we can be alone?"

"Of course." He folded my hand in his and led me out to the foyer and to the stairway, almost pulling me along. "Your suite?"

I nodded, not trusting my voice. How was I going to do this? I had no proof, even though I knew for sure that it was Lydia who had stolen the pendant from the museum. Would Antoni think I was trying to drive a wedge between him and his sister? Would he be angry with me? I considered how I would feel if Antoni accused my mother of a crime, asking me to believe him even though he didn't have any proof. Putting myself in Antoni's shoes made me feel even more miserable and my courage faltered as we reached my suite door.

"Antoni..." I tried to say it out loud but it came out as a husk of air.

He heard, and looked at me as we entered my suite. "Targa." His voice was soft, comforting. "You look terrified."

He put his hands on either side of my face, fingertips just touching the back of my neck. "What is it? You can tell me anything, you know that, right?"

My nod was more of a head wobble, because I was agreeing to something that wasn't true.

"I'm making up all kinds of horrible stories in my mind right now, Targa. Please put me out of my misery."

He released my face and we sat down on the couch in the sitting room. Antoni took my hand and held it on his knee. His eyes felt like laser-beams boring into my soul.

"I need to ask you for a promise first," I said.

"Okay, if I can, I will. What is it?"

"I need to tell you something that will be upsetting, and I need you not to ask me how I know this thing. I need you to trust that it's true."

His brow wrinkled as he digested this.

"Promise me you won't ask me how I know," I repeated.

"I promise," he replied. He took a deep breath and slowed down his speech. "I won't ask. Now what is it?"

I took a deep breath, too. "It was Lydia who broke into the museum and stole the pendant." It came out in a rush.

At first, his face did not change at all, but as the words sank in, he paled and looked as though I'd just hit him in the stomach. His fingers released the slightest amount of pressure on my own and the gesture sent a barb of fear through my heart.

"I'm so sorry, Antoni."

His eyes never left mine but his voice turned dangerous. "That's a very serious accusation, Targa."

"It's not an accusation, it's a fact."

He released my hand and got up, beginning to pace around the small coffee table in the middle of the room. He was no longer looking at me; his focus had gone inward and his eyes had gone hard.

"Whoever stole that pendant didn't do it for money. If they did, why wouldn't they take everything else in that showcase?" he asked.

Whoever stole that pendant...

He didn't believe me. I felt like I couldn't breathe, my hands and feet became cold and clammy. "Antoni..."

"Why would she do such a thing?" he asked, but he wasn't asking me, he was just thinking out loud, so I kept silent.

My heart gave a little leap of hope—maybe he did believe me. I couldn't quite follow his line of thinking and desperation to understand how this had changed things between us finally loosened my tongue.

"Do you believe me?" I asked.

His eyes flashed to mine as he raked both hands over his head and rubbed his scalp hard in agitation. "Of course I do. I'm just trying to figure out why she would be so stupid."

Relief coursed through my limbs, making them tremble. I closed my eyes for a moment and took a steadying breath. When I opened them, Antoni was striding toward the door. I sprang up from the couch.

"Where are you going?"

He halted suddenly and turned around as though he'd forgotten something on his way to a meeting he was already late for. He reached for me and kissed me hard and fast.

Putting his forehead to mine, he said, "Thank you for coming to me first, and not going to the police." He jerked his head back and his laser-like focus returned to my eyes. "You haven't told the police?"

I shook my head. "No, of course not. But it's only a

matter of time before they find something linking the break-in to her, Antoni."

"I know, that's why I have to find her," he said.

With another quick kiss he had the door to my suite open and was heading down the stairs, with me trying to keep up.

"What are you going to say?" I asked.

"What else?" Antoni strode purposefully into the parlor and grabbed the jacket he'd thrown over the back of one of the couches. "I'm going to ask her why she did it, and find out what kind of other trouble she's in." He thrust his arms into his jacket and zipped it up in one angry motion. "I don't know why she doesn't talk to me first when she gets these crazy ideas."

These crazy ideas? What other stupid things had Lydia done? The siren's curiosity surged through me, but now wasn't a good time to ask. Antoni looked like he was on the warpath, and I was reminded of the fierce expression I'd seen through his face protection during the hockey game.

It was on the tip of my tongue to ask if he wanted me to come with him, but I knew he'd say no, and I agreed. It was going to be a confrontational conversation and it would be better done in private.

With a last, tense kiss on my forehead, Antoni was out the front door and gone.

EIGHTEEN

Georjie's check-in call kept me occupied until late into the evening, but the next morning when I still hadn't heard anything from Antoni, I sent him a text. *Have you spoken with her?*

His answer came quickly. *No luck yet and she's avoiding answering her phone, probably because she knows it's me. Going to take off from work early to try some other places.*

I threw myself into my schoolwork for the morning, but the afternoon had me back up in Martinius's office and staring at the receipt.

I picked up the receiver of the phone sitting on Martinius's desk and dialed the museum. When I got an answer, I asked: "Could I speak with Mr. Trusilo, please?"

"One moment, please," returned the voice.

I waited, chewing my lip and considering the almost one-hundred-fifty-year-old proof of transaction sitting on Martinius's desk. As an afterthought, I opened the top drawer and retrieved a plastic cover, slipping the receipt inside so it was at least a little bit protected. With every fiber of my being I wished Martinius was here so I could ask him about the pendant, and the receipt.

"Hello, Abraham Trusilo speaking."

"Abraham, it's Targa. You said to call if I discovered anything about the stolen pendant." I was talking too fast, I realized, and took a bracing inhale. "Well, I did."

"Yes?" His voice filled with anticipation. "What did you find?"

I described the receipt to him in detail, and what Sera had translated. "I can send you a photo of it."

"Please, do, but I would like to ask if you would mind if the police came to pick it up? It is evidence they need."

I hesitated, but brushed it aside. I was being silly. Of course they needed it. "Absolutely, but I need to know I'll get it back."

"Yes, they'll take a copy of it and return it to you, undamaged of course. What did you say was the amount made out as?"

I told him.

He went silent.

"Abraham?"

"Apologies, I am doing a calculation because that number seems very strange to me."

I heard papers rustling and the scratching of a pen or pencil through the phone. Impatiently, I waited, shifting my weight from one foot to the other.

"Yes, it is very strange. What Mattis paid for this person, this Rainer Veigel, as you say, to find the pendant, is quite a bit more than the pendant would be worth."

"And you've taken inflation into account?"

"I've only done a rough calculation, but I'll get it checked by one of my historians. To me, it doesn't make sense that Mattis would pay so much for it. It would have been cheaper to have another made in its likeness."

"There must be something very special about that particular pendant, then." I turned to face the window and look at the Baltic in the distance, turning these revelations over in my mind.

"I daresay."

Movement caught my eye through breaks in the hedges bordering the side yard, near the mostly unused gate and pathway. As far as I knew, I was the only one who used that old gate, but there was someone here. I narrowed my eyes, trying to make out who it was, expecting it was one of the staff.

A pale face appeared over the top of the gate, the angular face of a man with wisps of black hair framing his cheeks. A dark, wine-colored hood was pulled up over his head.

"Abraham," I interrupted him in the middle of his conjecture. "Did you say that the fellow who was questioning your staff was pale and wearing a maroon hoody?"

"Yes, why?"

"I have to go," I said. "Sorry."

I hung up without waiting for his reply and dashed out of Martinius's office and toward the rear servants stair. Tearing down the stairs, I landed on the final landing in a squat and threw myself out of the narrow rear doorway. Flying down the path to the back corner, I again caught sight of the pale face.

He saw me coming and disappeared behind the hedgerow.

Fear that he would get away hit the back of my throat and spurred me on, hair flying. After tearing open the back gate, I flew through the opening and skid to a halt, eyes darting left.

He was walking fast with his back to me, down the sidewalk following the winding road along the waterline.

My siren voice swelled in my throat and I yelled, "Stop!"

It came out like a deep blast of brass instruments, rolling over him like thunder.

He froze.

Panting from my mad sprint, I walked toward him, calming my heart and preparing to speak.

Slowly, he turned to face me.

Then I was the one to freeze. His expression was one of deep shock as his eyes found mine and our gazes clashed. I was sure the look on my own face must have matched his. Our eyes darted around one another's features, to eyes and lips and cheekbones and hair and back again in a baffled mad dash to process the arrangement of features.

We approached one another, staring, and stopped a few feet apart.

When a siren gives a command in her siren voice, the effect on any hapless human within hearing distance is immediate. Their eyes go soft and unfocused, their face blank. This man did not have a blank face, far from it—his face was full of lucid intelligence. His alert if confounded expression was sharpened by a crafty kind of brilliance.

There was only one kind of human who was immune to a siren's voice, and that was those who had siren blood in their ancestry. I had learned this from my mother when we'd returned to Canada from Poland, and I'd wondered why she hadn't used her voice on Martinius to make him forget what he knew about our identities. She had explained that it wouldn't have worked on him anyway, because Sybellen was most certainly a siren.

I knew why I was staring at this man, mind a blur of questions, face a mask of consternation—but why was he looking at me this way?

"Who are you?" I asked, my siren sound gone and my voice a hollow husk as it cracked over the question.

"Who are *you*?" he replied, and I was shaken by the timbre of his voice. It was beautiful, smooth as cream and deeper than it should be for all his fine features.

White, almost perfectly opaque skin. Bright blue eyes. Black hair. High cheekbones and forehead, expressive wide mouth. I felt like I was looking at my male doppelganger. There were differences—his cheeks and jaw were sharper than mine, his nose longer, and his eyes were deep set, his eyelids large, giving him an intimidating face. But our coloring was the same, even if the blue of his eyes was more intense, almost indigo. Truly, this man was the son of a siren.

"You're one of us," he went on, taking another step closer, his eyes locked onto mine. I couldn't have looked away if I had wanted to. "I heard it in your voice."

I found my voice again, not without considerable effort. "You were at the museum earlier today?"

He did not deny it. "I was."

"And now you're here, at the Novak house, where the pendant used to be. You want it."

His lips softened and parted at hearing the name 'Novak'. His eyes now bordered on pleading and something in my heart warmed to him at this vulnerable, achingly human emotion. "Yes, I want it. Very much."

"Do you know Lydia?"

His brows pinched and the movement was so genuinely

confused that I knew he did not. He shook his head. "Who is Lydia?"

I thought it best to leave Lydia out of the conversation and redirected instead. "Why is the pendant so important to you?"

He seemed puzzled at this question, cocking his head and considering me. "You of all people, being what you are, ask me this?"

Now it was my turn to be confused. He thought I should know its value, its importance. "Up until it was stolen, I thought it was just another artifact from the wreck."

"You truly do not know the powers of that stone?"

These words unlocked a fresh realization—it was not the pendant everyone was after, it was the gem inside, the aquamarine. I shook my head. "I wish you would tell me."

He studied me, the black slashes of his brows down over those burning oceanic eyes. He stepped closer and we were now within touching distance. I could see the perfection of his skin, the stubble of a few days' worth of beard growth.

"I need it for my mother."

"Who is your mother?"

"Her name is Bel. Do you...know her?"

My breath hitched and I whispered, "Sybellen?"

He took in a small, shuddering breath and his eyes grew glassy with moisture as tears lined his lower lids. The blue of his eyes deepened. "Yes."

How could this be? My mind was reeling, the world around me was tilting and swaying. I clenched my eyes shut, processing what the existence of this flesh and blood person in front of me meant. Warm hands touched my shoulders and I opened my eyes and looked up into his familiar yet completely unfamiliar face, his impossible face.

I lifted trembling hands and put them on his upper arms and we stood there holding one another like that, gently, as though we were afraid the other would break or vanish like a ghost.

"You're a Novak," I said, my lower lip trembling. He wasn't just a Novak, he was a century and a half old Novak, and I had no doubt of his telling the truth about it. He oozed authenticity the way other people oozed perspiration.

He nodded and a tear slipped down his cheek. For the first time since my eyes were glued to his face, he smiled and it was a brilliant, dazzling smile.

My mind tripped over all the things I'd read in Aleksandra's Diary, latching onto the things she'd written about Sybellen's sons. She'd had twins. One was very much like her husband, Mattis, and the other...the one who had drowned the night of the wreck, the one who had been lost forever...

"You're Emun." Saying the name rose gooseflesh all over my body.

Another tear slipped down his cheek but he was still smiling. He seemed barely able to control his emotion, and that wide expressive mouth trembled at the corners.

"You don't know how long I have wanted to hear someone call me by my name, my *real*, given name." His eyes burned into mine and his hands tightened around my arms. "You *know* me."

I nodded, and a droplet of moisture tracked down my own cheek. Every beat of the heart in my chest was a juicy, aching pulse. This was the shock of my young life, never had anything so shaken me to my core, not even my own salt-birth, when it had finally come.

"*How* do you know me?"

"I read your grandmother's diary. She believed you

drowned along with all the rest, that night in eighteen-sixty-nine."

His face broke briefly and he struggled to regain control of it—it seemed as though his heart had been torn open by this statement. He nodded and the smile through the tears returned. "Yes, she would have believed that."

Here was Martinius's ancestor, the true last living Novak, the one Martinius should have found, rather than me and Mom. My own heart broke a little, wishing Martinius had stayed alive long enough to have met this miracle.

"You're Emun Novak," I repeated, and he nodded.

"But I still don't know who you are. Are you not a Novak, too? Looking at you is like looking at family. Who are we to each other?"

I shook my head. "We aren't related, at least there is no proof that we are, nothing linking us in my ancestry. I'm a MacAuley, of Canada, and before my mother was a MacAuley, she was a Belshaw."

"That explains your accent," he replied with another smile. "But you *are* a siren."

I nodded. "And you are the son of a siren."

He nodded. "I hope you don't mind me saying I'm a little overcome." He rubbed his fingers across his forehead, like he had a headache.

He wasn't alone in that. My temples throbbed to the beat of my heart.

"You'd better come inside," I said.

NINETEEN

Emun followed me through the gate and across the yard to the rear door I had come rushing out of mere minutes before, although it felt like a lifetime ago. Stealing a glance at him as we climbed the steps to the main level and passed through the foyer, I noticed his eyes had gone glassy and he was taking in his surroundings with a quiet internal shock on his face.

"Are you okay?"

"I haven't been here since my brother died." His voice was thick with emotion. "It has changed a lot, but it still feels like the place of my childhood."

He paused in the foyer, peering through the archway leading into the large front room.

"Go ahead," I said quietly.

He went to the archway and stood there, surveying the empty room—the enormous tiled fireplace, the mermaid crest over the lintel, the bookcases filled with classic stories, the wood furniture and sconces from which yellow electric light glowed.

When he didn't move for a long time, I came to stand beside him.

"We used to put a Christmas tree there," he pointed to the corner nearest the large front window, "so people could see the lights from the front yard."

"I'm failing to understand how you can be here, Emun," I said, my mind still whirling at this impossibility.

He looked at me, his lips parting to answer when a voice interrupted us.

"Hello, Miss Novak. I see we have a visitor."

We turned to see Adalbert standing across the foyer, a curious expression on his face. "Will your guest be staying for dinner, or needing a room prepared?"

Emun and I shared a glance.

"Adalbert, this is Emun," I began.

Emun smiled and gave Adalbert a nod, which was returned. There was nothing in Adalbert's expression other than an intention to offer pleasant hospitality to our guest.

"He will stay for dinner, and he will need a room as well," I said. "Thank you for asking."

"Very good." Adalbert continued on his way.

"Let's go to Martinius's office. It's private there, and we can talk."

Emun followed me up the stairs. "Martinius..." he said, thoughtfully.

"He would be your," I paused, wracking my brains, "great-great-nephew. The great-great-grandson of your twin, Michal."

Emun seemed to agree to this but his bewildered expression made me think I knew more than he did about his own family tree. I took Emun through the narrow stairway leading to the top floor where everything was smaller and older. Opening the door to Martinius's office, I flicked on the light. The fireplace was cold but the wooden box nearby was full of firewood, and I set about making a fire.

Emun closed the door and looked around the room. "This place has not changed either."

"Was this your father's office?"

He shook his head. "He worked out of the office at the port. This was more of a playroom for me and my brother, not that we spent a lot of time here after we could walk and run. We preferred to be outside on warm days, or in the sitting room with the rest of the family on cold ones."

Stacking the firewood, I took a match from the box and lit a piece of twisted newspaper. Holding the flame to the logs, I waited for it to catch.

"Let me help you with that," Emun said, coming to crouch beside me. "It works better if you stack some kindling underneath so the oxygen can circulate." He restacked the logs, making a kind of teepee shape and sliding thinner pieces underneath. Taking a fresh match, he struck it and lit the kindling. Coaxing it to life with his breath, the flames caught and grew, flickering and snapping.

"Thanks. I haven't made too many fires in my life."

He smiled. "It just takes a bit of practice. I've lit more fires on beaches from driftwood than one could count."

We retreated to the couch and sat in a silence that wasn't exactly awkward, but heavy with expectation nonetheless.

"I don't understand how you can be alive, Emun," I began.

The black slashes of his brows twitched with surprise. "Given what we are, I'm not sure what you mean."

"I knew that having siren blood gives male offspring

immunity from the influence of a siren's voice, but I wasn't aware they also inherited the long lifespan."

He looked at me askance. "Tritons are no different from sirens in this matter. Why would they be?"

The word struck me like a blow to the forehead. "*Tritons?*" The flesh of my arms felt cold as the hairs stood up.

His expression softened. "You were not aware that we exist. That's been true of most of the sirens I've met."

I shook my head, numb. "My mother explained that the gene is passed only from mother to daughter."

"Your mother is mistaken, but it is an error easily made. Only one siren I've met, a very old one, knew what I was. It was she who explained that what human fairy-tales call mermen, are in reality called tritons. I have never actually met another triton. We seem to be in short supply."

I had no words, as digesting this information appeared to have stolen my powers of speech.

"Who is your mother?" he asked.

"Mira MacAuley. We are Atlantic Canadians."

"I do not know the name. Might you introduce us?"

Oh, how I wished I could. "She's gone to the ocean, only a few weeks ago, actually."

"I see." He searched my face. "You mean, for a salt-cycle?"

I nodded, my throat closed. I wondered if I'd ever get over the urge to cry when my mother came up in conversation.

"I'm sorry," he said.

"Thank you." These simple words meant a lot to me coming from Emun. Emun's own mother had abandoned him and his family, and though Emun was supposed to have died and therefore not suffered from the loss, it was clearly not the case. "So, you survived the shipwreck?"

Emun smiled. "Yes and no. I did drown that night, just like everyone else on board. The difference was that I came back to life."

Dumbfounded, I gaped at him again.

"I was just a child, only six at the time. I had no idea what had happened. I thought maybe I had gone to hell at first. It was something my grandmother sometimes talked about. It wasn't until I was older that I pieced together what I could remember and came up with an explanation of what had happened." He paused. "Are you all right? You look unwell."

"You had to die to change," I replied, thickly.

He nodded. "Yes."

"Me too," was all I could manage.

"We are unusual, then," he said with a secretive smile, "and perhaps bonded in some way, no?"

I agreed. "Where did you go, what did you do?"

"That is a story long in the telling. Once I became accustomed to my new form, I searched for my mother, as any child would do. I understood that she was like me, that I was what I was because of her and not because of my father, unlike my twin who was like my father in every way. I had always been linked with her—we shared a melancholy longing for the sea and a withdrawn nature. Even when I was young, I understood her better than anyone else in our family did, even my father, who loved her greatly."

"But you never found her?"

"No, and I gave up looking for her sometime in my mid-thirties, a very long time ago now. I did not pick up the search again until a few months ago, when I had reason to try harder."

"To try harder? What changed?"

He gave a dry chuckle and rubbed the back of his head, mussing the glossy black strands of his long hair. "A chance encounter with a stranger in an American bar. He gave me a missing piece of the puzzle, and a swollen head and sore jaw to go along with it."

"You were in America?"

"It was my home for many years, and I have property there even now, on the coast of Maine."

I gave a delighted laugh. "We are practically neighbors! Or were, rather. My home town is across the border to the north, a little city called Saltford."

He didn't look surprised. "I guessed from your accent that you were northeastern. I have lived a great many places and done a great many jobs, but always my heart comes back to the Atlantic."

I could relate to this. In my limited life experience as a siren, I had swum in the Baltic Sea and the Atlantic. I could not imagine any ocean could rival the power of its dark and churning depths, its salty authority.

"One of my hobbies is vintage cars, and I had journeyed to Boston for a car show."

I wondered if he'd gone alone, and if he had family or children, but I didn't interrupt him.

"The evening after the final day of the show, I went to one of the collegiate bars in the Boston harbor for a drink. I was sitting at the bar when a stranger bellied up next to me. He smelled like a distillery and was unsteady on his feet. Nevertheless, the bartender served him and he proceeded to consume three more bourbons. Just as I was about to leave, he reached into the chest pocket of his shirt and pulled out a piece of jewelry. I could not look away from it, because it reminded me so much of a pendant my father had had made for my mother as a gift."

"The aquamarine pendant that was stolen!"

He nodded. "The very same."

"So it was Sybellen's, after all. The museum did not know to whom it belonged, although I just found proof it belonged to the Novak family."

"It is hers still, though I wish I had known the significance of it when I was little, it would have made all the difference. While the jewelry he had was not identical to the one my father had commissioned, it was similar enough that I felt compelled to ask him about it."

"What did he say about it?"

His expression became perplexed. "I am still trying to unravel what it meant, and how much of it was just the ramblings of a drunkard. He told me that he'd stolen it from a mermaid."

I let out a disbelieving breath and could not have torn my gaze from Emun's face if the mansion had caught fire.

"He was slurring his words but I understood enough to realize that I had to come back to Poland and look for the pendant. He told me that he'd taken the gem from the mermaid so that the siren's curse would come over her and she'd be lost to the sea, the way she deserved. You can imagine my shock at such a statement."

Could I ever. "On so many levels," I said. "The siren's curse? And what could she have possibly done to him to deserve the theft, and how could he have lifted something from any siren? Unless maybe she was asleep or drugged, no man would find it easy to steal from a mermaid."

"You are correct, but this particular man was immune to the siren's voice."

"The son of a siren?" That made it even more unbeliev-able. Why would he be so malignant to his own kind?

But Emun was shaking his head no. "Not the son of a siren, an *Atlantean*."

"Whoa, a what now?" My jaw had dropped in amaze-ment. "As in, a citizen of Atlantis? The mythical city Plato wrote about?"

Emun smiled. "What makes you think it is a myth? You're a siren, is it such a stretch to think that Atlantis was real, and that some of its people may have survived?"

"I guess if you put it that way, no." The experience in Saltford in the summer had done much to expand my perceptions of what was possible, showing me that myths and legends were likely based on something that might very well have been real at one point. "Okay, so this Atlantean stole a mermaid's necklace so that she'd be vulnerable to the ocean? Why?"

"It took buying him yet another drink, the poor sod, and a lot of patience, but the story I pried from his addled wits interlocked like a puzzle piece with something I recalled from my youth, which is important for you to hear first." He got up and put another log on the fire, as it was already dwindling. Sitting down again, he said, "My mother was a tortured soul. I didn't understand why at the time, I just knew she was in pain, and it was getting worse. I also knew that it was driving my father to desperation. One day, my father had taken me to the shipping offices at the harbor. Sometimes he did that because his employees liked to see us as we grew up, and my father liked to expose us to the busi-ness that we would one day inherit. Michal and I liked to watch the ships coming in and out of the harbor. On this day, Michal was at home, and I had gone with my father, who was particularly distracted. I was too young to appreciate all the stress he was under, but I could feel his agitation, that is until a man came into the shipping office. He was very excited, and asked to see my father immediately. My father was in a meeting, but this man demanded to see him and that my father himself would have the secretary's head if he was not let in at once. The secretary interrupted the meeting and my father came rushing out. The strange man gave my father an envelope and they embraced. My father's eyes were moist and he was so excited. It's why I remember the day so well. I had never seen tears in my father's eyes before. Some papers and money were exchanged and the man left.

"My father immediately dismissed the meeting and asked for his secretary to take me home. I was affected by all the excitement and I remember crying because I didn't want to leave. I wanted to go with my father wherever he was going because I hadn't seen him so happy in a very long time. I knew that something big had happened and I didn't want to be left out."

I knew what that felt like. I had hated it when my parents had shared whispered discussions or had sent me to my room to allow them to have an adult conversation. Nothing was more titillating for a child than to be in on things they were forbidden to know about.

"My father took me aside," Emun explained, "and showed me what the man had delivered. He opened the envelope and pulled out a small stone, an aquamarine. It was pretty, but it was rough and uncut and not all that special next to some jewelry that I had seen my grandmother wear. I didn't understand what the fuss was about.

"'This doesn't look like much, my son,' he'd said, 'but it will do wonders for your poor mama. I will give it to her tonight. The jeweler has made a special setting for it, just for your mother, and he will make it perfect so that she can wear it close to her body always. She'll be much happier from now on, you'll see.'

"He made me promise not to tell my mother what was coming, or anyone else in the family, especially my brother because he was terrible at keeping secrets. I promised, and I became excited too, because I could feel that my mother was growing increasingly unhappy. She hadn't been herself for a long time, wasn't speaking very much anymore, and was ill with sadness."

"Sounds familiar," I said quietly. "My mother suffered so much before she finally went back to the ocean."

Emun gave me a compassionate look. "It is a cruel thing, is it not?"

I agreed. "Go on."

"I allowed the secretary to take me home, since my father was insistent that taking me to the jewelers with him would only slow down the process."

"But he never did give it to her." I knew what came next.

Emun shook his head, eyes sad. "She disappeared that night, and by the time my father got home with the completed gift, it was storming. He went completely mad, and only now do I understand that madness better. Desperate to find her, he took me to *The Sybellen* and assembled as many sailors as he could as quickly as possible. My poor grandparents didn't understand his madness either, and it terrified my poor grandmother more than anyone."

I nodded. "I know."

He paused at this and cocked his head. "You do?"

In answer, I got up and went to the desk where Aleksandra's diary still sat. I returned to Emun and handed it to him.

He took it from me, running his hands over the leather. "I know this book." He was so quiet I could hardly hear the words. "I saw my grandmother write in it many times. How incredible that it has survived all this time. But then again, the Novaks were always good at keeping records, and this would be a particularly valuable one." He looked up at me. "You read it? Do you understand Polish?"

I smiled. "No. Martinius had the excerpt to do with events leading up to the wreck translated into English for me, because I very much wanted to know the story. He gave it to me as a gift before my mother and I left Poland the last time."

"What an extraordinary man he must have been."

"It seems like your family might have had more than its fair share of extraordinary men," I murmured.

"Perhaps." He let out a long slow breath. "I wish I could have met him."

"He would have loved that," I replied. "But please, continue your story before I die of curiosity."

Emun set the diary on the couch beside his thigh and continued. "Those events when I was just a child, my father going mad, the storm and the shipwreck, my mother going missing, they were traumatic in and of themselves, but I knew there was a piece of information missing. It bothered me when I grew old enough to think it through with an adult's rationality, why it was so important for my father to deliver the gift to my mother that he'd taken it to sea with him in a furious storm. Surely, if someone has gone missing and is believed to have drowned or become stranded somewhere, your first concern should be to get them to safety, not to deliver a piece of jewelry to them. It wasn't until I met the Atlantean in that Boston harbor bar that a piece of the mystery snapped into place. In his slurring and broken language, he told me a bunch of strange things—how Atlantis was real, that the ruins can be seen only by satellite if you look at the eye of Africa, and how their territory extended all the way out to the Azores. But what he said that was the most relevant centered around a legend about a triton who fell in love with a siren. Sirens being susceptible to the effects of salt-water, and at the mercy of their salt and land cycles, the triton made his lover a gift."

"An aquamarine pendant."

Emun nodded. "The legend doesn't say whether or not it was a pendant, but whatever form it came in, it was most definitely an aquamarine, one which contained a powerful magic. The magic, it was said, would protect her from the ebb and flow of the siren cycles, allowing her to be with the triton always, rather than having to leave him to go on land."

"That's why he called it the siren's curse."

"Yes."

"And you believed him—this drunk stranger?"

Emun's shoulders lifted. "Why should I not believe him? My father certainly did. I would not doubt that my father paid an inordinate amount of money for that man to retrieve that gem. Where he found it, I would pay an exorbitant sum to know myself."

"I found the receipt for it. The man who sold it to your father was a fellow by the name of Rainer Veigel, and you are right, Mattis did pay far more than it was worth."

"Do you have this receipt? I would like to see it."

I got up and retrieved it from where I'd left it on Martinius's desk. I handed it to him and watched as his eyes scanned it, lingering at the bottom.

"I haven't seen that signature in several lifetimes," he

said, his voice quiet and eyes sad. "How strange to see it now. My, what a lot he paid for the little stone." He shook his head. "I'm sure he would have given more for it. All he had, in fact."

"Do you think the mermaid the Atlantean stole the gem from was your mother? Seems quite a strange coincidence."

Emun's brows knit together. "I don't know. The jewelry he had was not the same as the one my father had made, so I suspect it was a different siren."

"Well, it at least explains why someone would break into the museum and steal this particular gem without stealing any of the other artifacts. They believe it to have power."

"Yes."

But why Antoni's sister was the one to have stolen it was something that made no sense to me whatsoever.

"So you were the one who made a mess of the wreck, looking for the pendant?"

Emun gave me a crooked smile. "You saw my calling card, did you?"

"Mom and I went to visit the wreck one night, and we noticed that it had been recently visited by someone who seemed to be looking for something."

"That was me." His expression turned sheepish. "I also have to apologize for breaking into the house. I had referenced an old article published not long after the wreck was salvaged and it said that the artifacts were stored in the old Novak mansion, so I thought they might still be here. I hadn't realized until later that they'd been transferred to the museum."

"So you went to the museum to ask around, but it was after the pendant had been stolen already."

"And I made the museum staff very uncomfortable and

suspicious. If your hearing is anything like mine, it means you can listen to conversations not meant for you. When I heard one of the staff calling the police, I got out of there posthaste."

I nodded. "It's how I knew to run after you when I saw you poking around the house from the gate. The curator had called me and described the man who was there asking questions."

"So what about you, then? If you're not a Novak, what are you doing here?"

I told Emun about how my mother had been a salvage professional and part of the team that worked on the wreck. "Martinius found a photo of my mom in the press and thought she was Sybellen. He lured her here by granting the salvage job to the company my mom used to work for—The Bluejackets."

"I see." His eyes combed my face. "Well, if you look anything like your mother, then she and my mother definitely shared similar features. Even you have a remarkable likeness to Sybellen, it's why I was so dumbfounded when I saw your face for the first time."

"My mom suspects that it's likely we do share common ancestry in some way, but there's no way of knowing how we're linked. Mermaids don't do a good job keeping track of these things."

Emun shook his head. "No, I should think not. But you and I could also be related, then."

I nodded. "It's not totally impossible." I had to admit that as I gazed upon his intense blue eyes, pale skin, and blue-black hair, if we weren't related it would be very surprising.

"What happened with the Atlantean after he told you the story? Did you try to take the gem from him?"

"It crossed my mind, I have to admit, but no. The more questions I asked him, the more I think it made him realize he'd made a mistake in talking about Atlanteans and mermaids as though they really existed. He didn't know what I was, but I was awfully interested in what he had to say. He became argumentative and aggressive, so the bar staff finally bounced him. I didn't want to seem like I was following him, so I waited a few minutes before I left. By the time I got outside, he'd disappeared and I didn't know which way he'd gone. But that night, before I reached the hotel, I was jumped by four men. They were surprisingly strong, but thankfully I have a triton's power and was able to fend them off."

"That's crazy! Why do you think they jumped you?"

He shrugged. "I don't know, but I wouldn't be surprised if it had something to do with the stranger. Maybe it was his friends trying to wipe out the human who knew too much. They got off a few good shots and I had a headache the next day and a stiff jaw. But I never got good looks at them and I haven't seen them since."

"Wow," I said, whistling under my breath.

"The stranger's story made me realize that my father knew my mother's nature and believed in the power of the gem. It made his actions make more sense. I had to find out for myself if the power of the gem was real, and the last time I had seen the aqua, it had been in my father's hand. I knew he was going to get it put into a setting, and I knew he had taken it to sea on a stormy night in a mad attempt to find my mother. He'd even taken me with him because he knew we were strongly connected and perhaps he was hoping she would hear my voice on the wind, or that just knowing I was aboard, she would want to prevent *The Sybellen* from sailing any further out into the gale. I surmised that the jewel had gone down with the ship and would likely still be there. I wrapped up my business in America and flew here as quickly as I could. I didn't bother to research the wreck, I had been there before and knew where it was. I hadn't realized there had been a salvage this past summer. When I saw the wreck, I could see there had been work done on it, so I tore it apart looking for the pendant just in case it had been missed. When I didn't find it anywhere, I thought it had to be here."

I wondered if I should tell him that I knew who had taken the pendant. I'd already said her name aloud to him while we were outside. Emun had a peaceable vibe about him, but I didn't know how he'd react if I reminded him of the clue I'd already given—that I knew who had what he was looking for. I decided to wait a little longer.

"What do you plan to do with the pendant, when you do get it?"

His expression said that he thought it would be obvious. "I would search for my mother with a renewed vigor, of course."

"You didn't find her before—what makes you think you can find her now?"

"I have no idea if I will see my mother again, Targa," Emun replied, "but if I ever do run into her again, don't you think that I'd regret not having the pendant to give her? Even if the pendant doesn't have the magical properties that Atlantean thinks it has, it would be wonderful to give her the gift my father thought it so important she should have. And if it does have the ability to stall the curse while she's wearing it, then maybe she could be rescued. I have seen a siren in a salt-flush state." He shook his head. "It's a horrible thing to witness."

I swallowed hard and my mouth felt chalky. Picturing

my mother with a vacant expression in her eyes, behaving like an animal with no self-awareness or logic, threw a fresh wave of terror over me. If I found her like that one day, it would be worse than losing a loved one to Alzheimer's, for her body would be strong and vital, but her mind would be lost to me. She wouldn't even know me—it was a sentence worse than death.

A new desire was being birthed in my heart, one that echoed the want that I could see in Emun's eyes for Sybellen.

I had proved that I had the ability to call my mother back to me. I believed that I also had the power to call Sybellen to me, but I kept that critical piece of information to myself.

Given the choice between it ending up in Sybellen's hands or Mira's hands, there was no question as to the only outcome that was acceptable to me.

I wanted that pendant for Mira. I wanted my mother back.

TWENTY

A knock at the door made me jump and a stealthy guilt threaded through my mind as I got up to answer. Thankful Emun didn't have Petra's mind-reading powers, I put a smile on my face and opened the door. Adalbert stood in the hall.

"Dinner is served, and the suite across the hall from yours has been prepared for Emun."

Emun got up from the couch and came to the door. "Thank you, that is very kind."

Adalbert nodded and retreated.

"Hungry?" I asked the 'guest' who actually had more right to own this mansion than I did.

"Famished."

We made our way to the dining room where the smell of fish, potatoes, lemon, and dill filled the air. Adalbert and the other staff had moved the large dining table over to make room for a smaller, more intimate set-up near one of the windows, after they'd heard Georjie crack a joke about feeling like she was sitting down to The Last Supper with Antoni and me. It was intuitive of them, and I appreciated it. As hard as it was adjusting to a life of having a staff, it was amazing to have simple desires like this fulfilled before I even knew I had them.

"You asked me before," Emun said as he tucked into the food, "if I knew someone named Lydia."

My heart sank to my stomach. I'd hoped he'd forgotten. "Mm-hmm."

"Who is she, and why did you think I knew her?" He put a forkful of fish in his mouth and watched my face.

"She's Antoni's—my boyfriend's—sister." I took a sip of water, mind racing for a believable excuse. "I just thought maybe you might have met at one point."

"But why?"

"It was just a feeling. I was mistaken."

He swallowed, his eyes seeming to burn into mine, but he didn't push further. He hadn't let it slide though, I could tell. It was grounds to think I was hiding something.

"Antoni, he is Polish?"

Relieved to be off the topic of Lydia, I nodded. "I met him in the summer, during the salvage project."

"He is...the one?"

I knew what Emun meant by this—was Antoni the guy my siren desire had targeted to be my mate. I swallowed my bite of potato. "He is."

The dining room went quiet. Most people would have said congratulations, or given some kind of best wishes, but Emun knew more than most people.

"He doesn't know?" Emun speared an asparagus shoot but didn't put it in his mouth, as he was more interested in my answer.

I shook my head. "Did any of your...mates?"

He rested the fork on his plate. "Actually, tritons are not burdened by the same vicious cycles as sirens. I've never felt compelled to find a mate because of the effect of salt on my system." He gave a chuckle and his eyebrows jumped. "I say 'tritons' but truthfully, I don't know if there are any others. All I can speak to is my own experience. But any romantic relationships I've ever had were entirely of my choosing. I can't imagine what it would be like to feel so compelled."

"You don't have the salt and land cycles? You can move through the world as you choose?"

Emun nodded. "Thankfully."

"Why do you think you haven't run across any other tritons? Have you not spent so much time in the ocean, perhaps, since you don't have to?"

He smiled, and his face became endearing, charming. When he wasn't smiling, Emun looked downright intimidating. "While it's true that I do prefer a life on land more because I like interacting with people, I have spent years in the world's oceans and seas, and a few years ago, I actually documented my experiences in a journal. But in all the time I spent underwater, I never did run into another triton. I ran into Atlanteans and sirens, but never another like me."

"That explains why my mother thought only females could become mer."

He agreed. "I read once that all crocodile eggs are inherently female, and that it requires a very specific and small window of temperature for a male to form. Because of this, only one in every five crocodiles that hatch are male. Perhaps it is something like that."

"Only with a smaller gap?"

"Maybe." He shrugged. "It would be nice to learn why it is this way. It can be lonely at times, being the only one of your kind."

"I'll bet." I cleaned my plate and took a drink of water. "So, you wrote your life story?"

"Parts of it, anyway."

I was about to ask him if I could read it when he said, "It's in no condition to be read by anyone other than me."

"You're not worried that the manuscript will fall into the wrong hands?"

He laughed. "It's locked in a safety deposit vault in a bank back in Maine, but if someone actually did manage to steal it and it was leaked somehow, it would be taken as fiction anyway. So no. I don't worry."

"Do you plan to publish it one day?"

He lifted one shoulder.

"You should consider bringing it here so it can be part of the Novak history. That way I'll have the right to read it," I teased.

He chuckled and wiped his lips with his napkin. "I would let you read it one day, after it has been polished."

"I'll hold you to it."

He grew serious. "I can tell you, as someone who has fallen desperately in love more than once, you really should tell Antoni what you are."

"You sound like my best friend," I murmured unhappily before taking another swig of water. "You don't know what's at stake."

"Oh, but I do."

We looked at each other across the table as the grandfather clock in the corner ticked away the seconds of our lives.

"Might I get to meet the lucky fellow?" he asked.

The way he said lucky made me narrow my eyes. I couldn't quite tell if he'd given it a sarcastic undertone, or if I was just imagining it.

"I don't see a way around it. This is your home now, as much as it is mine."

He blinked in a startled way, as though this hadn't actually occurred to him. "How would you explain to him who I am?"

That had me stumped.

"If you're not going to tell him what you are," he went on, "then it will be awfully complicated to explain who I am. Don't you think?"

My eyes narrowed again and my back stiffened. I realized now the danger Emun posed. "Am I going to have a problem with you?"

"Relax," Emun said soothingly. "Your secret is not mine to tell. I'm no threat to your relationship. We can tell him that my family is the original owner of the pendant, that Rainer Veigel actually stole it and sold it to Mattis. That way he won't be surprised when it is passed over to me rather than given back to the museum...once it is found, of course. I can choose a name from the manifest of sailors and manufacture a link to the family."

"You can do that?"

He waved a hand. "This is the easy part. I have had to create many identities in my long life. I have no intention of moving into this place." He looked around the room. "As much as it feels familiar, it long ago ceased to be my home."

"I understand."

Emun might be able to manufacture some right to the pendant that would satisfy the authorities well enough, but the pendant legally belonged to my mother, and that was how I intended it to stay. I said none of this, but my own secret plans had already begun to weave a web that would keep the aquamarine in my possession.

"Once it is found," I echoed.

I was already a step ahead of Emun. I knew who had stolen it, though not why. And, although I hadn't heard from Antoni since early this morning, I was hopeful that he had found Lydia and learned what she had had done with it. What I didn't want was for Antoni and Emun to start talking to one another, or my plans would quickly unravel.

THE SOUND of voices arguing in the hall brought us both to our feet, eyes wide.

"Targa? Targa!" The cry was desperate and not from a voice I recognized.

Adalbert's voice came next, trying to calm whoever it was who was having a fit.

Bolting from the dining room, I was in the front foyer in moments, with Emun right behind me.

"Lydia!" I exclaimed.

I hadn't recognized her voice because I'd never heard it sound like that before—hysterical. Her face was streaked with mascara and her expression was a rictus of terror. Adalbert was holding her by the shoulders as she strained forward. There was an awful keening sound coming from the back of her throat.

"Targa." She took a gulp and made an effort to stop crying. "They took him, Targa. They took Antoni. I didn't know where else to come. I didn't know what to do."

My skin felt coated with ice as her words took root. The feeling was like watching the earth heave at the base of someone's headstone, a burgeoning terror.

"Who?" I was at her side, an arm around her shoulder. "Who took Antoni?"

Lydia was crying and gulping too much to answer, black tears making tracks down her cheeks. Her beautiful eyes looked done up for Halloween.

"Perhaps if she sat down for a moment, took a breath."

Emun's voice punctured the hysteria like a foghorn on a misty night. "Whatever happened, you'll be able to tell us more clearly if you settle. Perhaps a drink of water?"

Adalbert was on it in a moment. "Right away."

I looked up at Emun, momentarily distracted by how his voice had changed. Its soothing qualities were amplified and though it didn't have any physiological effect on me, I felt the tension ease out of Lydia's body and her breathing regulate. This was a magic I did not have. In order to get Lydia to calm down, I would have to give her a command that would force her brain to evacuate whatever experience she'd had, which wouldn't do any good in this situation.

Lydia nodded and began to breathe more steadily, and her tears thinned. I escorted her into the sitting room and she perched on the edge of a chair, finally getting control of herself. I handed her a box of tissues.

"Can you tell us what happened?" Emun prompted with that same tone.

Lydia reacted like a cat under a soft touch, melting and leaning into the sound of his voice.

I wanted to send Emun away, fear clutched at my breast at what Lydia was going to say, but if Emun left, she might not be able to speak at all. I pinched my lips shut in frustration.

"Antoni confronted me earlier today," Lydia said, still taking gulps of air. Her tortured eyes found mine. "I'm so sorry, Targa. I can't tell you how sorry I am."

From the look on her face, I guessed that Antoni hadn't told her who had ratted on her, and she thought that I didn't know.

"I'm the one who took the pendant from the museum. I stole it."

Emun moved closer, his frame tense with a new energy, but he didn't say anything.

"But it wasn't my fault. They made me do it."

Emun and I shared a look.

"Who made you do it?" he coaxed.

"Adrian did, this guy I played cards against at the Leviathan. It's an underground gaming community, and it used to be so fun. I loved it while I was winning, but then I played against Adrian." She hiccupped and swallowed again.

Adalbert reappeared with a glass of water and handed it to her before retreating to clear the dining room table. She took the glass and drank three big swallows, a dribble going down her chin. She brushed it away.

Her words tumbled out in a rush, almost impossible to understand as her accent thickened. "I owed him a lot of money, more money than I had, and I was too embarrassed to go to Antoni and ask for help again; he'd be so ashamed of me."

Her face crumpled again and she fought for control.

"Slowly, slowly," Emun soothed her. "We're not going anywhere."

She nodded and took another big breath. "I begged Adrian for some other way to pay him back, a payment plan or a favor or something. He wouldn't let me pay it back over time, but he agreed to a favor—"

"Stealing the pendant?" Emun asked.

She nodded.

Emun looked at me. "Do you know this Adrian fellow?"

"Antoni named him when I saw him and Lydia together at the exhibition opening, but no, I don't know him." Even to my own ears my voice sounded harsh and angry. Would I have to be a century and a half old before I could sound as calm as Emun did when stuff went sideways?

"Go on, Lydia." Emun crouched down so he could look up at her compassionately. "We're going to do our best to make this right, but you can't leave out any details, okay? Tell us everything."

She nodded again. "Okay. Adrian asked me to steal the pendant in exchange for the debt to be wiped out completely. At first I didn't agree, but then he got scary, threatening to harass my mom, my brothers. It seemed like he wanted the pendant *way* more than he wanted the money. When I told him that the museum security would catch me for sure, because I'd never stolen anything big before and didn't know how to do it, he told me that the museum would be having an event soon, and that if I was smart, I could figure out a way to attend."

"That was why you wanted to come to the event," I said, "so you could scope out the pendant, not because you wanted to support your brother's girlfriend. Did you use Antoni's connection to me to get in?"

She nodded. "I'm so sorry, Targa."

"I know you are," I replied. "I can see that." *Now that your brother is in trouble.* I wanted to strangle the girl. If anything happened to Antoni...

"I've been so cold to you because I was terrified that you could see right through me."

"I understand," I said through a tight jaw. "Then what happened?"

"Adrian formed a plan. He had me meet with one of the museum staff who gave me the key to the display case, the code to the back door and information about how the security system worked."

I wondered how Adrian had "convinced" this poor

museum employee and would have guessed that it wasn't with his natural charm. But that wasn't the most important thing right this minute.

"It actually wasn't that hard," she went on, "but I have never been so scared in my life. I was to deliver the pendant to Adrian today. A couple of hours before we were to meet, Antoni confronted me and said he knew that it was me who had stolen the pendant. He was so furious." She squeezed her eyes shut and more mascara-tainted tears dripped from her eyelashes. When she opened her eyes it was to look up at me, pleading. "I love my brother, I love my family."

My heart had begun to pound and my hands and feet ache with the desire to start running. "I don't doubt that, Lydia."

"I told him everything...and he went to the meeting."

"Where?" Emun asked.

"At a small private airstrip. Antoni told me to stay back while he talked to them, he took money to negotiate with them. I couldn't hear what they were saying from where I was hiding but they had a conversation, and it even looked somewhat friendly, at first."

"Did Antoni have the pendant with him at this point?" Emun interrupted.

She shook her head. "No, I still had it. Antoni didn't want them to know where it was so that he could use it as leverage. He just wanted them to take the money and forget about the pendant, but he also wanted to know why they wanted it so badly. Apparently, it isn't even worth that much, and they didn't want anything else from the museum, just that, which made no sense."

"They never told you why they wanted it?"

She shook her head. "And I never thought to ask; truthfully, I was too scared to care. Everything was going fine until two more men came out of the small plane sitting on the runway. The three of them overpowered Antoni and held him down on the pavement and started yelling into the darkness that they knew I was there and if I didn't show myself and deliver the pendant, they would kill my brother." Her body began to shake as she came to this part of the story and I thought she was going to lose control again. My own core quivered with terror and anger at the word 'kill'.

"Easy now," Emun said quietly, as though soothing a spooked horse. "What did you do?"

"I came out, of course," Lydia cried out harshly. "I gave them the pendant and just wanted them to go away, but then..." her face collapsed again, "they took Antoni with them."

My throat closed up with fear and confusion, and I found myself lost for words. Thankfully, Emun asked the question for both of us.

"Why would they do that?"

"I don't know!" she wailed. "I don't know, I don't know! They got the pendant. I don't know why they took my brother! If I'd only hidden close by, I might have heard what was said before they put him on the ground, but I was too far away!"

"Did they fly away with him?"

My palms came to my eyelids and pressed there, blocking out the awful look on Lydia's face. *This is a nightmare, this can't have happened.* Anger shook my body, anger at Lydia, anger at these men, anger at Antoni for being so stupid as to face them alone, anger at myself for letting Antoni confront Lydia by himself. But larger than the rage was the debilitating fear that they would hurt Antoni, that they'd hurt him already.

I assumed that Lydia had nodded in the affirmative to

Emun's last question because he said next, "Do you know where they were going?"

I opened my eyes and saw Lydia shake her head.

"What were they flying? Describe it to me," he said.

"It was a small plane." She seemed lost for words.

"Did it have a propeller on its nose? Or maybe two on its wings?"

She nodded.

"Which one?" Emun asked.

"On its nose."

He nodded. "How many people do you think it could hold?"

"Maybe six or eight, not very many."

Emun took this in.

"What should we do?" Lydia drew a shuddering breath.

Emun's voice became an emollient balm, an extracting elixir. "Think back, Lydia, to any interaction you had with Adrian. Did he ever mention any place at any time, even in passing?"

Her face softened at his question, but never did she lose her look of lucidity. "Ponta Delgada." She looked up at me with a startled expression, like someone other than her had said it. "Where's that?"

"It's a long way out into the Atlantic, well off the coast of Portugal," said Emun.

Our eyes met.

"It's part of the Azores," he said to me, meaningfully.

I made the connection shortly after Emun had, though neither of us said it out loud.

Atlanteans.

TWENTY-ONE

"Hello?" A deep, drowsy voice answered the phone.

"Ivan? It's Targa. I'm so sorry if I woke you."

"Miss Novak?" The voice brightened. "You didn't, I was just reading a book by the fire, it calms me before bed."

"You haven't been drinking, by chance?"

There was a pause. "No, ma'am." He sounded a little startled, if not affronted.

"Sorry, I had to ask. I don't care if you like a nightcap, I just...well, we have an emergency. How soon can you be ready to fly?"

"Uh..." He droned for a moment and I heard noises in the background, fabric rubbing on fabric, and the sound of feedback as things banged against the receiver. "Sorry, let me just...I have to call ahead and get cleared for takeoff. If there are no issues, we can be ready in about an hour. Where are we going?"

"The Azores."

There was silence as he digested this. "Is everything all right, Miss?"

"I'll tell you more on the plane. Meet you at the airfield?"

"Yes, okay. See you there."

Emun waved at me desperately and was mouthing something at me.

"Wait, one moment, Ivan." I pulled the phone away from my ear. "What?"

"Ask him what model of plane he's flying."

I put the mouthpiece back to my lips. "What model of plane do we fly, Ivan?"

"It's a Gulfstream G650."

I relayed this to Emun and he nodded, looking pleased.

I put down the phone and looked at Emun.

"And so we are aligned," he said, quietly. "We need to move, now."

Lydia got to her feet. "I'm coming with you," she said shakily.

I rounded on her without tempering myself. "No you're not, you've done enough damage. You'll just get in the way."

She staggered back against the couch, her face pained, her lips parted to protest, but she didn't say anything. I called Sera and asked her to make up a room for Lydia, and to 'look after her.' Sera nodded in understanding.

Emun and I took a car from the garage and headed for the airstrip the company leased from, a different one from where Antoni had been taken.

"I'm having a hard time with...thinking," I said to Emun as we sped through the dark, wet evening, the lights of the city blurring by. "What are we going to do?"

"If they land before we do, we'll have lost him. It's our only chance."

"But they've already left. They're at least a couple of hours ahead of us."

"I know, but listen to me. I was a pilot in another life."

"Of course you were."

"Ponta Delgada is a little less than twenty-five-hundred nautical miles from us. According to the description Lydia gave, they're flying a turboprop. It can't go any more than a thousand miles on a single tank of fuel, and probably quite a bit less than that."

"They have to stop and refuel somewhere. Maybe even more than once," I surmised. Hope fluttered in my breast. "But we don't."

"That's right, but they could also switch planes in Nantes, or in Porto. If I were them, I would, because from Porto to the Azores is just under a thousand nautical miles, it would be foolish to take a turboprop from Portugal to the Azores, even on a day with favorable winds."

I pulled the car into the parking lot at the airstrip and we got out. We met Ivan on the tarmac and got settled into our seats as Ivan and the tower relayed information back and forth. The Gulfstream began to taxi.

Ivan's voice came over the intercom. "I hope you brought some food, there wasn't time to assemble anyone for the crew. It's just us."

"Bless him," Emun said across the aisle. "He sounds cool as a cucumber for someone who was about to go to bed an hour ago."

I nodded but wasn't really listening.

"You okay?" Emun asked.

"I don't like flying."

"Oh." Emun sat back in his seat and looked to be getting comfortable.

"Wait, you were a pilot?" What he'd said earlier finally sank in. "What insanity came over you that made you want to be a pilot? Doesn't flying make you feel sick?"

Our bodies pressed back into our seats as the plane took off.

"Sick? No, I love the freedom of flying, of seeing the world from above."

My bones were transforming into lead and his voice began to drone. My eyelids drooped, my head became heavy, and I fought to keep it from drooping forward. With effort, I leaned back against the seat instead and looked at Emun from under lowered lids.

"Targa?" His features were a blur of concern.

"I can't fight it..." I murmured, my words on a whispered breath. I led my lids drop as the ponderous darkness took me.

TWENTY-TWO

I came to as someone was shaking my shoulder. Opening my eyes, I saw Emun standing over me, his blue eyes dark with worry.

"Targa?"

I tried to tell him I was okay, but it came out a garbled mess.

"You slept the entire time. Are you all right?" Emun knelt beside me in the aisle. "Ivan told me you always fall asleep when you fly, but I've never seen anyone out so cold and so fast before. It was rather alarming."

He handed me an open bottle of water.

I took it and drank slowly, the haze beginning to clear. "Ponta Delgada? We're here?"

Emun nodded.

"What time is it?"

"Early morning, the sun isn't even up yet." He spoke very quietly, in case Ivan was listening. "Listen, we don't know how much time we have. We need to get into the control tower. Do you think you can do that for us? With your voice?"

I nodded and got up slowly, my head spinning. Emun put a hand under my elbow and steadied me.

We exited the plane and met Ivan on the tarmac.

"Emun told me what happened," Ivan said, brow creased with worry. "And that you've alerted the authorities."

I looked at Emun with surprise and I was gripped by a sudden panic. What had he told Ivan while I was sleeping?

"The police are waiting for us inside," Emun told Ivan in that soothing tone he'd used on Lydia. "We'd better not keep them waiting."

"You know how to reach me. I'll be ready to take you home when your business is concluded here, just give me as much notice as you can. God be with you."

"Thank you, Ivan." Emun took my elbow and we left Ivan to park the jet and headed for the airport control tower.

"What did you tell him?" I whispered as we approached one of the doors.

"A version of the truth," Emun answered before putting his finger to his lips and nodding at the two airport security guards who passed us going the other way.

"You're headed the wrong way," came a friendly voice and we turned to see one of the security guards had stopped on the tarmac and was pointing towards the arrivals building. "This is the air-control tower," he said. "That's arrivals, over there."

I was on stage.

My siren sound filled the air with its stringed instruments. "We need to see the planes scheduled to land in the next twenty-four hours. Get us the schedule."

"I'll get you the schedule," he droned, his face dropping

from friendly to blank. He walked past us like a zombie and disappeared inside.

"Wow," Emun said under his breath.

"You can fly without feeling like lead weights are attached to every joint, so consider us even," I replied, quietly.

The guard returned with a clipboard and handed it to us without question.

"Thanks," I said. "You can go about your normal business. We're approved to be here."

"You're approved to be here," he muttered, and walked away.

We watched him join the other guard and they exchanged a few words before going about their work without giving us another glance.

Emun took the clipboard from me and began to read it over in the glare of the airport lights.

Ponta Delgada was a long, kidney-shaped island, one of the larger ones in the Azores. The airport, known as Nordela, had a single airstrip which ran along the coastline. At the end of the airstrip were a cluster of small buildings, a car rental building, and a parking lot for planes.

According to the clipboard, three small planes, which seemed to fit what we were looking for, were scheduled to land in the next few hours.

The small airport was open with short grass, no trees or brush behind which to conceal ourselves. Fortunately, it wasn't light yet, so we chose to settle ourselves in the grass near a storage unit between the arrivals building and the refueling station. The first plane on the roster was scheduled to land in the next five minutes, but Emun pointed out its lights as they descended a few minutes early.

The small plane bumped along the runway, finally

turning into its parking space in front of the arrivals building. We couldn't tear our eyes from the plane as we watched three men come down the narrow steps. When they were followed by three women, Emun muttered that it wasn't the plane we were waiting for.

Twenty minutes later, the second small plane landed, and we watched it through greedy eyes as it coasted to a stop at the end of the runway nearest us.

To our surprise, the nose of the plane turned left rather than right—away from the arrivals building, and began to taxi toward the far edge of the runway.

A couple of the airport's employees began to yell to one another, noticing that the plane was behaving strangely as well.

"What are they doing?" I squeaked, watching the plane roll away from us and toward the rocky edge which seemed to fall off into the black oblivion of the sea.

Emun and I were on our feet, stunned, as a few employees got into a small motorized cart and buzzed after the errant plane.

We began to run.

In the distance, the lights of the plane came to a stop, seemingly on the edge of nothing. Shadowy figures emerged from the belly of the plane, dropping right onto the ground.

"That has to be them," I panted, speeding up. "Did they know we were waiting? What on earth are they doing on the wrong side of the airport?"

"They're going to the water, look!"

We sprinted across what seemed like miles of empty field and pavement, watching helplessly as the figures which had deplaned climbed onto the rocky shoal lining the coast, and disappeared over its edge, now completely out of sight.

My heart was wedged in my neck, throbbing painfully. My legs burned as I urged them faster. Emun was ahead of me now, legs and arms pumping like an Olympian.

We passed by the small plane, where the airport employees were in an argument with a man in a uniform who I guessed had to be the pilot. They didn't notice us as we ran by. The plane's engine still whirred and electronic sounds filled the air, while the sound of crashing waves grew loud. An emergency alarm wailed in the background. The noises together were deafening.

Reaching the dark boulders, we peered over the edge and saw lights bobbing in the water. Shapes picked their way toward the lights, and I recognized Antoni's silhouette as a flashlight beam came across his body from someone nearest the water.

"Antoni!" I screamed, my voice drowned out by the sounds around us.

"It's a submersible," Emun yelled into my ear. "Look!"

The dark shape with the lights in the water was not much to look at, just the suggestion of a much larger body invisible below the surface.

He was right. A hatched door was propped open and the small group of men, with Antoni second from the front, was climbing inside. We were too far away to catch them and my voice was useless if they couldn't hear it.

"Come on." Emun grabbed my arm and pulled me to where we could cross over the rocky border and pick our way down after them.

TWENTY-THREE

Bubbles and foam crested the water's surface as the sub sank from view. My heart was in overdrive as Emun and I ran for the water's edge. Without so much as a question between us, we stripped our clothes and left them in two little heaps hidden in the rocks.

The lights of the sub could be seen as a dim retreating glow, and I dove headfirst into the black water, legs melding and vision sharpening. I heard a splash as Emun entered the water behind me, but I barely noticed him. Antoni was inside a submarine! One that was quickly headed out into a dark sea. I was wrestling with a barrage of fear-based emotion, even as the salt plied at my mind.

Emun and I trailed after the submersible, keeping the lights in view and staying within its wake.

For roughly thirty minutes, at a depth of about fifteen meters, we trailed the sub in silence as it headed roughly west. The time passing, and the salt-water, did wonders for my frantic mind. I had been imagining horrible scenarios where the men on board tortured and abused Antoni, or worse, had already killed him. Seeing him well and moving under his own powers was a small comfort. But what did they have planned for him?

I became aware of Emun's presence, the powerful movement of his fins and his lack of talk. He seemed to know that I was too upset to make conversation. Glancing at him in my periphery served as a good distraction. The only other mer-creature I had ever seen was my mother. Emun was an entirely new sight and in spite of the stress I was under, I couldn't help but observe him.

I let him pull ahead of me slightly so I could take a closer look.

In the dim light, his coloring was difficult to make out because his tail was nearly as dark as mine was light. I couldn't tell if his scales were black or dark gray or blue, but they gleamed like they were made of resin. His dorsal fin and the ends of his tail had lighter tips that might have been red or rose colored, I couldn't tell in exact shade in the darkness. His tail was thicker and longer than my mother's, as he was broader at the waist and lacked the flaring hips Mom and I had. While his scales were smooth, cords and mounds of muscle could be seen moving under the surface, flexing gracefully as they powered him through the Atlantic. His pale skin gleamed, reflecting light and easily the most visible part of him, while his black hair blew out behind him, dark as onyx.

He glanced over at me, his eyes nearly all dark pupil to let in the light of the waning moon.

"Getting a good look?" His voice came out smoothly, without air bubbles or distortion. It was startlingly loud.

I nodded, unabashed. "Where do you think they're taking him?"

"I don't know, Targa, but it's going to have more to do with the pendant than it will to do with Antoni."

"It doesn't make sense that they've taken him. They have the necklace—what could they possibly want him for?"

Emun didn't answer right away. We swam in silence for a time, keeping the sub's lights in view.

"They might want insurance for a future plan," he ventured. "Perhaps they aren't done with the wreck, perhaps it's Antoni who has something they want, perhaps they'll contact you for ransom." He threw me a sympathetic glance, magnified by the way his pupils were so large and liquid black. He looked a little doll-like with those eyes, and those fine bones in his face. "We'll get him back, Targa. How many people do you know that can stand up to the power of a siren and a triton together? Just don't forget that we don't know who we're dealing with. If they're Atlanteans, then they'll have immunity to the power of your voice, but they won't be as physically strong as us. They won't be immune to the power of my voice, but if I use it on them, I'll hurt Antoni, and possibly you as well."

"I don't understand. What do you mean?"

"The powers of a triton's voice differs from that of a siren. I don't have the ability to erase memory or make irresistible commands, but I can force incredible volume, enough to burst an eardrum, break glass, or do other kinds of damage." He reached forward in the water and propelled himself with a graceful stroke, turning his head to look at me from time to time. "I don't want to have to use it if I don't have to, but a deaf Antoni is better than a dead Antoni, wouldn't you agree?"

"Let's agree not to use your voice, Emun," I replied. "A deaf Antoni is not acceptable to me or to him. I understand that it is better than a dead Antoni, yes, but that does not make it acceptable. There will be another way we can rescue him, even if my voice turns out to be useless."

He looked at me and I couldn't read his expression.

I grabbed his arm and slowed him down, desperation rising in my throat. "I mean it, Emun. Promise me you'll not use your voice if there's a chance it could damage Antoni's hearing."

"I don't know if I can make that promise," he began.

I squeezed his arm. "You have to," I hissed, and I felt my fins stand out erect and my face change. The points of my teeth became razor-sharp and pressed against my tongue.

The lights of the sub grew dim in the distance.

"Promise me or you go no farther," I snarled. "I'll go on my own if I have to."

I prepared myself to call on my elemental powers, bristling as I waited for him to comply. My fingers grew tense, curled in on themselves.

"I promise," Emun responded gently, his voice soothing, and he pried my fingers from his arm. "He's yours, I'll respect your wishes. You know why I am here."

We picked up speed again until the sub lights were bright. My defensive reaction eased and my hackles lay themselves down.

Yes, I knew why Emun was here. He wanted the pendant, but so did I. I liked him, but I didn't fully trust him. I would have given anything for my mother to have been at my side instead of him.

For a time we did not communicate again, and I was left alone with my scheming. If it came to a confrontation between Emun and me, who was more powerful? I could bend water to my will and break metal with my bare hands, but what kind of powers did tritons have? Triton, rather, since it appeared perhaps there was only one. It had already been demonstrated that they, he, was not just a male version of a siren, but a different creation with other abilities and powers.

"They're descending." Emun's voice brought me out of my musings. The sub's lights were drifting downward and its beams pointed into the depths where the tops of craggy mountains could be seen.

We followed, our bodies adjusting to the pressure as the depth increased. A jagged mountain range rose out of the gloom, sinister and with deep black abysses between the jutting spires and ridges. Silhouettes of sharks cast themselves against the rocks, and the beams of the submarine illuminated startled sea creatures, including a large squid which vanished into a crack in a craggy cliffside.

The sub leveled off for a long while, skimming over the tops of the mountains. Just as monotony settled in, it descended again and slowed considerably.

I felt Emun's hand touch my forearm as we slowed to watch.

The sub slowed to a crawl and its beams became brighter, as though someone had flicked to high-beams. The twin spotlights illuminated a huge cliff face, craggy and deeply shadowed.

The sub moved forward, slowly.

"They're going to hit the wall," I cried. "What are they doing?"

"No..." Emun's hand tightened around my wrist. "They're going *inside the mountain*."

He was right, and we watched, aghast, as the lights illuminated an entrance point large enough to accommodate the sub.

"This is unbelievable," Emun muttered. Both of our eyes were glued to the sub as it moved forward, penetrating the crack and disappearing from view inside the rock face.

The only sign of its passing was a dim glow lighting the cave from the inside.

Without another word, Emun and I followed the sub into the bowels of the underwater mountain. The sub slowed considerably, understandable since they were now locked in on all sides by rock faces and craggy teeth.

"They're insane," I muttered as we followed, worry for Antoni's life rising again in my chest. What if they crashed into the rocks? What if the sub had a malfunction? We were hundreds of feet down—not a problem for Emun and me, but a huge problem for a human reliant entirely on technology and superior piloting skills to keep them alive.

"They've been here before," Emun stated.

I nodded. Come to think of it, that was obvious. Whoever was piloting the sub seemed to know exactly where they were going.

We followed the sub deeper into the cave, which became tight in spots and opened out into huge caverns in others—caves which had to be crossed and the exit selected out of many options—some which likely led to a way out while others to more tunnels and caves.

A new problem began to rear its ugly head. We were following someone who knew where they were going, but the cave was a network, and we'd already passed multiple other entrances to different fingers and arms of the cave. If we didn't have a sub to follow, how were we going to get out?

I opened my mouth to bring this up to Emun but he had been pondering the same problem.

"Wherever they're going, they either need to hit upon a cave with oxygen to get out, or they have to have a robot to be able to interact with their environment. If they don't get

SALT & STONE   225

out, we can't rescue Antoni or get the pendant, and if they do..."

"We'll have a confrontation, which we have to win, but then we have to get Antoni out of here safely, which means we need the pilot."

Emun nodded. "Yes, so we'll have to subdue them somehow, and force them to take Antoni out of here safely."

"And if my voice has no effect?"

"We should assume that is the case. We don't know where they're going or what they're doing down here, or even why they have Antoni. Let's see where they go because we can't form a plan until we have more information."

Frowning, I agreed that this was the best we could plan at this point. Unless the men got out of the sub, there wasn't much we could do.

As we followed the sub deeper and deeper into the cave system, my mind wouldn't rest because of the fact that we had to rely on the men we were following to get back out again.

Putting my hand down at my side, I began to form a continuous column of ice as we swam. The ice crackled and drifted up to find the ceiling where it broke into chunks against the rock, but at least it provided a temporary thread in the direction from which we'd come. The water was cold enough down here that the melt rate would be very slow. For now, it was the best I could do. I supposed if I had to, I could use sonar to find my way out, but the deeper we got, the more exhausting it would be to get out that way. Sending sonic signals would tire me sooner than anything else.

Emun heard the sounds of the snapping ice columns

and looked back. I couldn't help the satisfaction I felt at the impressed look on his face.

"I've never seen that before," he said, watching the ice trail behind us as it drifted and made a strange looking tube against the dark rock surface. "I don't think that's a normal siren trait, is it?"

"It's an elemental trait," I murmured, continuing to form ice as we traveled.

"Element..." He paused, looking bemused. "You'll have to tell me more about that."

"Perhaps when my loved one isn't in mortal danger."

"Of course."

Emun had been right about one of his predictions. The sub slowed to a near-halt beneath a big black maw yawning over its hatch. There were buzzing and whirring sounds as the sub's previously dormant props in its belly came to life and propelled it upward through the rock.

The fissure in the rock broadened until its walls were no longer visible in the inky blackness. A huge cave had opened up around us, and the silver seam of the water's surface could be seen above our heads.

"You see," Emun muttered, and the sound of his voice had completely changed. No longer was it bouncing off the rock walls around us, but it expanded into the huge cavern we'd entered. "They're surfacing where there is air."

Emerging with just the tops of our heads as water sluiced from the sub's surfaces, the sound of sloshing water echoed off the distant walls and even more distant ceiling. Emun and I concealed ourselves behind one of the many rocky protrusions in the cave and waited for whatever was next.

The sounds of the sub's engines dying and the whirring sound of its hatch opening filled the cave. Men's voices followed, speaking a language I wasn't sure I could identify as it wasn't Polish, French, Italian, or Spanish.

Emun and I glanced at one another, listening, heads cocked.

"Dutch?" I guessed, only mouthing the words.

He shook his head and mouthed back, "Swiss German."

This revelation bothered me for a reason I couldn't put a finger on in the present stress I was under. Swiss German... This meant something, triggered something in my memory.

"Do you understand?" I mouthed.

Emun shook his head no.

If the circumstances hadn't been so dire, I would have asked him what the benefit of being one-hundred-sixty years old was if he hadn't used that time to learn the world's major languages.

Peeking over the top of the rocks, we watched as five men emerged from the sub. I was not surprised to see the finely formed jaw of Adrian. My attention was drawn to his hand where he held a small device from which emerged a faint teal glow, like a weak laser-beam. No matter which way Adrian turned, or how the device was jostled in his hand, the teal light pointed in one direction only, like a compass.

Antoni came out as the fourth man and I clamped a hand over my mouth to keep from crying out. Emun shot me a warning look and shook his head. He put a finger to his lips and I nodded in agreement, I knew I had to be quiet. The urge to come out from the rock blasting the men with my siren voice was nearly overwhelming, but if they were Atlantean, we would have given our major advantages away—the fact that they didn't know we were here.

I fought to control my breathing and watched Antoni,

combing him for any sign of injury or mistreatment. I let out a long slow breath when I could see that he was moving normally. He was being shadowed by two of the men, his every movement and position carefully monitored; he was under their control. He'd never fight against the men who held his only chance of leaving this cave alive.

The head and shoulders of the last man paused before getting fully out of the sub. He spoke to the others, gesturing with his hands. There was laughter, and the men sounded relaxed, almost jovial.

Emun and I shared a look at this. They were not worried about a thing, not even stressed or looking ashamed that they'd forcefully taken someone against his will. They appeared to have all the confidence in the world that they knew where they were going, they were perfectly safe and in control, and they were happy and maybe even excited to be in this freezing and deeply subterranean cave. The cold didn't bother me or Emun, but the men were bundled up in jackets, hats, scarves, and fingerless gloves. Even Antoni had been given a hat and scarf.

The last man disappeared into the sub's hatch and reappeared repeatedly, handing backpacks down to the others, one for each of them except Antoni. Finally, he too left the sub and jumped onto the cave floor as the rest of the men were fitting headlamps to their foreheads and turning on handheld flashlights. They heaved their backpacks onto their backs and began to move toward the back of the cave where a black crevice yawned upward. Adrian led, with that strange teal beam of light leading the way.

Emun and I shared a look of alarm. Where on earth were they going now? And on foot?

Keeping Antoni in the middle, they disappeared into

the crevice in the wall just wide enough for one man to go through at a time.

After Antoni disappeared through the crack, followed by the last two men, my fins returned to legs and Emun and I padded across the stone, naked and barefoot. At the tall jagged entrance we didn't hesitate, and darkness folded around us. Flashes of light and the sounds of conversation ahead of us were easy to follow.

The rock beneath our feet was damp and cold but smooth and in some places, a little slippery. The sound of dripping and running water was quiet but perpetual. The narrow walls of the passageway rose above our heads into blackness, making it impossible to see how high up it went. The sounds of the men's voices up ahead, their relaxed chit-chat and sometimes laughter echoed and bounced through the passageway, off endless hard surfaces, and through tunnels and smaller depressions and caves as we passed.

They did not appear to have intentions of killing or hurting Antoni at the moment, and the fear of this subsided enough that I was able to think. My mind tossed about various scenarios—picking off the men one by one from the back, silencing them, until we got to Antoni. Then, when he was within our grasp we could come between those in front of him to protect him. But how would we silently 'neutral-ize' the men behind him without alerting the others? Only if the party grew very stretched out might we have a chance to do it, and even then...it would require them not to be immune to my voice and we had no idea who these strangers were.

Emun was following behind me, neither of us bashful or self-conscious about being naked—one of the gifts of the mer. I was thankful to see that tritons had this same lack of embarrassment because if Emun had been squirming or staring, it would have been a distraction.

We began to ascend and the work of our toes gripping on the slick surface of the stone beneath us became arduous and slowed us down. How I wished for a pair of hiking shoes. My skin was now dry but my hair was damp and cold water ran down my back, tickling and annoying me. I stubbed my toe on something hard and bit my lip to keep from making a sound. Taking a step up, I stubbed the big toe on my other foot and halted, lips pinched in pain. Feeling gingerly forward with my toes, I realized something that stilled my whole body for a moment.

Emun tapped on my arm after a while and I looked back at him. In the near pitch, his pupils had expanded to fully black, as had mine, but his face and frame were a blur of pale skin and dark features.

I whispered a single word at him. "Stairs."

He looked down, then bent over and felt in front of his feet with a hand to find that I was right. We were no longer ascending on rough rock and the organic shapes of the cave floor. Someone had built stairs here—smooth-edged, worn and shallow, easy to climb. I braced myself on the walls with my hands as I began to climb. My hand found a smooth depression in the wall, long and straight and running parallel to the angle of the steps. A kind of banister?

The skin on the back of my neck seemed to crawl up and over my scalp.

Someone had been here long, long before us.

TWENTY-FOUR

I lost track of time as we continued to ascend. The men slowed as their legs were surely burning from the seemingly endless climb. Eventually, the stairs led to an open cavern with a high arched ceiling dotted with bioluminescent algae. Bright green and teal smudges of the stuff glowed from depressions in the walls, but didn't provide any helpful illumination. When looking back, I could see Emun's form a little better, a pale smudge in the darkness with limbs and a torso. The party of men ahead of us had grown quiet as they continued to hike, shoes scuffing against the cave floor and the beams from their headlamps and flashlight shooting around like spotlights from a nightclub. Probably, they were all breathing too hard from the exertion to talk.

We passed dark pools of water, and several waterfalls of varying volume, from thin streams to thick and quite power-ful. I wondered at where the water was coming from and longed to touch it, to discover its nature. I marveled at the nature of the network we'd found ourselves in, that it was not completely natural, but augmented by the hands of craftspeople. Emun had spoken of Atlantis whose territory the man in Boston claimed extended from Africa to the Azores. Were we in the ruins of Atlantis? We even passed what looked like a fountain, a tall womanly shape making a spire from a pool of still, black liquid.

The presence of engineered stairs disappeared and reappeared as we traveled. Here, I could not leave runnels of ice behind us, and the potential to get lost and wander for days in this complex city was very real.

The air had been cloying, humid, and dank since we left the cave with the sub, so when a gentle wind of fresh air brushed past our faces, Emun and I glanced at one another. Ocean air was coming into this network from outside, but it was impossible to pinpoint where it was coming from. It caressed my face, smelling of salt and sea and ozone.

The men's chatter picked up again, as did the narrow staircase, but this time the steps were short and curved before opening up into another huge subterranean cave.

Emun and I stopped at the entrance to the space and looked around with awe.

The entire cavern was illuminated by a soft golden and blue tinted glow. Hundreds of thousands of bright pinpoints—glowworms, I assumed—spread across the cavern ceiling. The surface of rock making up the jagged ceiling of the cathedral glittered like gold. Black pools and rivers of water spread out as far as the eye could see, snaking this way and that between rock steps and platforms. More curvy fountains could be seen throughout, some still spouting water and others grown still. The sound of water pouring filled the space like music.

More astounding than the unique setting was a thick tower of glittering aquamarine gems like the one from Sybellen's pendant. They had been collected into a glass cylinder set on the cave floor. It was as high as a man's waist and as thick as a human thigh. These aquamarines glittered and sparkled with their own source of light, throwing more illumination in all directions. Overtop of the cylinder of gems was a clear glass dome.

The men set their bags down and some of them crouched by the water's edge, reaching their hands toward it.

I gave a soft intake of breath when I saw how the water lit up at their touch, churning to life with a bright teal glow. At first glance, it looked magical, but I realized it was bioluminescent algae leaving the bright trails of light.

After concealing ourselves behind a thick stalagmite Emun and I watched quietly as the men took in their surroundings. My eyes found Antoni and swept him from head to feet. He seemed fine, and just as amazed by this wonder of nature we found ourselves in as everyone else was.

Emun tapped my arm and pointed to a cave wall beyond the cylinder of gems. I could see what appeared to be pieces of broken artwork on one of the far walls. Human figures, sea creatures, and possibly mer were depicted, but it was too far away and the art too ruined to make out much detail. These had to be the ruins of some ancient civilization and if I hadn't been so focused on rescuing Antoni, I would have been astounded.

My attention returned to the men as Adrian retrieved a tablet from his backpack, turned it on so the screen was aglow, and crossed over to Antoni. He held it out to Antoni and spoke to him, pointing to something on the screen.

Antoni took it and seemed to study whatever was on the screen for a short time, before handing it back with a shrug and a few words.

Adrian shoved the tablet back into Antoni's hands, looking insistent and jabbing at the screen. He pushed Antoni backward until he had no choice but to sit down on a mound of stone at the edge of a pool, then walked back to the others, muttering either to himself or to them.

Antoni set the tablet on his knee and interacted with the screen, sliding it back and forth and pinching to zoom in and out.

"What is happening?" I mouthed to Emun.

Emun made a doubtful face and shook his head.

We watched as all the men, aside from Antoni, surrounded the glass dome containing the gems. They bent beside it, feeling with their fingers around the base, wanting a way in. One of them knocked against the glass with a knuckle, and a blue ripple of light went across it, originating from the point of impact. The men looked at one another, surprised. Another man knocked on the glass, three times in three different places, and again the blue ripple of light shimmered outward from where he'd struck, in the manner of pebbles tossed into a calm, glassy surface of water.

One of the men put his hands on either side of the dome and exerted force, attempting to push it over or twist it off. The dome did not budge.

"There is magic here," whispered Emun, eyes glued to the dome. "They want to get at the gems and they don't know how." His huge-pupiled gaze drifted to where Antoni was bent over the tablet. "They think he knows a way in."

I could have laughed if the situation wasn't so tense. Antoni? Know the way into a dome protected by magic? The idea was absurd. Antoni knew spreadsheets and corporate management, not magic. They had to have the wrong person.

One of the men pointed out something, low, near the

floor. They bent to study where he was pointing. One of them called Antoni over and he joined them at the dome.

He bent over to look at where the man was pointing. I looked too, and could make out glyphs etched into the glass, almost hidden in the shadows.

Antoni spoke, shaking his head. He pointed to the glyphs one by one and seemed to be translating them. Straining, I finally caught one of the Polish words, one of the few I knew, and it made my blood run cold. The word was: Death

I knocked Emun on the shoulder, mouthing. "What are they talking about? Do you understand?"

"It is a curse, I think," Emun said, frowning as he listened.

Antoni straightened and the other men did as well, he was saying something to them while shaking his head and handing the tablet back.

The men seemed upset by Antoni's words. One of them threw up his hands in disgust and growled something to his mates. Walking to where he'd set down his pack, he opened it and retrieved something that looked like an ice-pick. He heaved it in one hand, turned, and began striding back to the men with purpose. Hefting it, he made as though to swing.

My whole body tensed for flight, my voice swelled in my throat. Emun put his hand on my arm and whispered, "Wait!"

The man swung the evil looking pick, not at Antoni, but at the glass dome. He struck it hard. There was a terrific cracking sound followed by the tinkle of broken glass as the dome flashed bright blue. The men cried out and covered their eyes. As the blue flash dissipated, the dome was clearly now spidered with fractures.

A few of the men applauded as the man with the ice-pick hooked the business end of the tool into the hole he'd created and began to yank the glass away from the aquamarine gems in the cylinder.

Emun's hand tightened on my forearm, his face visibly taut. "He shouldn't have done that."

There was the sound of wind moving through the cave, but no actual wind accompanied it. Everyone paused in what they were doing, as they heard it too. Heads with lamps attached looked around the cave, making a laser-light show. The sound of the wind increased until it was whistling, the whistling took on a keening sound, and the keen became a scream. The men bent again, crying out inaudibly and covering their ears. Emun and I covered ours as well.

The man with the pick dropped the tool and it thumped onto the cave floor as he clutched at his throat, eyes wide and bulging. His mouth opened, making a perfect O as though he was trying to scream—the sound, if any, lost in the sound of the intangible wind.

One of the other men went to him, reaching for him, trying to help him, but the moment he touched him he suffered a similar fate. Scratching at their mouths and necks as though they could not breathe, faces distorted in expressions of terror, they fell. For a time they writhed horribly on the stone floor, desperate for oxygen. The man who'd broken the dome rolled in his agony, tumbling into a pool with a splash of bright blue-green. The remaining men were too afraid to touch them, watching helplessly as their companions died. Antoni stared on in horror, but something in his face expressed a sad expectancy—he had tried to warn them.

My heart had taken up a thick energetic rhythm as the

scene played out in front of us as adrenaline coursed through my limbs. There were only three men left, Adrian, one other, and Antoni.

The screaming sound of the wind had stopped as the men died. The stunned silence in the cave was as loud as the shock on every face.

The glass dome had a large jagged hole large enough for a hand to reach in and draw out the gems, but neither Arian nor the other man moved. The scene was like something out of a movie poster—broken glass on the stone floor, a glowing cylinder of gems, Antoni standing behind the dome, and one man on either side. A body lay on the edge of a pool, hands still gripping the throat.

Adrian's remaining companion rounded on Antoni and began to yell, gesturing wildly at the dead men and the dome, as though it was his fault. He grabbed the front of Antoni's jacket, yanking him forward and almost off his feet.

Before I could think, my thighs flexed and I stood up, readying to spring to Antoni's defense. Emun grabbed my elbow and hauled me back down, but not before Antoni's eyes caught on the movement and locked for a microsecond on my gaze. His expression flickered from shock to deadpan, his face became ghostly as the blood drained. His eyes released me as I squatted again, cutting back to the man yelling in his face.

The man turned to see what Antoni had been looking at just as I disappeared behind the stone again, panting.

"Wait," Emun said. "They're not going to hurt him."

I wanted to scream at him, ask him how he knew that, yell that he wouldn't be affected if anything happened to Antoni.

Peeking out from behind the stone I watched as the man

hauled Antoni forward. My body tensed, and again I felt Emun's hand on my arm, begging for me not to do anything rash.

The man gestured at the gems, glittering in their cylinder, commanding Antoni to touch them.

Antoni seemed hesitant, and no wonder, considering what had happened to the others.

He glanced at where I was hiding and slowly walked forward, shoes crunching on the broken glass. Standing in front of the cylinder, he looked down at the sparkling jewels, face aglow with blue light. Adrian and his last companion looked on—their own little guinea pig, the cowards.

Antoni's eyes swept up, the only thing on his body that moved, he caught my gaze and I felt that he was trying to communicate something to me. His eyes begged me to understand something, but what?

I clenched my teeth, not knowing how long I could be still, my mind grasping for a plan for when the inevitable happened. It was very likely that these men were immune to my voice because how would they know about this place if they *weren't* Atlanteans?

With the speed of a viper striking for a kill, Antoni's hand darted through the hole in the dome. Snatching a handful of aquamarines, he sprang sideways and sprinted the short distance to a black pool of water, dropping gems as he ran.

The other man yelled, and Adrian fumbled in his jacket, probably for a weapon.

Antoni dove headfirst into one of the pools, with an explosion of bright green teal swirling against black as the water closed over him.

"Antoni." His name tore from my lips as I sprang from

our hiding place, and this time Emun's hands could not hold me down.

Sprinting, I crossed the stone floor in moments. Small cuts stung my bare feet from the broken glass. Ignoring the men, who were too shocked to react anyway, I dove into the pool behind Antoni. Water filled my ears, muffling the sudden sounds of shouting. I looked around in the dark water, desperate to find my beloved.

The pool seemed so deep as to be nearly bottomless. The bioluminescent algae that lived on the surface trailed after Antoni in the direction of a dark hole in the wall under the water.

My heart leapt into my throat and pounded so loud it was all I could hear. Why would Antoni swim into an underwater cave? He'd drown in just a few minutes.

My legs melded into a tail and propelled me into the cave.

Darkness closed around me and the sound of limbs moving in the water came to my ears. A moment later, a dim glow appeared ahead. Antoni's shape was a black silhouette against the glow. He was swimming smoothly and in places where the tunnel was tight he braced his hands against the walls and propelled himself along. He passed through the glow and into darkness again.

How long could he hold his breath?

"Antoni," I called out, my voice smooth and filling the space around us.

He looked back so quickly I couldn't register an expression. He immediately looked forward again and continued on. I followed, fighting my growing panic that he would soon lose consciousness. For a human, this was the most dangerous environment possible—underwater tunnels with no apparent way out, and Antoni had *chosen* this rather than staying with the men.

I reached his legs, preparing to pull him back to me and give him oxygen, but the tunnel was too tight. There wasn't room for the two of us to be side by side, we'd only become wedged.

I began to push him forward, and he went with it, lifting his hands away from the wall and making an aquadynamic shape. Ahead was another glow, and I prayed for an opening where we could emerge. We'd already been down here for too long for a human to survive unless they had Olympic level lungs. Did Antoni?

The glow ahead became brighter and the tunnel opened into another cave. The water's surface rippled overhead and I shot toward it, pushing Antoni ahead of me. Relief swelled in my heart, and amazement that he was still conscious. He was going to make it!

Antoni broke through first, then me, and suddenly we were side by side. A small cavern opened overhead, dusted with more glimmering glowworms.

"Antoni," I cried, my hands grasping at his shoulders. "Are you okay?"

He rubbed the water out of his eyes, opened them and looked at me.

"Targa," he reached for me. "How did you..."

As I began to wrap my arms around him, I saw something on his neck that made me freeze. Holding him still by his shoulders, I looked more closely. He continued to tread water and let me look, tilting his chin up. They were difficult to see, but there was no mistaking them: closing up, even as I watched, and seaming over with perfect skin—gills, just beneath his ears.

I looked at him with shock and he read my expression.

One hand emerged from the water and he held up a single jewel, glittering in the blue light.

"I wasn't sure if I could believe the legend," he said, "but when I saw you down here, I knew it had to work."

I peered at the gem, reaching for it. So it wasn't superior lungs which had helped Antoni survive the tunnel; it was the magic of the aquamarine.

He enclosed it in his hand, hiding it from view. "I can't risk losing it. I'll need it to get out of this place, unless you're going to do all my breathing for me. As fun as that sounds, I'm not sure it'll be very efficient in these tight tunnels."

"The gems give people gills?"

Antoni nodded. "Crazy, isn't it?" But his eyes drifted to my own gills, and then to where my naked torso and my long silvery-white tail swayed beneath us in the pool. "Maybe you won't think it's that crazy."

I gave a startled laugh.

He brushed my wet hair off my neck and back over my shoulder. He kissed my lips with his own cold ones. "When were you going to tell me?"

I took a breath, wanting to ask a million questions, make a million excuses, and pour my heart out to him. I was over-flowing with relief and shock, and was completely confounded at the lack of surprise I saw in Antoni's eyes. The only possible reason for that lack of shock—he had already known.

There was a muffled crack, distant but distinct.

We looked at one another.

"Gunfire," Antoni said, his jaw tight.

"Emun!" I cried. "I have to go back!"

"Emun?" Antoni's brows pinched. "Who is Emun? There's someone else here with you?"

"I'll explain later. Wait here, don't move. *Please* don't move until I get back."

"But…"

This was the last thing Antoni wanted and I couldn't blame him, but if something had happened to Emun, I would never forgive myself. I had blown our cover to go after Antoni, then left him to deal with the fallout all by himself.

"Promise me," I cried, desperate, squeezing Antoni's shoulders with my hands.

"I promise," he said, doubtfully, and then added, "I'll wait as long as I can."

This was the best I could ask for, I was out of time. I gave him a quick kiss and submerged, swimming back through the tunnels as quickly as I could without scraping my skin or scales against the rock walls closing me in.

TWENTY-FIVE

I emerged to a seemingly empty cavern. The broken dome and spray of aquamarines across the rock floor was untouched. My heart gave a high, frightened leap when I spotted a pool of blood, almost resinous and pitchy in the strange lights of the cave. It smeared across the rocks in the direction of a glistening black pool and disappeared over the edge. Was that Emun's blood?

My tail morphed into legs and I set my feet on the pool's base with my head just above the water line, looking around for some sign of life. I hesitated to use my voice to call out and draw the wrong kind of attention.

Movement in my periphery drew my view sideways as a human shape emerged suddenly from another pool. Adrian, water streaming from his head, rose from the pool like an apparition from a dream, eyes focused, hand lifting, the barrel of a gun coming to find its mark—me.

"Don't shoot!" My siren voice blasted from my throat like foghorn.

He froze, and his face went slack, the gun relaxed to his side. I let out a huge relieved breath. Not Atlantean, then.

"Lower the gun and be still," I commanded. Adrian's arm dropped.

Hopping out of the pool, I walked to the smear of blood, studying it. Looking into the pool where the blood trail ended offered no revelations. Slipping into the water I submerged and searched the pool, but it appeared to be vacant.

Emerging again, I glanced at where Adrian stood, body relaxed, face slack.

My eye was drawn to the spray of gems catching the light and glinting wetly. I knelt and picked one up.

It was my undoing.

Weakness flooded my limbs and I fell to one knee. Shock coursed through me, my vision blurred and a dull burning sensation flared and throbbed in my head, torso and limbs.

Someone knocked into me from behind, sending me sprawling toward the gems and onto the cavern floor. Landing on the jewels Antoni had spilled, they pressed into me like stinging insects, making me writhe and cry out in pain. My body would not respond to my desperate requests to get up, and my siren voice did not respond to my will.

Lying on my back, head swimming and body in agony, a blurry shape appeared above me. His shape spun as the cavern ceiling whirled and I wondered if I was going to be sick. The final member of the party, come out of hiding to finish me off. He spoke softly in Swiss German, his tone that of wonder. He nudged my hip with a booted toe, hard enough to rock my body. A tortured moan echoed in the cavern—mine.

The shape kneeled and he reached out of my view for something on the floor. I heard the dry clinking sound of a pile of gems being gathered into his hand, lifted over my helpless form. Almost lovingly, he lay the handful of gems down my torso. My body rocked in response to the pain, my muscles seizing and my mouth opening to cry out, a hoarse cry escaping. My tongue felt leaden, I tried to talk, tried to beg him to remove the gems, but my powers had abandoned me.

A blurry shape hit the man bent over me with a dull thud and I heard two sharp exhales of breath. Both of them disappeared from my view, but I could hear the sounds of a struggle, of fists hitting flesh, and grunts of pain. I couldn't lift my head or turn my neck but my mind screamed, *Emun!*

Two gunshots were followed by further combative sounds and a loud splash of water. Then nothing. Silence. Panic blossomed in every nerve as I lay there in agony, vulnerable and praying that Emun was alive. I felt as helpless as an infant, and just as weak.

Several agonizing moments later—moments that felt like hours—a face appeared overhead. The pale, angular face of Emun spun in sickly circles overhead.

"Targa! What's wrong with you?" His voice echoed a thousand times over, and pierced my ears and my brain like an ice-cold needle.

I tried to tell him the gems were hurting me but I couldn't speak. A strangled moan leaked from my mouth. Drawing breath sent tiny knives stabbing through my ribcage, my tongue had gone numb. Closing my eyes shut out the spinning ceiling, but my mind thought my body was still whirling. My stomach clenched. The stinging insects had penetrated, were drilling toward my heart. I had never known agony until this moment, and I wished for death to end it. I opened my eyes again, begging for relief.

Emun understood. His hands brushed over me as he pulled away the pile of gems on my torso. I heard him take a wheezing breath and knew he too was in pain. Rolling me off the gems I had been lying on, he made sure none were in contact with my skin. Immediately, the cave stopped spinning, my breathing eased. My limbs began to tingle. My tongue was still leaden.

"You need salt," I heard him say.

With a sharp gasp of pain and a grunt, he picked me up and carried me to the nearest pool, where he let me slide into the water.

The briny water touched all the places the gems had stung and the pain began to ease. My legs melded, but slowly, sluggishly, painfully. For several minutes I just drifted in the pool, letting the saltwater soak my gills and nurse my aching, weak body. My tongue and throat tingled, my gills greedily pulled the salt water through them, soothing with every inhale. I let out a long sad siren note, relieved to the point of tears that my voice had returned to me.

When I felt something like normal, I broke the surface.

Setting human feet on the pool's bottom, my legs trembled as though I'd been running sprints and overdone it. With a shaking hand, I reached for the pool's edge and gripped it, resting there. Emun had slipped into the water beside me and stood watching me, his face etched with concern.

"Feeling better?"

I nodded. "Thank you." My voice was a dry rasp. I couldn't take my eyes away from the beautiful aquamarines filling the column, how sinister and ugly they appeared to me now. "They were killing me." I dragged my eyes to Emun's face.

"The magic is real, just not in the way we expected."

"I thought they were supposed to help mermaids."

"But you're not just a mermaid," Emun said quietly, "are you?"

I didn't answer, but he was right. I wasn't just a mermaid, I was an elemental. Rare and powerful. But was I really so different, that the gems would help others of my kind, and yet kill me? I lifted a trembling hand and covered my eyes. It seemed I was not as impervious as I had once thought.

Adrian stood where I'd left him, in the pool, gun hanging at his side. Emun's eyes darted to him. "He's making me uneasy." Emun got out of the pool and went to take the gun from Adrian's lax hand.

He turned to me, gun in hand. "Where's Antoni?"

"He's through there," I gestured to the underwater tunnel. "I need to go get him. I told him to wait for me."

"I'll go. You rest," he said.

I shook my head. "I promised I'd be back for him."

Emun nodded. "I'll wait for you then."

It was only when he turned fully to face me that I noticed the blood oozing from a bullet hole just below his right rib.

"You're shot!" I beckoned for him to come to me. "Let me help you."

He put a hand over the wound. "It didn't hit any vital organs. I've been shot before. Hurts like hell but I'll heal."

I beckoned to him impatiently, frustrated that he would make me have to insist. "Get over here."

He slipped into the water beside me and we submerged together. Calling on the healing power of the salt water, I drew from the ocean and put a hand over his wound. The bullet had passed through, leaving a hole not unlike the one my mother had had after being shot with the speargun. Slowly, very slowly, the wound stopped bleeding and the muscles and skin drew closed and stitched themselves together. Emun blinked lazily at me, down at where he'd been injured, and back at my face. He touched my face gently, saying thank you.

Leaving Emun in the cavern to finish healing, I made the journey through the tunnel and back to Antoni. A dark shape coming toward me in the gloomy light told me he'd grown tired of waiting.

Stopping myself by bracing my hands against the tunnel walls, I reversed direction.

"That was quick," Emun remarked when both of us surfaced and climbed from the pool.

Antoni wrapped his arms around me and I hugged him back. He tightened when he saw Adrian, until Emun explained that Adrian was under my command.

"It was agony, waiting, and when I heard more gunshots I had to come," he murmured against my ear.

I just nodded against his shoulder, still feeling weak and too tired to waste my breath with unnecessary words.

When he released me, Antoni turned to Emun. "You're Emun, I guess?"

"Nice to meet you." Emun extended a hand to Antoni and the two men actually shook hands—here in this deep underwater world, with a still and vacant looking man standing beside them.

Antoni shucked off his wet shirt and draped it over my shoulders. I gave him a weak smile, wishing I had the energy to laugh. "I'm not embarrassed," I said.

"Clearly," Antoni replied, "but I am."

Emun chuckled and looked down at himself, naked and wet. "Sorry, unless you've got a spare set of shorts hidden somewhere, not much I can do about this business."

"Sorry, but how do you two know each other?" Antoni

asked, looking back and forth between the two of us. "Are you...the same?"

"More or less, although Targa's got abilities I sure don't have." Emun bent to pick up a gem. "And these don't affect me in the same way."

"What do you mean?" Antoni looked at me. "How did they affect you?"

"They almost killed her," Emun replied for me.

"What?" Antoni's arm tightened around me.

My eyes drifted to where Adrian stood, waiting patiently, almost sublimely. "We could ask him," I suggested.

***

"I'M GOING to ask you some questions, and you will tell me nothing but the truth," I said, my siren voice swelling around him, filling the cave.

"I will tell you nothing but the truth," he droned.

"What do you want the gems for?"

"To sell to the highest bidder."

"What do the gems do?"

"When held in the hand, they give a human the ability to breathe underwater."

"Do you already have buyers?" Emun asked from behind me.

"We have interested parties. They will be auctioned privately."

"Who are you offering them to?"

"All the major world militaries."

"Underwater armies," Antoni muttered, wrapping his arms around himself. "Unbelievable."

"Who do you work for?"

"The Group of Winterthür."

I looked at the men, questioningly. Antoni shrugged, indicating he'd never heard of them, but Emun said, "It's a think tank out of Switzerland."

"Switzerland?" A bell rang in my memory. "Antoni, do you remember Gerland Chamberlain?"

"The man we met at the museum?"

I nodded. "He was Swiss, and he was awfully interested in the jewelry case at the exhibition. He and Adrian must have been working together."

Antoni nodded. "Ask him."

"Who is Gerland Chamberlain?" I asked.

"The Group of Winterthür," he repeated.

"Is he Atlantean?" Emun asked.

Adrian jerked his head in a stiff nod. "Atlantean."

Antoni and I shared a look. Antoni just shook his head, amazed.

"How did you learn about the gems?" I asked Adrian.

Adrian droned out his story without emotion in his voice or on his face. "An archaeologist looking for Atlantis found ruins that told the story in pictures and a language that very few could decipher. It told of a sea god who made an aquamarine columnar for his lover, who had been cursed by an ancient enemy. The aquamarine lifted the curse for her as long as she held it in her hand or wore it on her body. It was discovered ages later that the same aquamarine gave humans the ability to survive underwater for as long as they wanted."

"But it lifts the salt curse?" Emun insisted. "It doesn't hurt mermaids?"

"It is said to free mermaids," Adrian droned. "This is what the ruins said."

Emun and I shared a look. "Why did it hurt this mermaid then?" Emun asked.

"I don't know."

I resisted the urge to choke Adrian for being so unhelpful. We guessed it was because I was no normal mermaid, but we were still only speculating.

"I might have something to add to this conversation," Antoni said, and when I turned to look at him, I was alarmed to see that his lips had turned blue.

"Antoni! You're freezing."

He nodded and his teeth chattered, his body tense and his arms around himself. "I think if we don't get out of here soon, I might become more of a burden than I am already." He nodded at Adrian. "Him too."

Adrian's lips were also taking on a blue-ish cast. Though he wasn't moving to warm himself, his skin was waxy and covered in gooseflesh. He had also begun to shiver.

"We are a long way from warmth," Emun said.

"There are warm clothes in the sub, if we can get back there as soon as possible, that will be a good start."

"Him too?"

"Well we can't just leave him here," I said. I looked at Adrian's face. "Do you know the way back?"

"Yes."

"Lead the way, and be quick about it."

With that, Adrian moved like he had an infusion of energy.

"Wait, what about the gems?" Antoni asked, through a tight jaw.

Emun, Antoni and I considered the pile of aquamarines.

"Adrian, does anyone else know about this place?"

"I don't know," he replied.

"I don't think we should just leave them here," Emun said. "They're too valuable, too powerful." He bent and retrieved a backpack, dumped out its contents and he and Antoni began to gather up the gems and put them in the bag. When they'd deposited every last one, Emun put the straps over his shoulders and gave me a nod.

"Lead on," I commanded Adrian.

By the time we returned to the sub, both Adrian and Antoni were shivering uncontrollably, teeth chattering so hard they could barely be understood. Adrian opened the hatch on the sub and retrieved dry clothes for himself and for Antoni. Quickly, they stripped out of their wet gear and pulled on the dry.

"What about the bodies?" I whispered to Emun once we were inside the sub. "Just leave them?"

"The most important thing is getting Antoni out of danger," he said quietly, as we watched Adrian at the sub's console. Antoni was seated in one of the six bucket seats, buckled over the shoulders and wrapped in a tin foil blanket. "We can talk about the bodies later, if you really want to do something about them. If it's important to you, I can come back and deal with them."

I gave him a look which I hoped expressed the gratitude I was feeling for this, and then went to sit with Antoni, wishing I had Saxony's powers of body heat. Dark smudges appeared below Antoni's eyes as his lids drooped heavily.

"So tired," he slurred.

"I need you to stay conscious for now, please love," I said, kissing his cheekbone. "Until you're warmer."

Antoni nodded slowly, laboriously.

Emun seemed to realize Adrian was in the same danger of slipping into unconsciousness. He slouched at the controls. Emun slid into the seat behind him and jostled his shoulder. "Hey, look alive, Adrian. No one else knows how to drive this tub."

I smiled. "Well, well, Emun has limits. You can fly a plane, but not pilot a sub."

He grinned over his shoulder at me. "Not this model, anyway." He flicked his fingers at the console in a disdainful gesture. "Too many electronics. Why can't they just make them like they used to?"

Adrian had straightened, but throughout the journey, Emun had to continuously poke and jostle him.

In a matter of hours, we had returned to the shores beside the airport of Ponta Delgada. The sun was blazing in the sky but the area was deserted as we emerged.

Erasing Adrian's mind of the events that had taken place, I suggested he find a hotel, take a hot bath, order a hot meal, and go to sleep. We took the small black device and tablet at Antoni's suggestion, then climbed out of the sub and Emun and I changed into our original clothing.

Poor Ivan was nearly frantic with worry after so many hours without contact, but within a matter of hours he had notified the airport in Gdansk and had us in the air.

My last thought before losing consciousness was that I couldn't wait to be alone with Antoni to discuss everything.

TWENTY-SIX

Waking in my own bed with Antoni beside me, my eyes fell on the strange black device and the tablet which Antoni had left on the bedside table. Reaching for the tablet, I pressed the home button, but the battery was dead. I slipped out of bed and took it to where my phone charger was plugged into the wall, grateful that they were the same brand.

"Does passing out on the plane have something to do with what you are?" Antoni asked behind me.

I straightened suddenly. "You're awake!"

He nodded and gestured for me to come back to bed. I plugged in the tablet and slipped between the covers, snuggling into the crook between his arm and chest. Suddenly, I sat up again. "Did you see Lydia? She'll be frantic!"

"I saw her. I sent her home last night after we arrived. I told her I'd talk with her later." He pulled me back down to settle in his arms again. "I wanted to talk to you so badly last night, but you seemed beyond exhausted. Almost sick, to tell you the truth." He kissed my forehead. "Just as I was feeling better, you fell apart on me."

"Yes. Sirens aren't good at flying. I think it has to do

with how far we are from the ocean." I described the sensations that came over me when I ascended in a plane, how they grew more severe with every thousand meters above land and sea the plane rose. "I really wanted to talk to you last night, too."

He gazed at me, eyes taking in the features of my face. "We both have some explaining to do."

"Can I start?"

"Please."

I rolled over and propped my head on my hand, tucking a pillow in front of my stomach and letting my other arm rest on it. "You don't know how much I wanted to tell you, to show you what I am. So many times, I condemned myself for keeping my secret from the one I love. I just couldn't, because..."

He waited, eyes one mine.

"Because my mother had drilled into me since childhood how important it was to keep her identity a secret, even from my father."

"Your father wasn't a mer... person? Like Emun?"

"No, he was just a man."

A narrow frown line appeared between Antoni's eyes. "I think I know how he would have felt if he knew. If you don't mind me saying so, I think she should have told him."

"Maybe she should have," I admitted, thinking that as much as I admired my mother, she wasn't perfect, and she had made mistakes in her life. "Mom loved him so much, and he loved her. In fact, their love was so powerful, it's why I'm able to do what I can do. Control water, make ice, or hot water, that kind of thing." I left out that I could stop a tsunami or make a massive whirlpool in the ocean; there was no need to brag...or scare him.

"It's magic." He rolled over onto his back and looked at

the ceiling, rubbing his temples with his fingertips. "Magic is real."

"Some is, I guess. Yes." I wanted to tell him what my friends were capable of, but one thing at a time. The poor guy had a lot to digest already. "You're not in as much shock as I thought you would be."

He faced me again. "That's because I'm pretty sure I met one of you before. I just didn't realize it until recently."

He had my attention. "Really?"

He nodded. "I did a semester of university in Warsaw, a kind of internship when I was in first year. I met a girl named Lusi." He knocked his shoulder up and amended, "Woman, not girl. She looked young and she was wild, but she was no girl. She had long, bright blond hair and dark eyes that seemed to change color with her emotions."

I ignored the tiny darts of jealousy searching for a target as Antoni talked about this girl from his past. I could tell by the way he spoke about her that they'd been more than friends.

"On New Year's Eve we went out together with a bunch of friends from Uni—a house party. It got pretty messy, and Lusi, who could be a bit of a hothead, got into a row with someone, so I dragged her out of there before things could get bad. We ended up going back to her apartment and having a few of our own New Year's Eve drinks." Antoni cleared his throat, clearly uncomfortable talking about this part of his past.

"It's okay," I said, "go on."

"When she took off her dress, I saw she had an interesting tattoo. Here," he pointed to his hip bone. "I asked her about it and she began to spin a crazy story. It was very entertaining and pure fiction. This was part of Lusi's charm, she rarely answered a question directly, and instead liked to weave a web of intrigue around herself. She told me she was a very old mermaid, one who swam up the Warsaw river in medieval times, became trapped by some merchant men, only to be freed by some local fishermen who felt badly about keeping such a beautiful creature penned up. She was so grateful for being rescued that she pledged to become a protector of Warsaw."

I absorbed this, in no doubt whatsoever that what Lusi had told Antoni that night, pretending to be in jest, was actually some form of the truth.

"Her tattoo was very old, she said, a glyph from a long-dead language, and that it meant 'anything for you.' She'd tattooed it on herself so she'd never forget about the love a triton had for a siren that was powerful enough to set all sirens free."

"It was the same glyph as the one on the pendant."

Antoni nodded. "Yes, the same. When I saw it in the museum, I was astounded by it, because I had always thought her story to be completely made up. Even after seeing plenty of artwork around Warsaw of a mermaid with a sword—the protector of the city—I thought she was very clever to take something from legend and make it sound so real. I just thought the statues and crests of that mermaid had inspired her, but it seems it was the other way around. I can still hardly believe it."

"When's the last time you spoke to her?"

"Not since University. We stayed in touch for a while, but communication with her became less and less frequent, until finally we lost touch completely. I don't even know if she's still in Warsaw. She's not one of those people who maintains relationships for a long time, and never claimed to be. She always warned me that she would break my heart if I got too close to her."

"And did she?"

The corner of Antoni's mouth twitched up and his dimple appeared. "A little. Though she and I would never have worked. She was far too volatile, almost scary, and you could never get a straight answer out of her. But after she told me the story of the mermaid, she saw that I was curious about the old language. I looked it up and couldn't find anything like it. She began to teach me a little. Not much, mind you, I didn't have time to learn a whole language on top of my studies, but enough to understand the principles of it."

"That's why Adrian and those men kidnapped you? They wanted you to interpret for them."

"Exactly. And what they found, Targa..." he shook his head. "It will rock archeology and history forever if it gets out. Especially now that I know you're real. The ruins they found suggest an entire underwater city with a rich culture and even a monarchy of some kind."

"What did they tell you about it?"

He chuckled. "Not much. They weren't interested in educating me, only in utilizing what little knowledge I already had."

"Do you think it was Atlantis? Where we were?"

"I don't know. It seemed like it could be, but there was a name in the glyphs and it wasn't Atlantis."

"What was the name?" I was almost holding my breath, and gripped the sheets with a fist.

"Okeanos."

I blinked. "Never heard of it."

"Me either."

"But Gerland is an Atlantean." I wrinkled my nose, confused.

Antoni shrugged. "I can't explain it, love. I can't even

tell you if Okeanos was a place or a person. What they showed me were photographs of mosaics that were partially ruined and had more to do with the legend of the sea deity who made this aquamarine for his lover. That was all they cared about, not the place."

"Just one aquamarine?"

Antoni propped his pillows against the headboard and sat up, snugging his back up to the wall so he could sit straight. "Yes, it didn't start out in a million little pieces like the way it was when we saw it. In the ruins, the mosaics depicted it as a six-sided column, huge, as thick as a man's leg."

"How did it end up being cut into all those gems?"

He shook his head. "I don't know. What they had me trying to read was just talking more about the effect the aquamarines have on mermaids and men. For mermaids, it lifts an ancient curse that was placed on them by a very old, angry sea-god of some kind. The glyphs described the effect it had on sirens in a strange way—a sort of 'waxing' effect on her."

"Waxing?"

"Yeah, like the moon."

What did *that* mean, I wondered? Considering the siren cycles, I wondered if it meant that if a siren was in a land-cycle, the gem would lock her there, and alternately, if she was in a salt-cycle, it would lock her there also. "Did it say anything else about the effect it had on mermaids?"

"Probably, but they didn't give me much time to look at those photographs. They moved me on to try and decipher how to get the gems out from under that dome, and the effect that they had on humans."

"Allowing them to breathe underwater."

"Exactly. This Group of Winterthür, they're a secret

association of the world's wealthiest. Emun told me a bit
about them on the plane. Their purpose is to acquire
powerful ancient relics for themselves, and exploit them
however they see fit without letting the world know that
they exist."

"The group, or the relics?"

"Both." He nodded thoughtfully. "You know what's also
amazing, is that Lusi had one of them."

"A gem?"

"Yes. I remember it well because I never saw her
without it. It was a ring. She wore a lot of rings, changed
them every day, they were kind of her thing. But there was
one that she never went without. It wasn't that pretty or
special looking, it was just plain silver with an aquamarine
held in a claw setting. It was small and unremarkable. But
now I understand the value it likely had for her."

I rolled onto my back and sat up, sitting against the
pillow beside him. "It would have been nice to know about
all of this sooner," I grumbled.

"For your mom?"

"I guess you've figured out by now that she's not
working for The Bluejackets."

Antoni nodded. "I never really believed that story,
you know."

I laughed, humorlessly. "You're not easy to fool."

"Well, Lusi had me fooled for years. It all came rushing
back when I saw the glyph at the exhibition. At first I
couldn't remember where I knew it from, but it bugged me
so much that I couldn't stop thinking about it."

"When did you figure it out?"

"Not until those men were shoving the tablet in front of
my face and demanding that I tell them what the glyphs
meant, did it come clear. Before that, I had thought that

maybe Lusi's ring and the pendant were made by the same jeweler, one of those old companies, you know. Like Novak, handed down through generations. But it was much bigger than that. And you know what else I figured out?" He took my hand, lacing his fingers through mine.

"What?"

"That I did drown that day on the Baltic, when we went sailing, and you were able to save me because of what you are."

I swallowed down the lump in my throat. "I'm glad you finally know the truth. And I'm glad you're not rejecting me because of it."

"You're crazy to think that I would. I'm in love with you, Targa. It doesn't matter where you come from."

"Siren allure can make men do things they might not do if they were in their right mind," I added.

"Do you think I'm not in my right mind?"

Slowly, I shook my head. "I'm sorry, Antoni. Sorry I didn't tell you the truth."

"I'm sorry you didn't either, but it's out now, and if it wasn't for the memories I have of Lusi, I'm not sure how I'd be taking it."

"But you're okay?"

He squeezed my hand and smiled in response.

"How did the men know about those caves?" I asked. "How did they know where to go?"

Antoni's face expressed a kind of respect. "The pendant led them there. That's why they wanted it so badly. According to the glyphs, because the gems were all one piece in the beginning, the individual gems are magically bound together." He gestured to the black device on the bedside table. "Hand that to me and I'll show you."

Retrieving the device, I put it in Antoni's hand. "This is

actually a camera of sorts. They took the gem out of its setting and put it in here," he lifted a little panel to reveal a pocket inside. "The camera inside took continuous photos of it using Kirlian photography. Have you ever heard of it?"

I shook my head. "What does it do?"

"Essentially, it captures a thing's energy and makes it visible. You can put whatever you want under this special camera, an apple, a shoe, or in this case—a gem. Its energy appears as waves of light. Every time they snapped a photo of it, its energy was pointing in a direction." He pointed to a little clear button on the side of the device. "The light came out here, all they had to do was follow it."

"So they'd never been in those caves before?"

"I don't know, we weren't exactly chit-chatting about it. But I don't think so."

I digested this, sitting back against the pillows. And inevitably, my thoughts came around to my mother. I had a way of calling her, and I had something to give her that would free her of the curse. But there was still so much I didn't know. What would the gem do to a siren who was in a salt-cycle? Would it free her immediately? Would it send her deeper into her salt-state? The gem had proven that it had different effects on different beings, and because of what it had done to me, I didn't trust it.

"Targa," Antoni said, softly, bringing me back to the present. I looked into his eyes and saw worry there. "Who is Emun?"

"Oh." I was startled by his question, though it was completely valid. "Emun didn't tell you on the plane? I thought for sure you would have talked all the way home."

"He didn't seem to want to talk to me very badly. I tried to ask him some questions, but he just kept telling me to wait until you were awake. He told me a bit about the

Group of Winterthür, but he didn't want to say much else without you being lucid."

Respect for Emun swelled in my heart. He hadn't had to do that. He could have spilled the whole story while I was unconscious, yet he resisted.

"Prepare yourself to be amazed again," I said. "Emun is a Novak. He's one of Sybellen's twin boys."

Antoni looked as stunned as I expected him to look. "He's a *Novak?*"

I nodded. "The one true heir to the Novak fortune."

His mouth opened and closed again. "But that would make him..."

"A century and a half old? Yes. I'm still amazed he even exists. Mom always told me that the mer-gene could only be passed down from mother to daughter, that there was no such thing as mermen. She was wrong, but perhaps not very wrong. Emun says he's never met another triton, which is pretty weird."

"A hundred and fifty years..." he murmured, stunned.

"He's a triton. They live a long time."

A shadow passed over his face. "They? You mean 'we'... 'we' will live a long time. You and Emun both, as will Mira."

"If something doesn't kill us, yes, I suppose so." My heart ached at the look on his face as he thought about this. It wasn't a happy realization for him, and one I had avoided thinking about, myself.

"Targa," he began, voice gentle, eyes downcast. "I will understand if you...want to be with one of your own kind. In spite of what Martinius believed, you are insistent that you are not a Novak. It would be convenient for you to be with Emun, if that was what you wanted. It would allow him to take his inheritance, and for you to be here too, without having to answer too many questions."

"You need to stop this line of thinking, Antoni. The only reason I am here is for you."

"Not for Martinius?"

"You remember how resistant Mom and I were to taking Martinius's fortune. We just couldn't see a way out of it, and didn't want it to go to the government. But now that Emun is here, I know what to do with it."

"That will be very tricky, legally, Targa. You'll be in for quite a battle. It would just be easier if you guys were...married."

"Don't be ridiculous. I'm in love with you, Antoni. I'm not interested in Emun in that way. And there isn't much a siren voice cannot accomplish, you know."

Still, he looked doubtful. I leaned over and kissed his lips, wanting to change the look on his face so desperately. He began to kiss me back, hesitantly at first, but as I persisted, and put my hands on his torso, he melted into me and I into him. In that moment, all I cared about was making him believe that he was the one for me.

The only one.

TWENTY-SEVEN

We found Emun sitting on one of the couches at the top of the main staircase. He was sitting upright, hands on his knees, and forward on the seat as though he was about to stand up and bolt into a sprint.

"Morning!" He smiled at us, face bright and hopeful.

"You're looking chipper," Antoni said. "I need a coffee or two to get that same look in my eye."

"I have a renewed energy, now that I have this," he held up one of the aquamarine gems between his thumb and forefinger.

"Where did we put the rest of them?" I asked, wary as I stared at the jewel.

"I put them in the safe downstairs," Antoni answered.

"And the tablet and camera?" Emun looked at Antoni.

"They're in my room," I replied. "The tablet is charging. I can't wait to see the photos on it."

"That'll be troublesome," injected Antoni, leaning against the wall. "It's locked and needs a code. I'll have to take it to someone who can get into it."

Emun nodded, but didn't seem all that interested in the

tablet. "I was just waiting for you to get up so I could thank you and say goodbye. I don't know how long it's going to take to find my mother, but I simply must not fail this time. No matter what. You can't understand the things I have been imagining about her since we got back, that she's in trouble, that maybe the curse has her in its grip. Maybe she's nothing but an animal right now."

He was talking without taking a breath and it was startling to see how emotional he'd become. Since I'd met him, he'd been calm, reserved, flinty in the face of danger. But thoughts of his mother in a salt-flush state had him full of anxiety. I understood perfectly.

Antoni and I glanced at one another. Sitting down beside Emun on the couch, I said, "I can make your search go much faster."

His indigo eyes darkened as he turned in my direction. "What do you mean?"

Antoni perched on the armrest and crossed his arms, listening with interest. He didn't know what I had discovered either.

"I think I can call your mother to you, instead of you having to go find her."

"I don't understand. How?"

"It must be one of my elemental gifts. I discovered it by accident one night when I was missing my mom. Through the ocean, I was able to pinpoint where she was and that she was okay. I called her name, and she *heard* me. She changed direction and began to come home. If I had let the connection between us continue, she would have come all the way, I have no doubt."

His eyes momentarily glazed over and his bottom lip trembled. Glancing up at me, he lifted a hand to his mouth, covered it, and then pulled it away and took a deep breath.

"Forgive me." He looked down at his own hand, watching the way the fingers trembled. "I had prepared myself to spend years at sea, searching. I thought I'd have plenty of time to be ready to see her again. I haven't seen her since..."

"The night of the wreck," Antoni finished.

Emun glanced up at him and nodded, his expression vulnerable and unsteady. "Yes. Since the wreck." He looked at me again. "You're sure this will work?"

"I haven't tried with anyone except my mother, so I'm not totally certain, no. I don't know if I could do it because we are genetically linked, or if I could do it for any siren, but all we can do is try. If that's what you want."

Emun blew out a breath and slowly nodded. "I can't turn it down."

"There's just one thing," Antoni said, raising a hand. "Something the glyphs in the ruins said."

"About the gems' effect on a siren?"

He nodded. "I'm certainly no expert in whatever language those ruins had on them, but from what I understood, the gems make a siren wax in a direction she's already headed in."

Emun considered this. "That's an interesting word. The way a moon waxes? Grows fatter?"

Antoni agreed. "Yes and in fact the glyphs did reference the moon as a metaphor."

"So, if she's in a salt-cycle, giving her a gem would only make her worse?"

Antoni shrugged. "Your interpretation is as good if not better than mine at this point."

I took Emun's hand and squeezed it. "All we can do is try. Why don't I call her and see what I can learn about her state. When I called my mom, I could tell she was in a salt-cycle, but she wasn't salt-flush. She only left a few months ago and from what I understand, salt-flush can take a while to happen. But I could *feel* her. Maybe I'll be able to do the same for Sybellen."

Emun agreed. "Yes, one thing at a time, right?"

"Right." Glancing out the window, the sun was already well on its way into the sky. "Shall we do it tonight? After dark?"

Antoni and Emun both nodded.

"Tonight, then." Emun put his hands on his forehead and tugged his hair back.

I couldn't imagine what it would be like to not have seen my mother since I was six, and to know I might get to see her for the first time in a century and a half.

Emun disappeared for the rest of the day. I didn't know where he went or what he was doing, but as the sun dipped below the horizon, he found Antoni and me sitting in the gazebo in the back garden. He wandered across the yard from the gate, hands tucked into his jeans, looking cool and calm again. Antoni and I were chatting quietly and holding hands, still adjusting to the new level of honesty that had opened up between us. We stopped talking and watched Emun approach.

"Are you ready?" I asked.

"I don't know how you get ready for something like this, but I guess I'm as ready as I'll ever be."

The three of us walked down to my favorite rocky promontory. Emun and Antoni stood behind me and waited while I went to the water's edge and sat down cross-legged, trying to replicate the way it had been when I had connected with my mother. I closed my eyes and breathed deeply, quashing the doubting voice telling me I had gotten Emun's hopes up for nothing.

Tuning in to the sound of the waves, the feel of the salt

in the air, the spray dusting over my body, I let my mind slip into the Baltic the way my body had so many times before.

I had never met Sybellen, but my imagination formed her easily as I knew she looked a lot like my mother, and I'd seen her countenance on the figurehead Mira had taken from the wreck. I imagined her swimming, and hoped that was what she was doing. If she was having a land-cycle then I wouldn't be able to find her, this I knew. Our connection would only work if she was in one of the world's connected bodies of water. I visualized her swimming alongside a whale, fingers brushing the slick surface of its body.

Sybellen.

My mind reached for hers, combing millions of square miles of salt-water. My elemental calling carried, rising and falling through layers of water the way music rose and fell on the wind.

Sybellen, your son is waiting for you.

Finding her felt like a warm and familiar hello with someone you knew you'd be friends with if given enough time. The tether between us was strong, inescapable, and impervious to distance or time. She was alive, she was in the ocean, she was in a salt-cycle but was not salt-flush, and now...

She was coming.

I had no sense of time passing, but when I opened my eyes, a feeling of completeness fell over me. Certainty. Sybellen had responded to my calling, just the way my mother had previously.

Looking back over my shoulder, I saw Emun and Antoni standing on the rocks, waiting patiently. They shared a look. Emun was glassy eyed.

"I've never heard anything like that," Emun said. "It

was like you were singing to my soul instead of to my ears. Is it done?"

"It's done." I got up, looking out at the Baltic, its dark waves churning and its whitecaps catching the moonlight.

"Now what?" Emun sounded nervous and his eyes darted about, skimming my face, the water's surface, and back again.

"She needs time to get here."

"Any idea how long?"

I lifted a shoulder. "I'll know. All you have to do now is wait. She's coming, Emun. Your mother is coming."

He blew out a breath but seemed lost for words. Moisture rimmed his lower lids. "The impossible is finally coming to pass."

I gave him a hug and he squeezed me tightly, whispering *thank you* in my ear.

IT DIDN'T HAPPEN the way I expected.

While my connection to Sybellen was strong when I had called her, as soon as I left the beach and went back to my daily life, I lost her. Emun asked me daily where she was, but unless I went down to the water and connected to her, I couldn't tell him.

She had been far south of the Canary Islands, had a long journey ahead, and couldn't make it all the way here without resting. I wondered what the experience of being called by an elemental was like. Had she heard my voice audibly? Or was it just a feeling? Did she, even now, feel a connection to me even though I couldn't feel it as I went about the day? Had her mind logically understood what was happening, or was it more like an instinct that drove her without any real rationality to it? I had so many questions to ask her, and as she drew closer and the days wore on, I became more and more excited, almost to the point that Emun and I couldn't spend time together because we would make each other anxious with our anticipation, me to meet another siren, and he to be reunited with his mother.

Emun went down to the rocks with me every other night and waited patiently while I found the connection between Sybellen and me. One night, I finally looked back at him from where I sat on the rocks and said, "She's so close now, Emun. I think maybe tomorrow."

He let out the breath he'd been holding in and just nodded his head.

Twenty-two hours later found Emun, Antoni, and me seated on the rocks together, Antoni huddled in a parka, hat and gloves. The wind lifted the water and buffeted us with spray. Whitecaps churned and in contrast the troughs between appeared black under the starless sky.

We waited, sometimes talking, other times just watching the restless Baltic for a sign of Sybellen.

She did not disappoint.

When her shining black head broke the surface, she was past the rocks where we sat and had her back to us.

"There," Emun croaked, spotting her first as he'd looked back over his shoulder.

We scrambled to our feet and raced over the slippery rocks toward shore as Sybellen's long black hair and bare back emerged from the slapping waves.

Something cinched around my heart as I stepped onto the beach, eyes glued to the siren now nearly fully out of the water.

She turned her head, eyes and face shadowed in the dark night. The three of us froze in shock. It wouldn't have mattered if we'd only had a single candle to light the shore-line that night, I would know that face anywhere.

Emun and I cried out at the exact same moment, mine a cry of shock and Emun's the heartbreaking sound of a small, lost boy finding safety again.

"Mom!"

TWENTY-EIGHT

She was not yet free of the salt, I could see it in the wary, untamed look in her eye. Her face was slow to register emotion. Her bright blue eyes were dark and focused in on mine, sharpening with recognition.

Emun was ahead of me, his hand reaching out toward her.

My blood curdled as I realized what he was doing, the faint blue-green glow now emanating from his palm flashed in my eye like the moment before waking from a nightmare.

My mother's wandering gaze fell on Emun as he reached her, and she did not step back from him. Her head only cocked to one side, her lips parted.

"No, Emun!" I called, my siren voice swelling. "Wait!"

Emun reached for her hand and put the gem in her palm.

In the next moment, her knees buckled and she fell, boneless and limp.

Emun barked in surprise but stepped forward to catch her as she slumped. He turned, her naked slick body draped over one shoulder. Emun's blue eyes were dark with terror.

"What happened?" His voice was a heavy rasp, almost a choke. His arm wrapped around my mother's waist and he picked her up properly, turning her to cradle her body like a child's.

I had tears flowing freely down my face and wiped at them to clear my vision, but the world was a blur.

I had called Sybellen, and Mira had answered.

"Martinius was right," I said, reaching him and brushing my mother's hair back from her face. Her eyes were closed, her face relaxed. I tried to pry the gem from her grip, but Emun pushed my hand away.

"Don't touch it, it'll hurt you."

"Take it from her hand," I cried. "Before it's too late."

Antoni tried to pry her fingers open but failed. The gem was locked in her fist as surely as though it was inside a vault.

"Let's get her inside, quickly," Antoni said, his voice steady and strong.

Emun had tears running down his face now, too, falling down his black leather jacket and landing in my mother's hair. Emun carried her easily but nearly stumbled on the rocks because he couldn't see where he was going. Antoni steadied him as I lurched along beside, fighting for my own balance through the shock. My mind was stuck on a loop.

Martinius was right. Martinius was right. My mother is Sybellen. How is it possible? Martinus was right? How? How? How?

Antoni held the door to the mansion open and Emun carried my mother up the stairs.

"Put her in Targa's room," Antoni suggested. "She'll want to be close to her."

Emun didn't respond, just carried my mother—*our*

mother—through the door as Antoni held it, and laid her wet body on the bed.

I drew the covers around her while Emun tried again to remove the gem from her hand. Even a triton's strength could not dislodge it.

Emun and I stood at the side of the bed, looking down at our mother, and Antoni stood at the foot, looking on.

"I'm sorry, I didn't know. I didn't know." Emun moaned and put a hand on my shoulder.

I turned to look at him and saw my own shock reflected in his eyes. He opened his arms and I stepped into them, salt-tears still streaming from both our eyes.

"Sister," he whispered, arms tightening around me.

A sound from the bed had me whipping around, Emun hovering right behind me.

Mom's eyelids fluttered and she gave a small sound in her throat, like she was fighting off a headache. A slash appeared between her brows as she frowned. Her lashes lifted and she was there. My mother was there, lucid, herself.

I gave a laugh of relief and wiped at the water on my face.

"Mom?"

"Targa," she said, her gaze holding mine. "What's happened? I heard you calling me and the next thing I knew I was just swimming. Swimming almost without stopping."

I bent and hugged her, kissing her cheek.

"The gem worked." Emun's words came out on a sigh of relief.

My mother's body went from pliable to still at the sound of his voice.

I pulled back and moved aside so she could see Emun.

He stepped forward, taking her free hand. "Mom?"

Her blue eyes locked on his face, devouring his features, his hair, his shoulders and torso, then back to his face again. She lifted her hand from his grasp and reached for him.

He bent so she could touch him. Her hand touched his cheek, her fingers traced his brow bone, his lips, his jawline, touched his hair.

"I know you," she said, finally. Her voice broke. "I remember you..."

Emun's tears ran unbidden down his face and dripped onto the bed. My mother's eyes welled up but did not yet spill over.

"I remember, now. I remember, and I'm so sorry."

Emun shook his head and sniffled. "You don't need to be sorry, Mama."

She nodded. "I do. I remember, now. I love you."

Antoni and I shared a look, astonished, sober, and mingled with happiness. Antoni stepped close and wrapped his arm around my shoulder. I pressed my head to his body, squeezing my eyes shut in silent gratitude.

Sybellen pulled Emun, her son, down and wrapped her arms around him. She began a siren's weep into his hair.

"My son," she rasped, her voice pregnant with sorrow. "I remember everything."

EPILOGUE

My name is Amiralyon—but Mira to my daughter and my human friends. I am a siren of the Okeanos, that sprawling, richly endowed, undiscovered underwater land of the Atlantic. I am the only 'maid of the sea'—as some once poetically called us—to have lived two childhoods, two adolescent lives, and two adult lives. I am the only siren to have two siren names. The two women I have been, may as well have been strangers for all they knew of one another...until now.

I had forgotten everything.

When Nike had sent me back into a state of youth, there remained not a shadow, not even a filament as fine as spider's silk to tether my second life to my first. Even Trina was of no use, her own mind addled by Nike's magic. How artfully the sorceress had etched upon the landscape of her memory. How little Trina had passed on to me. How thoroughly she had been erased. Now that my memory has returned to me, I am dazzled by Nike's powers, more so because she must surely be dead. If she were not dead, she would have found me and restored me to my former self.

Sybellen.

But I am getting ahead of myself.

In the early days of my first life (though one could argue that all sirens have many lives, no one could dispute that I experienced this in a way entirely unique to our kind, and perhaps to any kind), I was afraid of our sovereign. I think we all were, to some degree. Apollyona was fierce, powerful, sometimes ruthless. She was a natural born queen. Though any siren could have challenged her for our highest-ranking position, I don't think the idea crossed many minds. Apollyona was our champion, our protector, our war-lady, our defender, our provider.

She was also my mother, and Trina was her handmaid.

THE STORY CONTINUES IN...SALT & the Sovereign, The Siren's Curse, Book 2. Sign up to Abby's newsletter at www.alknorrbooks.com to be notified upon its release (early 2019).

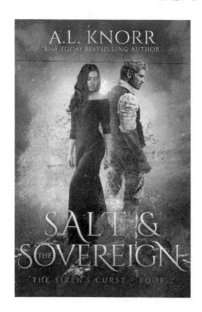

ABOUT THE AUTHOR

A.L. Knorr is an author of Urban Fantasy Fiction. She's a Canadian who is a true digital nomad and is constantly traveling with her laptop. A.L. stands for Abby-Lynn, but that's a lot of letters to fit on a cover. Abby is working on The Siren's Curse Trilogy which follows Targa and Mira back to Poland, and promises more twists and intrigue and a few huge surprises!

You can connect with Abby here:
www.alknorrbooks.com

ELY PUBLIC LIBRARY
P.O. Box 249
1595 Dows St.
Ely, IA 52227